THE HORNETS' NEST

THE HORNETS' NEST

NEIL MACKENZIE

Copyright © 2026 by Neil Mackenzie
All rights reserved. No part of this book may be reproduced in any manner whatsoever without written permission except in the case of brief quotations embodied in critical articles and reviews.
The story, all names, characters, and incidents portrayed in this production are fictitious. No identification with arthropods (living or deceased), places, buildings, and products is intended or should be inferred.
ISBN: 9781764426305
First Printing, 2026

For Vicky, Joal and Eve.

Prologue

From the top table, Vespa gazed out across the great Feasting Chamber as happy conversation bubbled around her. Butterflies chatted with mantises, mosquitoes gossiped with dragonflies, termites debated with beetles – representatives of every great house of insect, myriapod and arachnid brought together to celebrate her wedding.

Beneath the table, she squeezed her husband's hand and whispered in his ear: "It looks like my mother's plan is working very nicely."

Vespa had wanted a small family affair, but her mother, Queen Velutina, and the Council of Hornets, keenly aware of the young princess's popularity, saw an opportunity to modernise their image. Hornets should no longer be feared, but recognised as the gracious, caring, and hospitable creatures they truly are. And so, a grand state wedding was ordained, with invitations sent to all leaders far and wide.

Smiling, Vespa kissed her new husband softly. Love was something she had neither pursued nor expected. At first, she'd dismissed the gentle tickle in her heart as an adolescent distraction. Besides, she had little time for it, as there was too much to read and learn. But love had found her, and there had been no resisting it.

The last (and favourite) child of Queen Velutina, growing up Vespa never embraced the frills and flourishes expected of a young princess. As a teenager, she showed little patience for idle gossip and courtly chatter. Ceremony without logic frustrated her. Rather, she craved knowledge, insisting on a university education. While she read mathematics, biology and sociology, she sought the company of thinkers – even the group of intellectual radicals who whispered of ancient times when arthropods were a minuscule part of a much larger world.

"It certainly seems that way, doesn't it?" her husband replied, beaming at the overflowing plates and brimming goblets.

Indeed, a great deal of care had gone into the arrangements. Visiting royals from the worlds of termites, ants, bees and wasps were paired with local highborn who ushered their guests through the intricacies of hornet customs. The Household Guards, tasked with directing the swarms of visiting arthros angling for a glimpse of the bridal couple, dutifully followed orders to be unfailingly polite. The seating plan delicately balanced old rivalries, new alliances, and the prevailing socio-political currents. Even the menu was strictly vegetarian.

But of all the details, none had been considered more carefully than Vespa's gown. The subject of endless speculation, it exceeded all expectations. Earlier, as she walked arm-in-arm down the aisle with her mother, a collective gasp of approval had swelled through the Old Cathedral. The bodice, crafted from the lightest fabrics, mimicked the scales of butterfly wings. Sheer sleeves flowed into intricate silk webbing. Her glistening skirt was made of layered fabric, and the train, velvety as caterpillar fur, swept far behind. Crowning the outfit was a headpiece of myriad antennae that swayed gracefully with every step.

Turning her attention to a hidden pocket, Vespa slipped out her phone, glancing at the photo she'd posted of herself and her husband just after the ceremony. She smiled before discreetly replacing it. Of course, it had gone viral – most of the content she posted did – but this was her most liked and shared post ever. Vespa had been one of the first arthropods of nobility to embrace social media, and she became known not only for her ethical views on arthro equity and environmental management but for revealing her life as a princess. Her followers loved her authenticity, and her celebrity influenced well beyond the hornet world.

As her husband nudged her under the table, a flourish of trumpets rang around the chamber, followed by the booming voice of the Grand Drone.

"Your Majesties, Your Royal Highnesses, Blue Bloods, Leaders and representatives of the great Houses of Arthropods..." Formally dressed, wings neatly folded, the elderly administrator stood still, his head bowed, waiting, almost paternally, for the room to hush.

"On behalf of Queen Velutina," he declared, "I welcome you to the marriage celebration of Princess Vespa and the Very Honourable Zir Hal."

Polite applause rippled across the room.

"Pray silence for... the groom," he intoned, theatrically rolling the 'r' and stretching out the 'o's.

Vespa squeezed Hal's hand. As the page drew back his chair, Hal flashed his wife a reassuring smile, kissed her lightly on the lips and stood tall. A murmur of approval circled, for he was a popular choice of consort: grounded but fun, confident but not arrogant, modern without being radical. Standing before these most important arthropods, he appeared a fine statesman in the making.

With just the slightest trace of nerves, Hal welcomed the guests, easily remembering the names of key dignitaries. Turning to his left and right, he complimented the princesses on their dresses, thanked his best man, and acknowledged his mother's unwavering love and support.

Then Hal grinned. "I will be honest, though," he said, "when I first met Vespa, I had no idea what I was letting myself in for!"

A ripple of laughter.

"There I was, a simple soldier of the court, bewitched by a beautiful princess with a dazzling smile and the sharpest mind. I mean, who wouldn't be attracted to a princess writing a thesis on the possibilities of cellulose microfibrils serving as dense data servers."

Vespa flashed her husband a wry smile as the crowd chuckled.

"What strikes me most," Hal continued, "is that Vespa never accepts that things just are. She doesn't flatter for favour or follow rules she doesn't believe in. And yet, she is fiercely devoted – to her people, to her mother, to truth, justice, to her followers..." He frowned and shook his head theatrically at the guests who laughed back at him. "And somehow, miraculously, to me."

A hum of affection passed through the crowd.

"She could have chosen a thousand more sophisticated hornets. But she chose me. And a love grounded in respect, curiosity, and the occasional lively debate!"

Vespa nodded enthusiastically, as the guests chittered in amusement.

Hal turned to Queen Velutina. "To my mother-in-law, thank you. Not only for your blessing, but for raising a daughter with such conviction, grace and vision. I will spend my life, Your Highness, trying to be worthy of your trust."

The Queen was unaccustomed to displays of sentiment, but she blinked rapidly to hold back a tear.

"And thank you," Hal added, addressing the guests, "for allowing us to share this, our happiest day, with you who have come in peace and friendship."

"Hear, hear," called a bee dressed in the garb of a Senior Queen, and a warm chorus of agreement hummed through the Feasting Chamber.

Finally, Hal turned back to his wife. His voice softened. "My love, my heart, my fierce and fearless friend. I promise to stand beside you through every challenge. To love you without hesitation for all our days."

He raised a glass of nectar.

"To my extraordinary wife. May our future be full of love, purpose, joy... and just a little bit of mayhem. To Vespa!"

"To Vespa!" shouted back every guest as they drank deeply from the toasting goblets. Cheers, stamps, taps and clicks reverberated around the chamber in an outpouring of celebration. It wasn't just a toast to a princess, or a bride, but to a better future for everyone.

The guests returned to their seats, agreeing loudly that it was a splendid speech. And what a marvellous couple! But in the prevailing jubilation, no one noticed when one of the senior princesses on the top table slumped forward, then slid back in her chair, clutching her neck. When the husband of another princess started retching, there was good-natured giggling from the front tables – he had a reputation as a bit of a drinker. But when the best man leapt up shrieking, grabbing his throat and kicking out violently, sending plates and goblets crashing, a ripple of unease crept through the room.

Something was wrong.

Conversation paused as the guests exchanged nervous glances, trying to make sense of what was happening. Then all eyes were on the top table. Another princess collapsed, vomiting violently. Then another, and another. An elderly hornet shrieked. The guests began edging backwards, slowly at first. Then faster. When comprehension dawned, panic erupted, and everyone surged for the exits.

Vespa stared, stunned. All she could do was watch, transfixed, as her world went into slow motion. The heaving, the crumpling. She turned and saw Hal's mother clutching her thorax, convulsing, struggling for breath. Further along the table, her sisters and their husbands were either slumped, still, or writhing in pain. For the first time, fear rushed through her.

Hal?

She whipped round. He was jerking violently. His face blue, eyes bloodshot, wide and confused, he clutched his throat, desperate to speak but unable. And then he was still.

Vespa lunged for her husband, grabbing him with two hands, frantically shaking his still form. She wrapped her antennae around him, tapping and prodding. Nothing. No vibration, no pulse.

She grabbed his face, screaming his name. His eyes were completely red now, devoid of all life. She tried to kiss him – but someone held her back.

"Leave me alone!" she shrieked, lashing out at the hands, desperately clinging to her husband. But the grip on her was unyielding. "You mustn't touch him, my princess," a voice insisted. "It's poison. He's been poisoned. They've all been poisoned."

1

The Gig

Anton was late. As he burst through the door, a wall of warmth hit him, welcome relief from the frigid weather outside. He paused momentarily, steeling himself to brave the crush.

The crowd bubbled with good humour, their conversations blending into a continuous hum, punctuated by bursts of laughter. The Cave was heaving – a school had hired the venue for their annual rock concert, so the prittle-prattle of students droned around the room, competing with the DJ's bass-heavy beats.

Standing on tiptoes, Anton strained over a sea of heads that wore an exotic assortment of haircuts. Some were reduced to bristle, others dyed bright, a few carefully trained to stand tall. The school punk band was playing, so quite a few intimidating characters were hanging around, but behind all the piercings and body paint, Anton knew there were young hearts of gold.

Thanks to his false ID, he'd been to The Cave before and liked it. The style. The authenticity. Multi-species. While other venues had surrendered to modernisation, virtual reality pods and holographics, this place still had soul. Memories hung from its walls, vintage artefacts gathering dust on busy shelves. A few living relics clothed in various fades of black sat on stools, doggedly unmoved by the kids zipping excitedly around them.

There were two routes to the back room, and he needed to get there quickly – preferably unnoticed, because he knew how easily he could be distracted. Anton chose the less crowded route and pressed on, head down, irrationally hoping if he didn't see them, they wouldn't see him. He felt a few eyes looking and noticed a few pointing him out.

He pulled his phone from his back pocket and shook his head. Still late.

He pushed on, squeezing through gaps in the crowd that weren't really there. Insects turned, frowned, put out. *Too bad.* He needed to get there. They'd be angry and he'd apologise. He was used to apologising, and they were used to forgiving. That's how it worked in his life. He was late again; he said he was sorry again; they'd forgive him again.

It wasn't that he meant to be late. But the truth was, he was pretty disorganised, so if he actually remembered to add events and reminders to his phone, he'd more likely forget to charge it. Or it wouldn't have credit. He also found it hard to say he had to go. Never wanted to let anyone down. Maybe some supernatural force would whisk him through space and time, land him early for a meeting or catch-up or whatever he was inevitably late for.

He managed to push through the front room and found a bit of space under the arch. Beyond was the band room. No fancy décor. No umbrellas hanging from the ceiling. No seats. It was just a box – resplendent with walls of colourful, mostly illegible graffiti – with a stage at the end. Stretching up high, he scanned the crowd, looking for anyone he knew and the best route to avoid them. He wiped his brow with the back of his sleeve. *Nearly there.* He set off on the final push.

"Hiya."

He recognised the voice immediately. If he had a league table of the arthros he most wanted to avoid, she'd be at the top. But he knew he couldn't ignore her.

"Hey, Ems! How are you?" She was in her usual black. Lots of silky lace, stilettos; more holes than material in her tights. She wore a strip of black mascara above and below her piercing, unusually large green eyes. With closely cropped peroxide hair, pierced nose, ears and lips, she always stood out in a crowd.

"You look well," he said, nervously glancing at his phone again.

He and Ems had had a relationship. He thought she hoped they still might. He had treated her badly. Hadn't always been on time, had occasionally even forgotten to turn up at all. She couldn't understand why he hadn't called, and he couldn't understand why she'd made such a fuss. Anton had a way with girls. They liked his scruffy good looks, his defiant outlook on life. His I-don't-have-a-style style. Band tee-shirt, ubiquitous leather jacket.

Ems' friends thought him arrogant. She would remind him of the time they'd been discussing hooking up with other species. Anton said he had no problem going with a spider or a caterpillar or whatever, but described a body type he wasn't attracted to. Her friend had said he was describing her body type. "That's why I'm not attracted to you," Anton had said, immediately regretting it.

"I'm great, thanks," Ems said assuredly. "Looking forward to tonight?" But before he had time to answer, she was waving to someone else. "Great! I'll catch you later," and she was gone, disappearing into the throng. Had she given him a signal? Maybe they'd hook up later.

He turned his attention back to the room. He could see the others. *Come on. Quickly!*

The room was packed shoulder to shoulder, a steady hum of patient anticipation filling the air. Unusually for a school concert, though, it wasn't only students waiting for the main act. There were older brothers and sisters and friends; some with no link to the school at all. They hadn't come for the student band but the main act – a young local outfit that was causing a stir around town. They hadn't been together long, but their reputation was growing. Grungy garage guitar fused with unexpectedly great melodies, said one review. The buzz in the room sharpened as the **crack** of the snare drum snapped against the **dum, dum, dum** of the bass guitar. Two musicians were in place, poised and ready, but the space for the third, centre stage, remained empty.

That space was for him.

Bag slung over one shoulder, guitar case clutched to his chest, Anton made his final push towards the stage. And then a knee pressed into the back of his thigh. He stumbled, whipped around, ready to have a go – but in an instant, recognition melted his irritation. Smiling, they clasped hands and pressed shoulders.

"Hey, man!"

"You made it!" Anton replied, genuinely happy. "Did you see those Black Jackets?"

"Yeah. Who were those guys?"

Anton shook his head and shrugged. "Look, man, I've gotta go. Talk about it later, yeah? I'm so bloody late!"

He was in mid-seeyalater hug when a spider, exotic in tight black leather, enormous bubble sunglasses, and a shock of wild curly hair grabbed him by the collar. "What the hell! Where have you been? Like, we've been waiting for ages!"

"Whoa! You better go, man," the friend said, slapping Anton on his back. "I wouldn't mess with her."

The diminutive mass of crazy ringlets turned and looked him up and down, and then, with a voice full of sassy disdain, said: "Listen, idiot, why don't you just go and play with yourself, yeah? And it's not 'her', it's 'them'. Got it?"

As his friend held up his hands in submission, Anton stumbled onto the stage, shaking his head. "Sorry, guys. Got held up. You won't believe what happened to me," he said, frantically unpacking his bag as the ball of angry black leather climbed up behind their drum kit and took out their anger on the snare and kick drums.

"Glad you could make it," smiled the composed bee, a bass guitar slung around her thorax. There was just a hint of irony in her voice. She hovered calmly in front of her amplifier, a red tartan miniskirt and dark blue top set off with a white Peter Pan collar and cuffs. Dark hair, cut in a severe fringe, hung just above her eyes.

"Hey, Hon!" Stopping what he was doing for a moment, Anton smiled at the bee. "You look cool." He meant it. Friendship aside, he couldn't deny how striking she looked. Honey flashed him a demure smile.

Anton returned to his equipment. "I'm sorry, guys. It's been a hectic day. I lost all track of time. I'll tell you about it later." He plugged in. Amp to pedalboard, pedalboard to guitar. Head down, he kicked a few switches and started tuning.

He strummed. Nothing. Checked the volume. Fiddled with his leads. Hit a foot switch. Good.

Another strum. More silence. He scratched his head, confused.

"For God's sake, man!" The drummer ripped off their sunglasses, fixing him with a glare. "This is exactly why we do soundchecks!"

"Hang on," the bass player said calmly, reaching behind his amp. She flicked a switch. "Probably best if we turn it on."

He strummed again. This time a loud *grrring* rang out from the speaker. An ironic cheer erupted in front of the stage. He smiled ruefully to his bandmates, the first eye contact of the night. They were ready.

Up until now, his back had been to the audience. But now he was forced to face them, and confront his biggest demon. Despite all the cool swagger, Anton got super-nervous before playing. It would start as a quiet tickle in his chest, then an ever-increasing tightness would build through the hours before, until he became a pit of heaving anxiety.

He fiddled needlessly with his tuning and adjusted the mic stand, all the time his heart pounding. He knew everyone was watching him. Later, he'd flirt with them, and they'd love him and the music. But for the moment, he just wanted them to disappear.

He turned to the drummer, who, anger now dissipated, gave him a reassuring raise of their eyebrows and a faint nod of approval. They knew about his anxiety. The bass player met his glance with a quiet, knowing smile. She mouthed, 'okay?' He 'okayed' back. He had this. He always did. He leaned forward into the mic.

"H-hello." He turned away from the mic, coughed and swallowed, strummed a chord. He could feel the tightness in his chest disperse slightly. "Thanks for coming out tonight," he said. The lights dropped. Another strum. A round of whoops and whistles. "We hope you enjoy the show." A small cheer. Heartbeat normal, throat clear, brain in gear. From behind, four quick taps of the drumsticks. On what would have been the fifth tap, the band exploded into their opener, and the room went wild. High energy, impossible to stand still, any attempt at conversation futile. It was loud, raw and catchy, and the crowd was swept along on a wave of adrenaline that lasted the entire set.

Although they didn't realise it, each of them exuded an effortless cool. Spyder, their head often turned to the side in concentration was in complete command. Four corkscrewing limbs beat out a dancing, driving rhythm that, from time to time, brought out the widest of grins – as if she was celebrating being possessed by some dark melodic presence. Honey stared out to no one and everyone, in control. And then, suddenly, one leg would plant in front of the other. She dipped and recoiled in emphasis to the music before returning upright, statuesque and detached. She wasn't seeking to charm, but the audience was charmed anyway.

And then there was Anton. As the set went on, he played with ever more frantic energy – urgent and unfiltered, his right knee keeping the rhythm while he slammed his guitar, as if the music was trying to burst out of him. Anton wasn't interested in polish. He snarled and shouted with fire, veins bulging, sweat flying, eyes burning with passion.

But beneath the anger was purpose. Anton's songs were both poetic *and* political, and he wasn't scared to share his views. Tonight, he told the audience of his experience at the march and the aggressive Black Jackets – his performance almost a rallying cry.

"Thank you! Thank you very much!" he shouted over the applause, out of breath and buzzing. "You've been an amazing audience, and this has been an amazing night."

More cheering and clapping mixed with whooping and shouting rattled around the room. As the front of the stage chanted, 'we want more,' he couldn't help but beam. He glanced over at the rest of the band. They grinned back at him, a little overwhelmed by the fervour of the reception.

Turning back to the crowd, he raised his arms to quieten them. "Before we play our last song, I want to introduce the band," he announced. "First, on bass guitar, please put your hands and anything else you clap with together... for Honey Beeee!"

The crowd cheered and clapped in time as they shouted, 'Hon-ey! Hon-ey!' In return, Honey B gripped her guitar to her chest, bowed slightly and flashed a bashful smile from beneath her fringe. No one would have guessed she felt out of place in a sweaty club packed with punk rockers.

When the cheering died down, Anton continued. "And on drums, please show your appreciation for..." But before he could finish the sentence, someone shouted, 'We love you Spyder', and that started a chorus of 'Spy-der! Spy-der!'

Spyder wasn't one for shy glances and modest curtsies. As the applause swelled, they leapt from their stool, punching the air in time with the chants. Unashamedly out there, they vaulted over the drumkit and grabbed the microphone.

"Thank you! Yeah! Hey, y'all." They slung an arm around Anton's shoulder. "Hey, you guys, what about putting your hands together for the guy who brought us all together? Give it up for Ant-awwwn!"

The impassioned applause told it all. They knew Anton had a rare talent – a voice full of storytelling, sometimes gritty and angry, other times soft and vulnerable. His guitar playing was raw and stripped of airs and graces – just perfect for the music he wrote.

"Thank you! Thanks again," Anton said, waving. "So, this is our last song of the evening." He chimed out a riff that the crowd immediately recognised. "Thanks for coming tonight. We are Them Creepy Crawlies," Anton shouted, his words punctuated by an increasingly loud staccato guitar: "And this is... Them. Creepy. Crawlies!"

The band launched into their eponymous track, and the crowd went wild.

Them Creepy Crawlies
Crawling through my hair
Their tickle-tickle
I find it hard to bear.

An arthro mosh pit is a terrifying place. Tightly packed legs, arms, pincers, wings, antennae and mandibles shook and pogoed, leapt and lurched. The ants and beetles at the front of the stage shouted the words back. Dressed in black or brown, they moshed with excited good_humour. It wasn't for the fainthearted. You could get hurt if you didn't commit yourself. Crowd surfing, an ant was hoisted high, passed around, only to drop unceremoniously to the ground, capsized with legs and arms grasping helplessly.

Back from the chaos, a cross-section of more mature arthropods swayed and tapped, enjoying the music but taking a bit more care with their outfits. Ladybugs, dramatic in their red polka-dotted cloaks. Dragonflies, iridescent in blue, violet and purple. Earwigs with clippers securely bound. Caterpillars, outstanding in orange pants and yellow or rose jackets. They all stood tall on strong back legs, singing along with verve.

Further back, bumpy locusts and wide-eyed grasshoppers in green and tan jumpsuits bounced out of time like poorly coordinated trampolinists.

And right at the back, butterflies and moths provided the most colourful of backdrops – a kaleidoscope of pink, crimson, gold and violet. Of course, everyone was there for the band, but everyone liked to see their glamorous outfits.

Locked in the moment, the band played as if on autopilot. Unencumbered by their instruments, they were lost in the music. And Anton? Well, it was hard to look away. Eyes closed. A right leg rhythmically stomping. Infected, the arthropods gyrated, shook and sparkled under the spotlights, long ago having surrendered to his spell.

Back out in the front room, the rhythm pulled the grumpy regulars out of indifference and forced a twitch or a tap. Outside, even the cicadas couldn't help but scrape their wings in time.

And beyond the venue, where no one had heard of Them Creepy Crawlies, arthropods of all classes and species got on with life's ups and downs, all bound by something mysterious and arcane. This wasn't swarms of disorganised insects, myriapods, arachnids and crustaceans – small, insignificant or weak. This was life, most advanced. Organised and strong. Evolved and intelligent.

As the instrumental part of the song came to an end, Anton opened his eyes, smiled at the crowd, and prepared them to yell out the final chorus of their most popular song:

Creepy, creepy, creepy, creepy, crawlies
Creepy, creepy, creepy, creepy, crawlies

Creepy, creepy, creepy, creepy
CRAAWWWWLIIIIEEEES!

2

The Split

When the applause finally subsided, the band lingered on the stage, tied together in a post-performance bond, before, exhausted and elated, they allowed themselves to be enfolded by a sweaty swarm of backslapping, hugging well-wishers. There was no time for conversation, just for friends and fans to show their solidarity. "Best gig ever! Really excellent show! You guys were *great!*"

Spyder was a ball of kinetic energy, bouncing from one fan to another, blathering, high-fiving, and vibing all their free hands. Of all the band members, they were the most comfortable among the evening's exotics – super-friendly, hamming it up for selfies. "Oh, darling, you look fabulous," swooned two butterflies. *Click, click, click.* "Smile. Oh, gorgeous." *Click, click.* "This way. Oh, wonderful!" *Click, click, click.*

Honey, usually reserved, couldn't help feeling high on exhilaration, struggling to keep her feet on the ground. Surrounded by a swarm of sister bees, hover-hugging, she was happy to pose for the social butterflies, albeit without Spyder's theatrics. There was a hint of a blush, a twitch of a smile – no teeth, though, just intense eyes peering out from beneath her fringe.

While Spyder and Honey B were enjoying the post-gig elation, Anton felt less fulfilled. On stage, he had gorged and indulged. But now the thrill had dissolved, he didn't know what to do with himself. He was strangely uncomfortable with the attention, feeling that the adulation was, maybe, a lie and that everyone was just being polite. He said thanks and smiled, but a sense of disquiet – of unworthiness – gnawed at the back of his mind. In the end, he slipped away to the garden outside, where he sat quiet and alone with his secret self-doubt.

After a while, he was joined by his two bandmates. Spyder, still wired, fidgeted, legs and arms twitching. "Awesome! Man, I enjoyed that," they bubbled. "Best gig ever. Best gig eh-ver! What do you think, Hon? Don't you think it was great? You were great, babe."

Honey B's wings were still vibrating involuntarily. She brushed her fringe forward and tried to be calm. "Thank you," she smiled. "You, too! Weird when they sing back to you. What do you think, Anton?" Sighing, she pulled her legs up and crossed them under her, losing herself for a minute in some personal contemplation.

Anton sipped his drink and smiled at Honey. He was tired, emotionally and physically. He invested everything on stage, and while he didn't jump around, his performances were intense and draining. "Yeah, great. Tight."

Honey and Spyder exchanged a knowing look, rolling their eyes. Along with his nerves and petulance, they were used to his post-gig flatness.

Anton listened while Spyder and Honey gabbled about how they played, the crowd, the venue, the sound. Everyone who came out to the garden could see how comfortable they all were in each other's company. A few came over to offer best wishes and thanks. One or two close friends sat down and joined the conversation, until a voice they didn't recognise interrupted: "Hi, guys. That was a truly great show. Those kids really loved you."

Spyder looked up to see a slightly older praying mantis – definitely not part of their gang – in sensible shirt and pants. The mantis was tall and slender and slightly stooped. His wings were held neatly behind his back, and a couple of long, very thin antennae swayed as he moved. Oversized eyes sat atop a long, angular face, orange and protruding. There was nothing extraordinary about this praying mantis to make him stand out.

"Thanks, man. Appreciate it," Spyder replied with a polite smile.

"Sorry. I should've introduced myself. I'm Marty. From Creative Records. You may have heard of us?" He held out his hand.

"Creative Records? Sure! How do you do? I'm Spyder," said Spyder, shaking his hand and inviting him to join them. The gang squeezed up to make room for the mantis, who slid behind the table. Spyder had indeed heard of Creative Records, a new record label gaining a reputation for signing up fresh, young bands.

"Pleased to meet you." Marty shook hands with Anton and Honey and smiled at their friends. "You guys certainly have something. Something raw. How'd you think the evening went?"

"Great, man!" Spyder said, instantly taking on the role of spokesperson. There were nods and noises of agreement from around the table.

Marty smiled. "And you, Anton?" he asked, turning his attention to the singer, who was still slouching; indifferent.

"He bloody loved it, didn't you, darling!" Spyder exclaimed, flinging their upper arms around Anton, giving him a theatrical kiss on the cheek. Anton remained unmoved.

"Look," Marty continued, "I love you guys. I reckon you'd be a perfect fit for Creative. You'd focus on the music, and we'd take care of everything else. Would you guys be interested in meeting up for a chat?" He looked at Spyder and then Honey before addressing Anton. "What do you say?"

Before Anton had a chance to answer, Spyder burst out. "Are you serious? That would be totally cool, man!"

"Excellent," Marty said with a smile, eyelids sliding over his gleaming eyes. He explained that details would need to be worked out but suggested they start with a coffee and a chat – get to know each other better. He mentioned a café and suggested a time before standing up and shaking everyone's hand again. He offered round his business cards. Most of the gang hadn't been given a business card before. They read it. Turned it over. Read the back, nodded, and generally felt important.

Marty sidled off towards the exit, side-stepping the growing groups of youngsters looking for a bit of quiet in the garden. A few peered down their mandibles at the straight-looking mantis. At the door, Marty turned around and lifted an imaginary phone to the side of his face and mouthed, 'call me, yeah?'

The table waited until Marty had gone before erupting into a chorus of backslapping, 'well dones' and 'fully deserveds'.

The only one not sharing the excitement was Anton, who still sat back, unmoved and aloof. He knew it had been a great evening; they'd all played well and his voice had been decent. When a few of their singles had made it onto a few editorial playlists, he'd been pleasantly surprised. Yet tonight, face to face with those who seemed to love his music, it felt a bit weird. It was one thing to know that people were streaming your tunes – quite another to see, hear, and feel the adulation.

Ask Anton why he was in a band, and he'd talk about the art, the satisfaction of creating, his love and passion for the craft, the desire to grow and improve. He wanted to use his songs to comment on things that mattered. It wasn't about validation or recognition, or streams, or money (although he did occasionally let in a dream of success on a sleepless late night). He also harboured a healthy disdain for industry suits.

As the table found some composure, Anton said loudly enough so everyone could hear: "I just don't think we're ready yet, guys. And I don't trust that mantis."

Everyone fell silent. He had their attention. "Not ready? Ha, ha! Good one, dude," Spyder retorted, assuming he was joking until Anton gave them a suggestive eye-raise that clearly said he was serious.

"What's that supposed to mean?" Spyder countered. Anton's condescension wound them up, and they weren't going to let him sit there unchallenged. The gang shifted uncomfortably, and Honey sensed an argument brewing.

"Don't you think we should do the meet anyway? There's no harm, yeah?" Honey suggested, and the hangers-on nodded in agreement.

"Nah," Anton replied. He might have conceded if it had just been Spyder and Honey, but the gang's opinions only made him more defiant. "I'm not happy working with Creative – I've heard some bad stories about them."

Spyder took the bait. "Stories? What stories, Anton?"

Anton didn't respond, just checked his phone.

"Anton! Come on. Tell us," Spyder pressed, unwilling to back down.

Anton ignored the question. "Anyway, they're my songs, and I don't want to work with Creative." His tone was belligerent.

"I'm sorry, Anton," Spyder said, their anger rising. "Could you repeat that?"

He did. Slowly and quietly and very defiantly. Realising it was time to let the band sort out their own business, one by one the hangers-on made their excuses and left.

Spyder glared at Anton, who'd suddenly become animated, farewelling everyone like he was the reasonable one: "Goodnight! Seeya! Thanks for coming!"

Now it was just the three of them, Honey tried again. "You know, Anton, this could be an opportunity. Surely, we should hear what the mantis has to say. And if we don't like it, well, no harm done. We might even learn something. Come on, what do you say?" She put an arm around him, but Anton sat up, shrugging off her playfulness.

"Hey, man! Don't push her!" Spyder shouted. A few insects turned towards them.

"Oh, get lost, Spyder," Anton snapped dismissively. But Spyder wasn't going to be shut down. They sprang from their seat, leaning angrily towards him until their faces were almost touching – challenging, seething. More insects turned towards them, so Anton let Spyder dominate, daring them to take it further, until Honey wrapped an arm around the front of her friend, gently pulling them back as a few insects approached the table.

"Hey, guys. Come on, cool it. Spyder? It's not worth it. He's not worth it," someone said.

Spyder finally relented, their heart pounding as they brushed themself down. Throwing an ironic smile at the singer, they calmly said: "You know what, Anton? You're pathetic. You're selfish and arrogant and misogynistic and... I quit. There you go – that's what you wanted, wasn't it? Well, I can't be in a band with you anymore."

They turned to Honey and kissed her on the cheek. "I'm sorry, babe. I've gotta get outa here. I'll see you at home, yeah?"

Honey offered her friend an exasperated smile and watched the now ex-drummer of Them Creepy Crawlies shoulder their bag and push through the throng towards the exit.

She turned to Anton. "You really can be a dick."

But Anton just shrugged. "I suppose you'll quit as well."

Honey's wings quivered and she looked at Anton with frustration, shaking her head. "Is this really what you want?"

Anton remained cold and unmoved, arms wrapped tightly around his abdomen, refusing to meet her gaze.

"Fine." Honey picked up her guitar case and, without so much as a goodbye, she departed.

#

Most of the kids had left and now only a scattering of the older 'hardcore' remained. Two ladybugs, their polka dot gowns now casually off-the-shoulder, sat in futile conversation with a pair of jewel beetles, wings twitching and heads nodding. At the other end of the room, a beetle with a rockabilly quiff and grooves of experience etched into his brow, explained his tattoos to a young termite, who clearly wasn't listening. A group of cicadas argued about nothing and everything.

Anton sat at a corner table. When Spyder and Honey left, he lingered, distracted, with his old school buddies. One moment, he was one of the boys, high-spirited and flirty; the next, quietly serious, discussing politics, social welfare, and the march he'd been on earlier that day. An impartial observer might have wondered if he was simply being friendly – or gathering sympathy for when the inevitable gossip about the band split began.

All his friends had gone now. He was left with a wasp he didn't know sitting to his right, arms crossed in front of a too-big, threadbare yellow and black-hooped jumper, head tilted back at an impossible angle, mouth open, snoring gently.

To his left sat a centipede. Two saucer-sized black eyes flanked her aquiline head that seemed too big for her body. Anton thought she was attractive, if a little glazed. She was dressed in a suit of bondage armour, orange at the front, black at the back, from which a line of little horns protruded.

"So, what do you think?" she asked Anton, who was now sitting with his chin in his hands, feeling glum.

"Sorry – what do I think about what?"

"About myriapod suffrage. I saw you there."

Anton looked at her, confused.

"At the march. The demo, last week? Should animals like me be allowed to vote?"

"Well, of course," Anton replied, a little too eagerly. He had only just met the centipede and he was trying to be nice. "And it'll come. Arachnids have been enfranchised, haven't they?" The centipede nodded. "So," Anton continued, "it's only a matter of time before you get the vote as well."

"Arthropods together, eh!" she said, raising her arm in salute. "It's not going to be easy, is it?"

Anton shook his head sympathetically.

The centipede stood. "Right, gotta go," she said. Leaning down, she kissed Anton on the cheek and whispered, "Do you want to come back to my place?"

Anton leaned back and eyed her. It was tempting. "Maybe some other time," he replied.

"Suit yourself," the centipede said curtly. As she slinked away, Anton gazed after her, immediately regretting his decision, and made to follow. But before he had a chance, an earwig sidled into the free chair.

The last thing Anton wanted now was another conversation. He wanted to go after the centipede or, failing that, go home. He was exhausted and was sure he had a busy day tomorrow. The earwig just sat there, looking at him. *Great. On one side, I have a snoring wasp and on the other, a mute earwig.*

"H-h-how's it going?" Anton could barely hear the earwig, so, ignored him and made to stand up.

"H-h-how's it going?" the earwig repeated, a little louder.

Anton sighed and wearily sank back into his chair. "Good. Look man, I'm really tired, yeah? Gonna go in a minute."

"Oh, that's cool," said the earwig. He paused, wondering if he should let Anton leave. But as Anton stayed seated, he continued. "I'm Edward but m-m-my friends call me Wiggy," he continued. "You can call me Wiggy if you like. I know we're not friends or anything, but we're the same age, I think?"

Anton nodded.

"And it's only mum and dad that call me Edward. And another friend. And you're not my mum or dad. It would be funny if you were, us being the same age. So, er, that's not, ah p-p-possible." The earwig abruptly stopped talking, closed his eyes tightly and squeezed his hands together to calm himself.

"Sorry. I can get a bit…"

"Lost?" Anton suggested.

"Yes, lost," the earwig chuckled. "Sorry. I just saw you sitting there. I wanted to say how much I enjoyed the gig." He brushed his floppy fringe back up over his eyes and stuck out a hand.

"So," he announced formally. "Hello. My name is Wiggy."

Anton took it. "Hello Wiggy, pleased to meet you. My name is Anton."

"I've been listening to your music for a while now. I really like you."

"Thank you, Wiggy." Anton swept his phone up and into his pocket. He smiled at the earwig and glanced around the room. Only the cicadas now remained. "Now, if you don't mind, I really have to get some sleep."

Wiggy ignored him. "But, you know, on Fashion Queens, I reckon it would sound better if…" Anton was only half listening. His guitar was there. So was his bag. He patted his top pocket – phone – and checked his back pocket: wallet. *Right, let's go.*

He didn't get up. He couldn't help catching bits of what the earwig was saying. Some of it resonated. He tried to ignore the monologue, checked his pockets again, swiped his phone again and then resigned himself to listen for a bit longer. The earwig hardly drew breath. He moved on to another song, and then another, each time describing how he would add a guitar here or a keyboard there. He talked about drum machines, synthesisers, backing tracks and backing vocals.

Bloody hell! My drummer and bass player have resigned, and now a complete stranger is telling me what I should do with my songs.

He tried to be agitated or take exception, but he couldn't. He just sat and listened to the earwig. And then, extraordinarily, he found himself warming to both the strange creature and his ideas. He started to pay a little more attention, imagining a new guitar riff here, or how a keyboard might work there.

Any nervousness or stuttering was gone as the earwig hit his straps. He spoke quickly and clearly, right to the point, with a singular and authentic passion. There was definitely something unusual about him. His tail was thin and wound in a complicated tangle beneath the chair. His long limbs seemed out of proportion with his body, and he gesticulated so often that he looked unbalanced.

"Stop!" Anton exclaimed. "Hold it, please... Who are you?" he demanded, with ill-disguised incredulity.

"My name's Wiggy," the earwig replied. "I just told you."

"Yes, I know that. But who *are* you?" repeated Anton, sitting up straight. "What do you do? How do you know so much about our music?" He shook his head disbelievingly and held out his top two sets of arms, palms open. "I mean, who sits down, as a total stranger, and tells a songwriter what to do with his songs?"

Wiggy's confidence faltered. He swept his fringe back again. "S-sorry. I can get a bit c-carried away. Intense."

Anton laughed. "I'll say. Look man, I really do have to go to bed. But the things you suggested? Well, some of them make sense... I've also got some stuff to work out with the others."

Wiggy looked at Anton inquisitively.

"Yeah, well, you know... But, give me your number and maybe I'll give you a call. See if we can fix up a jam? You can play some of the stuff you've been telling me about..."

"Why, sure," Wiggy replied matter-of-factly, tapping his number into Anton's phone.

Anton got to his feet and yawned. "Thanks. Good. It's been... interesting." He collected his equipment and waved thanks to the staff clearing glasses at the end of the bar.

3

The Morning After

The next morning, Anton woke early after a fitful night's sleep – he never slept particularly well after a gig. He took some time to open his eyes, preferring to keep the day locked away for a while longer.

Usually, he liked to go over the set. Think about each song. It wasn't about the crowd's reaction but about who had done what. Clips on a cymbal or a delicate rebound on the bass. He was particularly good at remembering the little details. To an audience, the band may just play a song, but in truth, they were always making subtle changes – little tweaks that only happened when they really trusted themselves. About halfway through last night's set, the band had switched to automatic. Then they hadn't had to think about the words or the chords or the beats or the notes. They just played.

Yet even as last night's gig replayed in his head, Creative Records kept trying to force its way in. Anton had attempted to shove it away somewhere at the back of his mind, locking it in a drawer, in a room, in another place, another world. But the technique wasn't working so he let it gush in. He hadn't warmed to the praying mantis, but he knew he hadn't really given him a chance. Marty had been civil, polite and friendly, but Anton just didn't trust any record company execs, and the band shouldn't trust them either. They were opportunists and exploiters, scouting for the 'next big thing'? *Yeah, right!* If it wasn't Them Creepy Crawlies, it would just be someone else.

And, seriously, a praying mantis? Of all the insects! A predator. These record companies are stupid. They should have sent a hot butterfly or someone like that centipede last night. Anton was wholeheartedly indie. Release your own records. Organise your own gigs. Remain honest and true to the art.

Honey's and Spyder's aspirations clearly differed from his own, so maybe a split was for the best. *But why hadn't they discussed it?* Anton was sure they'd remain friends. Catch up at each other's gigs. Go for coffee. Of course, he'd miss their conversations, the mundane stuff you only talk about with really good friends. Like what to wear and where to buy it. Spyder was the band's fashionista – they knew all the best charity shops.

His mind wandered to last week, the day after their previous gig. As was their custom, they'd all met at their favourite café, The Bee's Knees. Honey was expounding on why bees were producing less nectar than ever. They'd talked about the weather, alarming recent shifts in the seasons. Anton had spoken about Ems and inter-species relationships.

The latest influencers. Spyder's shop. Just ordinary stuff. He would be sad if they drifted apart.

Anton finally dragged himself out of bed and checked himself in the mirror. He looked tired and small bags had formed under his coal-dark eyes. His face was thin, which made his chin appear longer than usual, and the high cheek-bones made it look as if he was sucking in. Anton wasn't scrawny, but he was definitely not athletic. He pressed his biceps, sure they were harder than yesterday, and shuffled to the kitchen area, where he put on the kettle. As he gazed absentmindedly out of the window, the earwig popped back into his head. That odd earwig. *What was his name?* He liked him. He was a bit unusual, telling Anton what to do with his songs. Anton tried to remember some of his ideas. There were some good ones, but who learns all the songs of a small indie punk band?

Edward. Wiggy! That was it.

Thoughts and questions jostled around his head. He was sure Honey and Spyder would have liked Wiggy. *How would they feel about a new member in the band?*

He wound the top off his biscuit tin and pulled out something brown. He munched, the sweetness a brief antidote to his lingering headiness. Through the window, he watched the morning sun trying to force its way through a blanket of cloud.

What now, then? He'd have to put the word out for a new bassist and drummer and come up with a new band name. Would they play old Them Creepy Crawlies songs?

They were his songs, after all. *Will Spyder still help me choose my clothes?*

He was still at school when they had met. A couple of earlier attempts at forming a band had come to nothing so he'd posted an ad in one of the online muso communities. He had only been a little late to their first catchup. *Ha!* He remembered his first impression: *if they play as good as they look, we're going to be superstars.* They had hit it off immediately. There was some talk of influences at that first meeting, but really, they'd just talked about themselves. They all left happier than they arrived.

At their first jam, Spyder and Honey were already set up and playing when Anton appeared. They sounded tight. Anton apologised for being held up. The others stopped playing while Anton got ready. He appreciated that, as he'd always hated others playing when he was trying to set up.

"Everybody ready?" Spyder had called, giving him an encouraging look. He began strumming around a couple of chords, and the others locked into an easy rhythm. As the afternoon unfolded, they began to stretch themselves beyond their comfort zones and, by the end, they had two songs. In their very first session!

Anton sipped his tea, smiling at the memory. Afterwards, they went for coffee and talked more about each other's backgrounds. Anton had never met a non-binary creature before. Or someone related to royalty, however distant, for that matter.

Everybody ready? That question now resonated. Ready for what? He hadn't given much thought to where the band might go, nor had he considered what Spyder and Honey wanted. He was up for writing songs and playing pub gigs and maybe even gaining a bit of a following. The extent of his ambition was to support a well-known touring band. And if they got some playlisting – well, happy days! But record deals? Large venues? Those weren't for him.

Anton washed his cup, winding his hand around the inside of it over and over again. He felt discombobulated and decided to go back to bed. He couldn't remember if he was supposed to be doing anything that day.

#

Honey and Spyder were at The Bee's Knees. The café was right at the heart of the Central Market, which boasted – with some validity – that you could stay here from dawn to dusk, without running out of things to do. Indeed, the sprawling market building overflowed with curiosities. A labyrinth of narrow alleys crisscrossed the ground floor, and a gallery on the first floor looked down on the teeming, noisy life beneath, where merchants and customers of all classes and species chatted, haggled and traded.

Over time, as demand outgrew the space, the market had spilled outside, less regimented and more chaotic. The entire area was a place of now and then. Traditional hand-made products – jewellery, baskets, ornaments, clothing – sat alongside the very latest technology. AI shopping assistants provided product origins, sustainability scores, and allergy warnings; drones and robots were on hand to help with home deliveries; info sensors sent sales records and product details to your personal cloud.

Of course, there was also food everywhere. Shops selling exotic spices and herbs mixed with vendors promoting locally farmed produce like fungi-of-the-forest, perfumed elderberry pips, and toadstool essence. But it wasn't all free range and natural. You could find ethically produced meats and dairy made from cultured cells and plant-based sources, as well as probiotics and nutraceuticals tailored to your genetic profile.

A stall on one side of the café sold 3D-printed edible flowers – just tell the robot your favourite shape and flavour, and a few moments later your snack was ready. On the other side, a dessert stall, where nearly every treat featured freshly collected nectar from free-range robo-bees.

Spyder and Honey watched this life humming and hustling around them. There was no dissection of the previous night, the music, the gossip, and the next show. They sat in silent contemplation, the future – for the band anyway – clouded with uncertainty.

"Cheer up!"

Spyder and Honey were shaken out of their melancholy by a plump, jolly-faced woodlouse. "Mind if I join you?"

Without waiting for an answer, the louse, dressed in a battered green apron, slithered into the seat opposite them.

"Winnie!" Spyder grinned. "How are things?"

"Oh, you know, petal, worked off my feet." Winnie reached down to massage her wobbling calves. "I really am getting too old for this."

"Never," replied Spyder. "What would the committee do without you? What would *I* do without you?"

"Mmm," replied Winnie, before ordering a cup of nettle tea from the waiter hovering over her.

"Just the two of you today? Where's that handsome young ant you're usually with?"

Winnie listened as Honey explained what had happened.

"Oh dear, luvvie. What a shame," Winnie said with genuine affection. She reached out and took the hands of the two young arthros. "But you two are my specials." She sniggered. "I still giggle when I think about how you two met."

Spyder snorted, leaning back and wrapping all eight of their bangled limbs around the chair's arms. Even when they dressed down, Spyder looked exotic. A tight orange jumpsuit hugged their athletic frame, and their usual mop was coiled into a tightly braided crown, each strand knotted with brightly coloured beads. "Oh, here we go," they said, a little irritated.

"Honey, dear, you seem to have a firm grip on that pretty bag of yours."

Honey's bag was indeed tucked tightly under a forewing, which she clasped to her abdomen. She was dressed in a pair of yellow shorts with a black crop top that showed a series of piercings she had had done recently.

"Once bitten, twice shy, Winnie," Honey winked.

"Yeah, yeah," Spyder tutted with just a hint of impatience.

"If I remember right, I was sitting just over there in my school uniform, munching on a sandwich," Honey continued, enjoying her friend's embarrassment, "when, bam, my bag's gone, and a spider is vanishing with it into the maze of the market.

"You didn't think I'd chase you, did you? Let alone catch you!"

Spyder rubbed their blushing face with her top hands.

"And what a mess you both created, as you careered around my market, food carts flying, clothes racks toppled, shoppers scared out of their wits."

"Bloody boarding-school bees with something to prove," quipped Spyder.

"Ha – you're right there!"

Spyder and Honey couldn't have come from more different backgrounds. Honey was raised in comfort: a large home, servants, a posh boarding school. In that landed world, it was all she could do to suppress her inner rebel. She never sought solace in boys or drugs because she was too practical; but all along, Honey knew she didn't fit in. Bright and versatile, she excelled in academics, sports, and music. Her mother, a distant cousin of Queen Bea, made her learn the cello, and while she appreciated its graceful poise and intensity, Honey was drawn to the bass guitar, which matched her introspective personality. And of course, she loved the fact that her mother disapproved. With an increasing desperation to forge her own way, one holiday evening over dinner, Honey announced that she was dropping out of school, leaving home, and going to live with a spider.

Spyder, on the other hand, never went to school, never had a home, and never owned anything expensive. Abandoned by their mother, they were forced to fend for themself on the street – begging, stealing, surviving in a community that society ignored. The younger street spiders were drawn to Spyder, and Spyder was glad to take on the role of older sibling. Given their situation, it was natural that Spyder developed a simmering anger, often taking it out on a pot or pan or another innocent receptacle. As they grew older, Spyder was able to channel their rage into a refined sense of rhythm, learning to create beats and pulses that made their brood dance, or drift off, hypnotised, to sleep.

"I'll never apologise for doing what I had to do to feed the kids," Spyder said belligerently, shifting a little in their chair. They turned to Winnie.

"That's why I can never thank you enough for what you did. You literally saved my life. Those centipedes... I can still hear their words." Spyder shivered at the memory: *'Thief! Thief! String her up, string her up!'* "Thank goodness you were able to convince them to let me go."

"But you were brave." Winnie's voice was gentle. "In that crowd of angry arthros, you didn't beg or plead. You stood up proud and told them who you were. I've never forgotten that. And I'll never forget when you asked them: 'Would you steal to keep your child alive?' The faces of those insects!"

Spyder grinned. They glanced down at an empty mug, then out at the bustling shoppers. "I was just tired. Tired of everyone pretending we didn't exist. That we weren't even part of this world."

"I had no idea what your life was like back then," Honey said quietly. "I was... well, I was angry too, but not for any good reason. Just at life. My parents. Their expectations. That day was the first time I did something *real*. I mean, me... chasing you, getting into a fight!"

"Well, it's funny how things work out," Winnie said, smiling at Spyder. "And now, all the stallholders love you."

Spyder brushed a stray braid behind their ear, then leaned forward and planted a big kiss on the woodlouse.

"Well, my dear, I couldn't just stand by and do nothing," said Winnie. "Given that we were between contractors, the timing was perfect, and you've certainly delivered on your promise: the market's never looked so good."

Spyder grinned proudly. "Well, we have an awesome crew who are always prepared to work hard. They take the job of cleaning the place very seriously."

Winnie dabbed her mouth with a napkin. "And of course, the committee have done their bit for the empowerment of our marginalised groups." As she rose to leave, she winked at Spyder. "Everyone sleeps a bit better now."

The three of them laughed as Winnie said her goodbyes. Outside, drones zipped overhead, children darted between stalls, and somewhere, a busker began to play. And as the time shifted towards lunch, a wave of cleaner spiders swept through the market.

Spyder and Honey returned to their thoughts. It had been nearly a year since Spyder had stolen Honey's bag and faced the prospect of a public lynching. It had been nearly a year since Winnie talked down the centipedes. Now, Honey remembered the look of disbelief on Spyder's face when, the angry shopkeepers having dispersed, she invited her thief for a coffee. And as they rearranged their bangles, Spyder remembered not really knowing why they accepted. Whatever. Nearly a year later, they were best friends.

"Do you remember the chemistry of that first jam we had together?" Honey asked. "We'd just moved in with each other, and I showed you that post from Anton looking to form a band."

"So?" Spyder replied abruptly.

"Well, we've worked so hard to get to this point, I'm not really sure I want to throw it all away..."

Spyder raised their eyebrows. "Anton's a selfish, up-his-own-arse, arrogant prick. His behaviour last night was..." They paused, searching for the right words. "Totally unacceptable."

"I agree. And don't forget, he can also be flaky and disrespectful! But... he can also be caring and kind. And he does apologise when he's late. Do you think he has some sort of confidence issue?"

Spyder shrugged and shook their head. "He's certainly got issues, babe."

Honey kept at it. "You know, I'm sure there's a genuinely decent insect in there somewhere. I'm sure we can help him find it."

"Honey, girl, you may be right." Spyder's head bobbed feistily. "But do I look like his mother?"

Honey laughed as Spyder returned her look with theatrically raised eyebrows.

They fell into daydreaming and people-watching for a while until Honey piped up again: "You know, we've never really talked about where the band was going. What we all wanted."

"Fame and fortune, girl," Spyder suggested.

"Yes, well, indeed." She grabbed Spyder's hand. "Honestly, I don't think I'm ready to call it quits just yet. And I know you're not either."

Spyder sighed deeply. "Gee, you don't give up, do you!"

Honey B mimicked Spyder's insolence. "Do I look like a bee that gives up?"

#

Anton had spent the morning in bed, listening to records and thinking. Ants were supposed to be good at working stuff out and Anton had two major problems to solve: (1) where to go musically, and (2) how to maintain a post-band relationship with Honey and Spyder.

He had revisited Them Creepy Crawlies' back catalogue. He didn't often listen to their music, but when he did, he was always pleasantly surprised. Now, again, he consoled himself: *If I wasn't in the band, I'd defo be a fan.*

As he listened, Wiggy's suggestions kept resurfacing in his mind. He replayed some of the songs several times, trying to imagine how the extra vocals and instrumentals might sound; the more he listened, the more excited he became about Wiggy's ideas. The band had come so far from their first, raw EP and he loved the groovy rhythms coming from the bass and drums. In the beginning, he'd been the main songwriter, coming up with the melodies and the words, the beats and basslines, but as time passed, he'd let Spyder and Honey run with their own ideas. Listening now, he could hear how much life they fed into the songs.

Yes – a bit of unbalanced guitar just there. Yes – an hypnotic synth line there. Yes, he's right. I can see just what he means! Wiggy's ideas were already motivating him. But a wave of conflicting thoughts were also gnawing at him, and he was having difficulty putting them in order.

In one respect, he was relieved. He'd spent a lot of time sorting stuff out for the band without any support, or thanks, from his bandmates. It was he who posted on their social media. He who had designed (and paid for!) their website. He who'd promoted tracks on Insectagram (he's paid for that as well!) He had arranged all the gigs. He was the driving force. And if he was being honest, he was a little bitter about it all.

The split is their loss! He held onto the thought, glowing with a newfound righteousness. He was the band's backbone, after all. Yet a persistent, irritating voice in the back of his mind hinted that maybe he did bear a little responsibility. How many discussions had been cut short because he'd been unreasonably determined to do things his way?

When he started the band, he was bursting with ideas. Song after song poured out. They weren't just songs, they were his babies. Each line and riff was personal and captured something too rare and intense for anyone else to touch. But as the band grew, so did the resentment – although he couldn't quite pinpoint how or why. Was it jealousy that his bandmates enjoyed the spotlight without having to write a single note? Or was it something else?

Thinking back on his behaviour, maybe at times he could have been more sensitive. He knew he hadn't always said the right thing, but they rarely challenged him. They were both strong-minded individuals: Spyder especially, and Honey, so diplomatic that she always found a way to press her point. He knew he could cut off conversations and insist on his way, but what did they expect? *I'm the one who does all the hard work: songwriter, gig booker, weight carrier.*

If he didn't think they were ready for the next step, then they weren't. *And surely, they could see the exploitative nature of record companies.* He was sure he was right about that! Was that arrogance? How much of that was really him and how much was... other stuff?

Anton had never talked to anyone about the challenges he had faced growing up, although he was sure they'd made him stronger. He remembered visiting a friend one Sunday afternoon, only to be sent home because the family was about to have dinner together. He had gone home in tears, wishing that he, too, had a model family.

He would miss them, particularly Honey, for whom his feelings were becoming more confused. They weren't just excellent musicians; they were excellent friends. Would it take much to swallow his pride and call them up with an admission: '*Hey guys, maybe I went a little too far. Maybe I can be a bit of a pain.*' But admitting he was wrong would be like peeling off his skin, like losing the little bit of control he had over his emotions. He just couldn't do it.

Starting a new band would be easier. He could find new musicians and build new relationships. He'd be different this time: more patient, more democratic. *I'll make sure everyone's on the same page right from the beginning.* But he couldn't shake the feeling that he'd still be the same person, wrestling with the same issues, the same frustrations, the same insecurities.

Come on, Anton! The answer's obvious. Apologise, you fool! Talk to them. Open up a little. Be more... egalitarian!

Then Arrogant Anton was back in his brain. *It's my band. I formed it; I want it to go my way.* He sighed. It was all making his head hurt.

There was another thing to consider. Even if he said how much he regretted his behaviour – *which I don't* – or how determined he was to change – *which I won't* – Spyder and Honey might still walk away. He knew they'd easily find a new band. One where they could have more input, more ambitions, one that trusted the corporate path. *The split is obviously best for all of us.*

Anton sat up and looked around his studio apartment. It wasn't very nice, but it was all he could afford. *I must get a job.* The record player was off, and the heavy silence pressed down on his anger, his resentment, his pride, his insecurities.

He stood up and paced aimlessly, rubbing his temples to try and help his mind work better. *I'm an ant, for goodness' sake! I'm supposed to be good at working stuff out.*

The doorbell rang.

It made him start... he wasn't expecting anyone. "Coming!" he called, shuffling across the room to open the door.

Honey and Spyder!

Spyder's hands were buried deep in their pockets as they leaned against the door frame, oversized sunglasses pulled onto their forehead, revealing their I'm-angry-so-don't-even-mess-with-me eyes. Honey, on the other hand, wore a gentle, reassuring smile.

Anton barely had time to speak before Spyder pushed past him into the bedsit. "Hello," Honey said gently, "we've come to talk."

Anton closed the door, and for a moment, the three stood awkwardly in the cramped room. "Anyone for tea?" he offered.

Spyder folded their arms in defiance. "We don't want tea, Anton, we want to know what the hell's going on in that little atom-sized brain of yours. We want to know why you're such an idiot, Anton. We want to know why you think you should be making decisions for us. And we want to know why you don't respect us."

Anton could feel his hackles rise. Sure, he loved Spyder's forthrightness, but he wasn't going to take this abuse in his own home. But still, he bit his tongue. *Let's just get this over with, and then we can all move on.*

"Right, I'll just put the kettle on," he retaliated, retreating to the kitchen area.

"And we want to know, Anton, what you really want from the band," Honey called after him.

Bloody hell! Honey too. Suddenly, all the thoughts that had been spiking in his head all day slowed and came into focus. He could see how everything fitted together, and, finally, he could see the future. While pouring the tea, he gathered his courage. He had to say what he felt, regardless of the outcome.

He placed the three cups of tea on the little coffee table and sat on his bed. The other two faced him from the settee. He composed himself.

"Guys, I'm sorry. I'm sorry about last night. I should have agreed to meet the mantis. I shouldn't have been..."

"... such a moron."

Honey shot Spyder a look.

"Well, he was," Spyder replied innocently.

Anton smiled. "Thanks for that, Spyder. I can always count on you to tell it as it is."

I am doing the right thing.

"I've been thinking about you guys all day. And about me and the band," he confessed, sipping his tea as his eyes shifted between his two friends. "Look, I don't want to lose our band, but more than anything, I don't want to lose you two. You guys are a huge part of my life."

Spyder shifted their posture ever so slightly. "Okay, man. Good start. But what about the 'creative' thing? Last night you just dismissed the idea of signing without a second thought."

"Spyder's right, Anton," Honey chipped in. "You assumed the decision was yours to make. If the band has any chance of carrying on, we have to make our decisions together."

"Absolutely," Anton replied.

"Good," said Spyder, taking a mouthful of tea.

"And we can't have you showing up late all the time," Honey continued. "Last night was embarrassing."

Spyder was about to launch into another tirade when Honey placed a hand on their knee and looked kindly at Anton. "If we can't tell you now, no one else will, yeah?"

Spyder gave Honey her hand back – they weren't going to be contained. "Mate, you're starting to hack everyone off, you know? There's nothing cool about being late all the time. People are tired of your attitude. This image you put out about not giving a toss. Frankly, it's just boring – and disrespectful. You gotta grow up a bit, man."

Anton held Spyder's gaze as a prickly moment of silence passed. But Spyder hadn't finished. "Look. You're a cool guy, Anton. You're intelligent, kind and fun. But..."

Honey broke in. "I guess what we're saying is that..."

"I know what you're saying," Anton said abruptly, looking away from his friends and rubbing his face. Honey wondered if Spyder had been too blunt.

Anton stood up and stared out of the window. No one had ever been this upfront with him before. He knew he had faults, that sometimes he couldn't help himself. He watched the tree outside for a moment, shaking softly in the breeze, then he sat back down on his bed, leaned forward, with his elbows resting on his knees, cupped his chin before sweeping the back of a hand across his eyes. There was a mix of respect, love and honesty in his expression as he looked from one friend to the other.

"Thank you. I needed that. And you're right – I can be a disappointing friend. But I'm going to try to be better...

a better friend and a better person." He smiled at Spyder, "And you'll tell me when I slip."

"Look man, we're always here if you want to talk," said Spyder softly, with a rare flicker of compassion.

"Thanks," said Anton simply.

"So, the band." Honey moved the conversation on.

"Yeah. The only way we can continue is if we all want the same thing," Spyder said, glancing at Honey, who looked at Anton.

"I think you know what we want."

Anton nodded. *Decision time, then. It's been an odd day.* Everything that had been bubbling away inside him had been forced to the surface, making him question who he was and why. He was glad that, no matter what, Spyder and Honey would always be his friends.

Last night, the band was over because Spyder and Honey wanted more. *Or was it because I wanted less?*

He looked at his two friends on the couch. "I'm in, guys. All the way. I'm still wary of the big players, but I'm willing to give it a go. All in. See where we can go. But there's a few things from my side, yeah?"

"Let's hear them," Honey said.

"First, I can't do all the organising anymore. I'd like us to look for a manager. I'll be honest, I wasn't drawn to the praying mantas, so let's see who's out there?"

Honey looked at Spyder, approvingly. "Done. Let me look into that."

"Second. Social media. I don't really know what I'm doing."

"Man, you've been pretty good so far!" said Spyder. "But, fair enough. Maybe the social butterflies can help out."

"Cool," said Anton. He stood up. He liked to pace when he was thinking.

"So... there's one more thing. Last night after you'd gone, I met this earwig. You'd like him – he's a bit, uh, different. Anyway, we got chatting. Well, he got chatting. Basically, he went through our entire set and told me how to make the songs better.

"I tried to ignore him, but, like, some of the things he suggested seemed to make sense. And this morning, in the clear light of day, they still do. So," Anton continued nervously, "I was thinking that we could invite him along to a practice?"

"I don't see why not," Spyder said.

"Sure. Invite him along," Honey said. "It can't do any harm."

They all sat back, satisfied. What needed to be said had been said and now there was a plan.

"I'll put the kettle on again then, shall I?" Spyder skipped off to the kitchen.

#

As Them Creepy Crawlies agreed on their future, the earwig Anton had just mentioned turned his chair ninety degrees and slid across to a bank of touchscreens. He tapped a trackpad, typed in a few numbers, and checked the changes on a chart on a neighbouring monitor.

Wiggy spent most of the day holed up in this dark room, lit only by the glow of screens and the blinking LEDs on rows of servers and hard drives. He sat in front of a laptop clad only in a pair of loose pyjama bottoms. His thin, almost emaciated frame gave the impression that he needed to be fed. Wiggy wasn't great with food. He lived off a constant stream of nervous energy.

Wiggy was a hacker and tragic computer nerd. He'd spent much of his young life trying to gain access to external networks and systems, not because he wanted to cause any damage but because he couldn't resist the challenge. He'd started off cracking his school management system, changing grades for his classmates – sometimes for money, sometimes for revenge; often just because he could. He dabbled with fixing competitions (too easy), phreaking (too boring), even simulating cyber-attacks so corporates could fix their weaknesses (too benevolent). At his most bored, he had broken into the defence system of a small insect sub-species. As part of the game, he purposely left a trail back to a cybercafé terminal and watched, amused, as various agents came and went, checking the hard-drive and asking questions.

He did it again. And again. The final time, while watching from across the café with an air of bored superiority, he felt a tap on his shoulder. Almost relieved to finally be caught, he turned around only to be surprised.

It wasn't an investigator or a cyber agent, but the representative of an organisation that tested security systems. They were always on the lookout for new talent and wanted to hire him so long as he didn't tell anyone about his work.

Wiggy didn't know or care who they were; why would he if they were paying him lots of money to do the stuff he did anyway? He didn't care that much about the money, but he was happy to be gainfully employed detecting weaknesses and improving the response capabilities of whichever organisation the contact sent his way.

As he grew more experienced, Wiggy discovered he had a talent for identifying issues no one else seemed to have thought about. Then, he developed software solutions and wrote code. Lots and lots of code.

Wiggy never met anyone else from the organisation apart from the contact, which didn't worry him. He liked the contact, and could tell the feeling was mutual. Wiggy didn't have many friends. His work contact was the first arthro to truly appreciate his skills.

Wiggy's parents, on the other hand, couldn't hide their disappointment in him. They'd wanted a son who would play football, have a nice girlfriend, get a good job, and eventually give them grandchildren. They didn't appreciate his computer skills or why he locked himself away in his room for hours on end. In an attempt to distract him, his mother gave him a guitar. She played the piano, so he assumed she wanted them to play together. But she never asked. Wiggy couldn't understand why; he assumed she was just embarrassed by him. Which was okay because he was used to letting down his parents. Besides, the guitar gave him another thing to be good at.

Wiggy knew he could be obsessive and over-enthusiastic - that's why he was bullied at school - traits he'd long presumed meant something was wrong with him. That is, until he met the contact. The contact admired Wiggy's unique talents and told him so. No one had ever paid Wiggy such compliments before.

Later the contact arranged an appointment with a doctor who informed Wiggy he was neurodivergent. They mentioned a couple of acronyms, which Wiggy promptly forgot. But the diagnosis came as a relief, helping him understand that he wasn't simply weird, difficult, or awkward. He was an earwig with a unique set of skills and strengths.

He could quite easily lose hours of his life locked in his work, but today his mind wandered. He thought about last night. He'd actually done it! He had gone up to Anton, and they had talked about the band. He was sure Anton liked some of his ideas. He hoped – prayed – that Anton would call.

Smiling to himself, he turned away from his computer screen. Wiggy lived in a big house now, one that the contact had helped him buy, saying it would be a good investment. There were way too many rooms, and far too few pieces of furniture. He used a bedroom, obviously, and the big lounge to watch TV. It opened onto a swimming pool that he never used, and a view he rarely looked at. The basement, however, was the place he felt most at home. Accessed from the TV room by a spiral staircase, it was a windowless cavern, lined from ceiling to floor with screens, hard-drives, and other paraphernalia. The rest of the space was filled with music equipment – guitars, amplifiers, keyboards, and more computers. A big white leather sofa ran along one wall, and on the table in front of it sat four coffee cups, several dirty plates, and a pile of take-out trays.

Wiggy rose from his chair, walked towards the music area and picked up an acoustic guitar. He began to strum absentmindedly. He loved the echoes of different harmonics and how they made him feel. Sometimes, he'd record his improvisations, then switch to a keyboard to see what counter melody he could come up with. Or perhaps he'd put on a record and play to it. Not mimicking the licks but inventing his own. He might feed them through the synthesiser to experiment with sounds. This was how he came up with the ideas for Them Creepy Crawlies.

So, yes, his legs might be a bit too long for the rest of his body. And sometimes they seemed to work at cross purposes, as if one pair had forgotten where the others were going. Yes, he was a bit gawky and uncoordinated. His antennae curled up at the end as if someone had squeezed and scrunched them when he was younger, and his hair fell over his eyes, forcing him to sweep it back all the time. His clothes were old and uncoordinated. He bought them ages ago from the sort of high street shop that looked permanently empty, and they always looked too short or too baggy.

But no one knew security systems like Wiggy. No one could develop software solutions like he could. And no one could play the guitar quite like him.

He was about to pick up another instrument when a shrill beep rang from one of the computers. In an instant, thoughts of Them Creepy Crawlies and music vanished as all his attention snapped to the noise. He rushed to the screen, clicking the mouse and tapping the keyboard. The noise stopped but he continued to click and tap and examine readouts until he picked up his phone and pressed a speed-dial number.

"You n-need to c-come over," he said into the phone.

4

The Way Forward

"Hiya, Anton," the two butterflies sang out in unison. "Oh! We just love your outfit, don't we, Blake?" They sat down at Anton's table inside The Bee's Knees.

"We certainly do, Brie! He's just so..." Blake held a hand to his mouth and looked Anton up and down. He was wearing what he usually wore – nothing special.

"... street," Brie finished her partner's sentence. The two butterflies nodded in agreement.

"Thank you," Anton replied. "You two look pretty good yourselves."

Blake and Brie always looked good. It was their thing. They were fashion influencers, and they took their appearances *very* seriously. Today, Brie's wings were clad in the flimsiest, lightest silver lace. Tiny gold flecks were scattered across their insides, and they shimmered when they caught the light. She wore a tight, velvet-like suit, black with hints of lime green, and had a white scarf wrapped around her neck. She tinkled with umpteen leglets, and her long face, accentuated by prominent cheekbones and enormous black-as-night eyes, was hard to forget.

Blake wasn't blessed with the model looks of his partner, but he was the most delightful and kind insect and had exquisite taste. His wings were dressed in a harlequin pattern of pale yellow, sky blue, and soft pink. His body was loosely wrapped in a rich, golden-brown robe with a bronze tie, and he'd accessorised his antennae with pearl-like dots. Thick, turtle-shell glasses sat upon his nose.

Together, Blake and Brie made a memorable couple, and they were, very obviously, in love.

"Oh, it's just some simple stuff we threw on this morning, isn't it, Brie?" Blake replied, picking up the corner of his robe and sashaying it back and forth.

"I bought the antennae sparkles at Spyder's store, didn't I darling?"

"You did! Aren't they fabulous?" Blake reached up, pulled each one down and then let them rebound. They glittered as they caught the light.

"Gorgeous," Brie whispered to herself.

Blake turned his attention to Anton. "Now, darling, what can we do for you? By the way, we absolutely loved your show the other evening, didn't we, Brie?"

"Yes, we certainly did. So full of energy. Oh, I simply love Spyder. They're so..."

"... gorgeous?" Blake teased.

Brie shoved her partner playfully. "And that Honey B. Oh, my goodness! Such understated style. She should be a model, you know. Blake, could we use her?"

"I think we could, my lovely," he said, reflectively. "Tall, strong, boyishly feminine. She'd work perfectly in Proudlove, wouldn't she?"

"Do you know, I think she would," Brie agreed.

"Excellent," Anton interrupted, with just a hint of sarcasm.

"Sorry! Sorry, darling. We sometimes get waylaid, don't we, my love?" Brie leaned over and kissed her partner on the cheek, leaving a great dollop of red lipstick.

"Now. Anton. What was it? We're all ears," Blake said, blushing.

"The thing is, we, I mean the band, are going to try to, ah, reach the next level," said Anton. "You know, get a manager. Tour. Try to make a living from it."

Brie clapped her hands together vigorously. "Oh darling – what fabulous news! Isn't it Blakey?"

He grinned. "Oh, just fabulous! Bravo, Anton. I'm sure everything will work out. Now, sweetie," he leaned forward, "how can we help?"

"Well, we really need support with our social media. Up to now, it's been me handling everything but..."

Brie held up her hand. "Yes! We'd love to do it, wouldn't we darling?"

"Of course we would," Blake replied.

Anton sensed a slight hesitation in Blake's tone.

"Obviously, we'd pay you," Anton assured.

"Oh, darling, thank you! We can sort all that stuff out later when you become famous. We totally love Them Creepy Crawlies, don't we Blake?"

Blake nodded enthusiastically. "And do you know, Anton darling, there's something else we might be able to help with."

"Oh, do tell!" Brie turned to Anton. "I love it when he has an idea!"

"Well, we could..." Blake was bursting, "... help with your wardrobe! I'm sure we could source outfits. Proudlove for a start. And we'd put you on our Insecta page and our Antenna channel. What do you think?"

"Oh, yes sweetheart." Brie clapped her hands again. "An absolutely marvellous idea! Oh, do say yes, Anton!"

A big smile spread across Anton's face. "That sounds great, guys. I'll have to check with the others. Honey may need a bit of convincing, but Spyder will definitely be up for it. Listen, could you pop by The Basement this evening, and we can chat about everything?"

"We can do that, can't we Brie?"

"Oh, yes! Yes! Wonderful, wonderful! We'll be there." Brie got up and gave Anton a smothering hug.

"So gorgeous! Blake, honey, come on, let's go. I've already got a plan percolating."

"Excellent! Yes, let's get going. Remember, we have an unboxing and try-on for Eve later."

The two butterflies glided out of the café, poised and graceful, confident and sexy, knowing that, as always, everyone was watching them.

Anton's phone alarm beeped. He downed the last of his coffee. As part of the band's 'way forward', as Spyder liked to call it, they'd agreed that they needed a helper – a roadie. He had arranged to meet up with Spyder and one of their brood at the store just around the corner, and he didn't want to be late.

#

Anton arrived at Spyder's store to find them busy with a customer. He took a seat and waited.

"Is it worth anything?" the customer, a beetle, was asking eagerly.

Spyder held the round, flat object up to the light. It was heavy – they needed two hands to lift it – and bigger than their head. And filthy. You'd think they'd shine it up before trying to sell it, Spyder reflected. One side was engraved with a shape resembling a face, although it wasn't an insect, an arachnid, or any arthropod. There was a series of squiggles around the edge, and on the other side, the imprint of a flower they didn't recognise.

They made an offer. The beetle made a counteroffer, but without much conviction, so Spyder stood their ground. The customer handed over the payment and sidled out of the shop. Spyder would polish the object up and either sell it for a small profit or have one of their brood fashion it into some sort of sculpture.

Spyder's store specialised in vintage clothes, but also sold trinkets and knick-knacks. Much of the stock was donated, but they were happy to invest in any items that promised a profit. Spyder employed a small army of helpers – mostly orphaned young spiders adopted by the Abandoned Spider Youth Scheme, an initiative they'd established with Winnie and the Central Market Management Committee. The program taught them values and morals from an early age, sent them to school, and then provided job opportunities.

"Anton!" Spyder looked at their phone. "You're on time – amazing!"

"Yeah, yeah," Anton replied, accustomed to such greetings now.

"Come in, hon. Had a good day?"

Anton loved Spyder's store. He started to amble around, picking up odd items and examining them. "Yeah, great, thanks. Just met up with the social butterflies."

"Oh. How'd that go?"

"Ha! You know Brie and Blake," Anton chuckled, rummaging through a clothes rack. "They were super-keen to get involved. And, you'll like this..."

"Sy, honey! Can you come up here a minute!" Spyder called. They turned back to Anton. "What will I like?"

Anton explained Blake's idea. When he'd finished, Spyder grinned widely and punched the air as if they'd won the lotto.

"I think they mentioned a brand called Proudlove?"

Spyder let out a muffled squeal.

Sy appeared at the top of the stairs and watched, bemused, at Spyder's dance of joy.

"Sy, great." Spyder patted themself down. "You remember Anton from the band?"

"Hey, man!" Sy drawled, turning to Anton. "Enjoyed the vibes at the Cave, yeah. Real cool."

A fit and lithe spider, he wore sliders, beach shorts and a vest. He was training his hair to mat together into dreads that were contained by a red, yellow and green cap. A pair of sunnies perched on his brow.

"Thanks, Sy," replied Anton. "Are you a musician?"

Sy smiled at Spyder. "Tryin', dude. They got me learning the drums, of course."

"Got talent this one," Spyder said, bumping fists with Sy. "Laid back, but good at loads of things, aren't you, hon?"

Sy perched on Spyder's desk. "So, man, what can I do for you?"

Anton explained the 'way forward' – they needed an assistant they could rely on. Someone to help move equipment, run errands, work the door. Maybe later, learn to mix and manage the lights. Sy listened, nodding slowly.

"So, you want me to be the band roadie? Cool, man. And what will you pay me for that work?"

Spyder explained he would receive the same as he was paid now. But as soon as the band started to make some money, he would get more.

"Sweet! Sounds like a plan. I'm in, yeah?" Sy replied.

Anton looked at Spyder. "Great. If you're free later, pop round to The Basement and meet the gang." Sy said he'd come by after work and disappeared back down the stairs.

"Great! Shall we go now?"

Spyder grabbed their coat and the two friends set off for the charity shops.

#

Honey held her phone to her ear as gentle jazz played in the background. Honey loved jazz. She had first encountered it at school, where it had helped her concentrate during her exam revision. Of all the band members, Honey had the most eclectic taste in music. Jazz, country, folk, prog, pop – she actually liked a bit of everything.

Since their big meeting, Honey had been busy looking for a manager. She posted on several musician pages and received a bunch of applications. Three candidates stood out, and Honey had arranged to meet them at The Bee's Knees.

She had also gotten back to Marty, the praying mantis from Creation, who had put her on to his colleague Charli. This was who she was waiting for on the end of the line.

Finally, a bright and professional voice answered. "Hi. This is Charli. How can I help?"

Honey introduced herself.

"Hey, Honey! Marty said you'd be calling. How are things your end?"

"Yeah, really good thanks," Honey replied, a little nervously.

"So, what can I do for you?"

"Well, we met Marty after our last gig. He said he wanted to sign us, so I'm, like, following up on that."

"Cool! So, tell me a bit more about the band."

Honey put the phone on speaker and started pacing around the room, explaining.

"That sounds awesome," Charli said. "You know, of course, that this industry is not easy. A lot of young bands think they're ready, but few are. Do you have any experience dealing with touring and the business side of things?"

"Well, no – that's why we're talking, isn't it?"

"Absolutely," Charli replied. "We're looking for bands with something really unique. Let me ask you: what sets Them Creepy Crawlies apart?"

Honey was facing away from her telephone, gently tapping her foot. "Well, the music, of course. You have listened to us, haven't you?"

There was silence.

Feeling the need to assert herself, Honey picked up the phone. "Charli, can I ask you why we should work with you rather than another agency?"

"Oh, Honey," Charli replied condescendingly, "that's not how this works. There are hundreds of bands out there hoping to be the next big thing. Look, what I could offer you is a four-record deal. We'd pay for the studio time, of course. We'd expect you to go out on the road... don't worry, we'd provide the vehicle! I'm thinking... forty shows in year one? We'd handle all the publicity and your socials. Once the costs have been covered, you'd receive ten percent of net revenues. Naturally, we'd retain the rights to all your songs. How does that sound?"

Honey had no idea what a normal deal for unsigned bands sounded like, but she knew this wasn't for Them

Creepy Crawlies. "You're joking, right?" Honey scoffed. "You'd own all our songs?"

"Look, Honey, we could stretch to twelve-and-a-half per-cent, but only because Marty likes you. Maybe chat it over with the other band members?"

"I don't think so, Charli," Honey replied quickly. "You definitely won't be right for us. Thanks for your time though. All the best."

Honey rang off abruptly, shaking her head in disbelief. Anton was right – these agencies were all in it for them-selves. Frustrated, she headed to the coffee machine for what felt like the umpteenth time that day. After her bass guitar, it was her most prized possession. Espresso spluttered into the mug, and as she leaned against the bench, she surveyed the room – a generous space provided at a discount by her mum. Honey and Spyder lived in the flat above, owned also by her mother. The apartments were part of an ancient nest that had petrified over time and had been developed into an estate of modern living and co-working units. The location was now quite sought after, with charity shops among high fashion outlets, offices and cafés, one of which was Honey's current part-time workplace.

At the far end of the space, drums, amplifiers and guitars were set up so everyone could see each other. Earlier that day, Honey had shuffled stuff around to leave a space for the earwig who was coming to try out.

Coffee in hand, Honey took her laptop to the other side of the room. She tucked in her wings and sat down on the sofa, hiking her legs up on the coffee table in front of her.

She'd done enough work for the day. The others weren't due for a bit, so she had time to see what was happening on Insectagram.

There was a knock at the door. Honey looked at her phone. She must have nodded off. She rolled off the sofa and floated over to open it. There stood a gangly earwig with two bags slung over his shoulders, another bag hanging from an upper forearm, and two other smaller ones gripped beneath. His fringe hung over his eyes, and he kept trying unsuccessfully to flick it back into place.

He smiled awkwardly. "Hello. Er... you must be Honey B? I can see that because you're a bee. Well, of course you are. Hi. Sorry. Er... you're not a spider so you're not Spyder. And you're not Anton cos I've met Anton. Sorry..." Wiggy paused, feeling a little embarrassed, then tried to shake her hand, but as he stretched, his bags tumbled down his limbs. He attempted to hoist them back into place, but as one settled, another resisted. In the end, he gave up and shuffled past her with bags dangling.

Honey watched bemused as the awkward earwig carefully parked his luggage in a corner. He turned and offered his hand again.

"Pleased to meet you," he said, shaking Honey's hand vigorously. "I'm Wiggy. I'll just get the rest of my stuff," he said, retreating back outside.

"Sure you don't want a hand?" Honey called after him, but receiving no answer, she shook her head in mild disbelief.

Honey went around the room switching on all the lamps. The band had spent time making the space warm and inviting – posters, rugs, fabrics and soft lighting all contributed to the mellow atmosphere.

Wiggy returned with two keyboards, two guitars, and a spider. He'd bumped into Sy at the top of the steps, who had introduced himself as the band's roadie. Begrudgingly, Wiggy handed over one of his bags.

"G'day!" Sy said brightly, "I'm your new roadie." He smiled apologetically, carefully placing Wiggy's bag on the floor with the rest of his stuff before following him back outside. The two soon returned with a selection of stands.

"I hope there's enough room for you!" Honey said.

"Oh. Sure. Sure. This, er, should be fine," Wiggy mumbled as he began setting up his equipment. Sy watched, unsure what to do, as Honey returned to the sofa.

A few minutes later, Anton and Spyder bounded through the door. Anton dropped a stack of shopping bags onto an easy chair. He pulled a jacket from one and held it against his chest.

"Look what I've got!" he announced triumphantly.

"Cool," Honey nodded. "So, you guys have been op-shopping?"

Anton nodded excitedly, tossing aside the jacket, then grabbing a pair of pants to show her, followed by a shirt. Spyder looked on maternally as Honey responded with sardonic 'ohs' and 'ahs'.

The mini fashion show over, Anton turned his attention to the others. "Hey, Wiggy, good to see you! You've met Sy?

Welcome to The Basement, both of you. You got enough space for all your kit? This is Spyder."

"Hey man, how's it going? Really pleased to meet you!" Spyder navigated the bags to shake Wiggy's hand. "Anton's told us all about your ideas. Can't wait to hear 'em."

Wiggy smiled nervously and, unable to think of anything to say, returned to setting up.

Spyder then turned to their flatmate. "How's it going, Hon?" The two embraced and Spyder flopped onto the sofa, stretching. "Phew, busy day. And then Anton wanted to go shopping. How'd it go with the manager stuff?"

Honey sat beside Spyder. "I've shortlisted three. Agencies are a no-go." She opened her laptop and began to show her friend the details.

"Anyone want a coffee?" Anton called from the kitchen as the machine ground out a fresh cup. "Wiggy?" There was no reply – Wiggy was absorbed in his set-up.

Armed with an espresso, Anton plonked down on an easy chair, throwing his feet onto some magazines on the coffee table.

"What do they look like?" he asked.

"Yeah. Interesting," replied Spyder.

"What about Creative?" Anton asked, sipping his espresso.

Honey gazed back at him, shaking her head. "Unbelievable." She recounted the conversation with Charli and the deal she'd offered.

Anton shrugged. "Told you, didn't I?"

Honey smiled back at Anton. "Yup... anyway," she continued, "Everything's set for tomorrow at The Bee's Knees. 2 pm, Anton. Don't be late!"

Anton pulled a friendly ugly face at Honey and made to get up. "So, guys, super-exciting to have our first jam with Wiggy, yeah? I've been working on some new songs, so I thought we could learn them together."

Honey and Spyder nodded their approval.

"And then maybe we could hear some of Wiggy's ideas on the old stuff?"

"Sounds good to me," agreed Spyder, making their way to the drums.

"Oh, by the way, I've asked Brie and Blake to call by. They're super-keen to take on our social media, Honey. Might even get us to dress up for their Antenna channel."

"Mmm, okay... that sounds interesting," Honey said cautiously. "Great about the socials, but dressing up...?"

"Nah, babe," Spyder said. "You'll love it!" They turned their attention to Wiggy who stood behind a bank of keyboards. "So, Wiggy man, are you happy to do some new stuff first?"

With a guitar wrapped over his shoulder, computer sparkling and keyboard flashing, Wiggy had transformed. "No," he said purposely. "Let's play your setlist from the other night and we'll see if you like my ideas."

Spyder squinted back at him, impressed at his bluntness.

"Fair enough." Anton turned to Honey, who nodded.

"Right. What was the first song we did?" Spyder asked.

"Phonographique," Wiggy replied without a pause.

"Phono it is! Everyone ready?" Spyder paused, their sticks in the air. "One. Two. Three. Four…"

The band worked through the setlist. Wiggy added extra guitar fills here and keyboard embellishments there, sometimes looping parts or suggesting a new rhythm. At the end of a song, they'd chat, agree or not, try something new, or simply smile or giggle with enthusiasm.

During the third song, Brie and Blake appeared. They'd dressed down for the evening, both now clothed entirely in black. "Don't mind us," they waved after the song had finished, so the band continued as the butterflies snapped photos and clips. They even press-ganged Sy into holding lights as they slinked around the musicians, mostly staying out of their way.

When Anton suggested a break, they all retired to the sofa and easy chairs. Sy, having discovered the fridge and coffee machine, took orders while Brie and Blake reviewed their work on the kitchen bench. Soon, conversation turned to social media plans, campaigns and clothes. The gang buzzed with excitement as everyone shared their ideas.

After a coffee, they returned to try out some of Anton's new tracks. Brie suggested capturing the songs' incubation would create great content, while Blake suggested that when they were famous, the footage could be used for a 'making of' documentary. No one doubted he was serious.

At exactly ten o'clock, Wiggy abruptly announced that he had to go. He said he hoped that his audition had gone well, asked if he could leave his stuff until later, and swept out of the room. After a few more songs, Brie and Blake said their goodbyes, which was the cue to call it a night. Sy did his best to clear up, and with everyone else gone, the three original Them Creepy Crawlies collapsed onto the sofa.

"Well, what do you guys think of Wiggy?" Anton asked his bandmates.

"Dude, I think it was completely *crazy*," Spyder replied, stretching out every limb as they relaxed. "I mean, he's a little *different*, isn't he, but some of the stuff he was coming up with was totally whack, man. What did you think, Hon?"

Honey, uncharacteristically animated, agreed. "He brings so many possibilities, and I think he'll fit easily into our little band of diverse souls."

"Okay. So, it's settled? We'll ask Wiggy to join the band?"

"Absolutely!" Spyder agreed, stifling a yawn.

"Honey?"

"It's a yes from me."

"Cool," Anton said. "I'll call him tomorrow."

"Right. We'll leave you to lock up, Anton. See you tomorrow at two."

Anton watched his two bandmates take their leave. He leaned back, as happy as he'd felt in quite a long while.

5

The Manager

Anton called around midday. When Wiggy saw who was ringing, his heart jumped. He'd been sitting at his computer all morning trying without success to concentrate, waiting for the call. He literally squealed with excitement when Anton broke the good news. He knew the jam/audition had gone well and had felt nervously confident they had liked what he'd done. He just wasn't confident that they had liked him. But that was all okay now.

Anton asked him if he'd like to come over to The Bee's Knees to help interview the potential managers. Wiggy said that he appreciated being asked, but he was too busy. That he was working on a security system for a client that he had to finish asap. That it was super-important, and he couldn't let them down. That he really wanted to be there, but...

"It's really okay," Anton said with a giggle. "Don't worry. Seriously, man. We'll catch up with you later, alright?"

Wiggy apologised once more and thanked Anton again before ringing off. He threw his phone on the workbench and twirled his chair round and round, silently punching the air. He was in a band! He was in Them Creepy Crawlies!

From being a bit glum, Wiggy was now totally wired. He marched over to a guitar, threw it over his shoulder, flicked the switch on the back of the amp, turned the volume up and hammered out a chord over and over again. The chord became a screeching solo, his fingers running up and down the fretboard at a million miles an hour. More thrashy chords. Lots of feedback. Then he sang out the words to an old standard he'd learned years ago. Then another. And another.

Finally, exhausted but still elated, he dumped the guitar on his sofa and collapsed beside it. He sat there for a while, beaming with the biggest smile and then, after some more uncoordinated punches in the air, he got up, went to the other side of the room and dropped into the big seat in front of his main terminal. He had work to do.

He grabbed the takeaway cup that had been sitting on his desk for a couple of days and sucked up some of the flat but still sugary liquid. He went to work on his keyboard while keeping his eyes firmly on the screen, watching things change. Distractedly, he grabbed a handful of two-day-old popcorn from a bowl in front of him, most of which fell onto his lap before he could swallow it. Kept tapping, watching, over and over.

He squinted, then pulled his chair over to an adjacent screen, crushing a scatter of popcorn. He tapped, and the new monitor came to life, displaying a maze of connecting lines and formulae. He nodded at the detail and, content with what he found, punched a key from another keyboard, and a third screen lit up, allowing the display from the second to stretch between the two. He sucked on the drink. It gurgled. He pushed the straw further down, but after a moment the gurgling stopped, so he dropped it into the bin under the workbench. He splashed another handful of popcorn around his mouth and carried on tapping and watching.

Then he stopped.

He scratched his head. Hit some keys. Nodded. Smiled. Wiggy pushed his chair back and stretched. He examined the screen again. Everything seemed as it should be.

"I may actually have done it," he said out loud. He looked at his watch. It was now mid-afternoon. He'd lost all track of time. "I may have just built the world's most brilliant cybersecurity framework."

He'd built it like a game. Anyone who wanted to access the data would need to find a key to each of the four levels of scaffold. But the process didn't happen on a screen. Oh, no – that would've been far too simple. That was the beauty of Wiggy's system. He'd designed it to operate *in the subconscious*. The first password was hidden in a memory, the second in a dream, the third in an emotion, with the final key hidden in imagination. You could tell you were getting near the password because you'd feel warmer, colder as you moved away. When a key was found – and Wiggy was particularly pleased with this – everything would reset: a new memory, a new emotion, etc. The password was updated each time someone passed a level.

Wiggy knew it was brilliant. Theoretically, anyway. He had to test it. And for that, he needed an interface between his subconscious and The Cloud, the place the contact had told him where the data he was tasked with defending was stored.

With his heart beating a little bit quicker, he twisted his chair towards a flycase and flicked the latches, lifting off the top section. Instead of a guitar amp, the container housed a homemade neural resonator that would act as the connector.

He lifted it carefully and, turning, examined it closely. It looked like something between a crown and a piece of experimental audio equipment – an intricate mesh of glinting filaments and flexible circuit tendrils. He pulled a tiny trigger, and it began to pulse softly.

Wiggy placed it on his head. The bioluminescent panels shimmered faintly along the rim as it locked to his neural frequency. Fine, whisker-like antennae then rose gently from the sides, twitching as they began to capture his brainwave patterns.

Of course, it was a super-basic resonator. He had substituted artificial polymers for chitin memory plates, and the conductive threads were organic – but he was pretty sure it wouldn't fry his brain.

He adjusted the angle until it felt right, then touched the right side of the cranial loop. Thin filaments slid through his hair and fastened themselves to the other side. He paused for a moment, then tapped the Bluetooth pairing button.

His vision wavered, his basement dissolving into strips and segments, like analogue film from a reel. It settled on an image of the previous night's band practice. He was on the first level.

#

While Wiggy was exploring his memory, Anton, Spyder and Honey sat around a table at the back of The Bee's Knees. They had just interviewed the second candidate.

"Wow! Phillip would be brilliant," Spyder said, excitedly.

"Absolutely," Honey agreed, looking at her notes. "Better than Mary?"

"Definitely!" Spyder and Anton replied in unison. Mary, a mosquito, had turned out to be totally unsuitable, but Phillip, a mayfly, had ticked all their boxes. Leave the music to the band... tick. Don't interfere creatively... tick. Experienced with social media... tick. Operations... tick.

"He obviously has a passion for the business of music," said Honey.

"And he won't suck the life out of us," Spyder added, prompting a fit of giggles from Honey and Anton. They didn't, therefore, notice the final applicant arrive.

"You must be Them Creepy Crawlies? Good afternoon. My name is Terry. May I take a seat?" he said, taking a seat.

Quickly pulling themselves together, they looked up and were surprised to see an overweight termite who was probably their parents' age. Dressed formally in a dark suit, Terry sported slicked-back hair over a plump, well-lived-in face, with heavy dark glasses. He leaned on a white-tipped stick.

"You must be Anton? And you're Spyder... and Honey?" Terry turned to each in turn, then very deliberately, removed his hat and set it on the table in front of him.

"Pleased to meet you all."

Honey cleared her throat, smiled, and invited the termite to share his background. He spoke slowly and confidently with an inner-city drawl that was thick as treacle. He chose words easily – to the point, nothing wasted. He explained he had originally served in the armed forces and that, demobbed, he'd opened a boxing club and gymnasium. Now, he mainly undertook small projects for private clients.

Anton thanked him for sharing this, said that it was very interesting, and could he talk a bit about his band management experience, to which Terry calmly replied that he'd never managed a band. This prompted confused glances around the table.

"But your resume shows a list of bands and what you did for them," Honey observed, scrolling through Terry's resume.

"I made it up," Terry replied, matter-of-factly.

"Excuse me?"

Terry returned Spyder's stare and repeated, "I made it up. You wouldn't have invited me here if I'd had no experience." He fixed his gaze on Honey. "Am I right?"

Honey frowned. "Well, yes, of course." She didn't know whether to feel intimidated or tell him her life story. "Well...

thank you, but I think we can bring this interview to an end." She began shuffling papers.

But Terry remained in his chair. "I like to invest in people and projects that I think will provide me a return." Terry paused and very deliberately looked at Anton, Spyder and Honey in turn before continuing. "Before I leave, can I say how much I enjoyed your show the other night? I saw how much the crowd loved you."

"You were there?" Anton asked, surprised.

"I was. The way I see it, if you can generate that sort of love in your hometown, you can do it anywhere in the world. My network of contacts is extremely wide. I can help you do that."

"Okay, I'll bite," Anton said, intrigued. "How?"

Terry walked the three young musicians through his resume, discussing various projects and clients and explained how his skills and connections were transferable – how he could use them to help the band.

"But let me ask you this, Anton, what are the goals of Them Creepy Crawlies?"

Anton looked at Spyder, who immediately said 'success'. Then Honey mentioned touring, and then added that she just wanted to be happy. Anton offered a few personal dreams – a new guitar, somewhere nice to live.

"Most of these are personal," Terry said when the three friends had finished their wishlists. "Think about where you want the band to be in one, two, or five years. New guitars or fame and fortune will follow once you achieve those goals. Do you understand?"

Honey looked at Spyder, who looked at Anton. They all started to nod.

"Good." Terry reached into his briefcase and handed Honey an envelope.

"I've taken the liberty of booking you all into a planning workshop. I've emailed you the details." Before they could respond, Terry continued, "And I assume you want to cut a new record?"

The band looked at each other, pursed their lips, and raised their eyebrows as you do when you're thinking 'well... yes, obviously'.

"Of course you do! So, I've booked Ant Hill Studios for you from next Friday for a week."

Spyder's eyes narrowed. They held up a hand. "Whoa, mister! This is supposed to be our interview. First question, yeah? Like, who's paying for this?"

Terry replied coolly. "Me. Like I said, I invest in things that will make me a profit. You will repay me when you are doing well. Honey, you understand business and money, don't you?" He opened his briefcase for a second time and withdrew a second, larger envelope. "This is a business plan for Them Creepy Crawlies. Go through it carefully. Show a lawyer. Show your parents. And then get back to me and let me know if you want to move forward."

Terry closed his briefcase, replaced his hat, stood up and said, "Anton, Honey, Spyder, it's been a pleasure." With a final tip of the hat, he shuffled out of The Bee's Knees and disappeared into the market, leaving the band speechless.

Spyder puffed their cheeks out and slowly blew out the air. "What a blooming liberty. Who does he think he is?"

"He'd certainly done his homework. I sort of liked him," Honey remarked, flicking through the proposal. "I mean, he's no-nonsense for sure, a bit scary, perhaps. But underneath his plain speaking, there was a warmth. Didn't you think so?"

Anton shook and nodded slowly. "Yeah... maybe. But he lied his way in here, didn't he? Do you think we can trust him?"

"But isn't that the sort of insect we want?" Honey asked. "Someone with initiative? A go-getter?"

As evening drew in, the market stalls began their closing routines and customers drifted away to their various sunset tasks. In The Bee's Knees café, however, three musicians remained huddled at a corner table deep in conversation. Honey voted for Terry. Anton was adamant they should choose Phillip, while Spyder remained on the fence. They all appreciated Phillip's industry insights. He was passionate, likable, and experienced in managing bands. Honey said he might lack the hunger they desired. Spyder worried that Terry's experience lay outside the music industry. Anton repeated his concern about Terry's honesty. It was just a feeling, but there was something 'off' about him. Honey read out extracts of his business plan, which seemed to make sense. What finally convinced Spyder was the fact that Terry had invested his own money in them. In the end, by a two-to-one vote, they agreed to give Terry a chance.

Anton stood up and stretched. "Democracy rules! Come on, then, let's head out and celebrate."

6

The Rise of Them
Creepy Crawlies

Planets aligning. Cosmic convergence. A confluence of factors. A culmination of events. All these phrases imply a variety of elements and circumstances, not always positive, can come together in a weird way to produce something significant.

It took only six months from the *big meeting* for Them Creepy Crawlies to become one of the world's most talked-about new bands. But as any successful outfit will tell you, while luck plays a part, you have to have talent, you have to be hard-working, and you have to have a plan.

Whiteboards, sticky labels, and coloured pens? Critical success factors and strategic planning frameworks? It wasn't very rock 'n' roll, but the four band members approached their planning workshop with good humour. Anton, Honey, Spyder and Wiggy all agreed that if they wanted to be full-time musicians, they needed money. To make money, they needed stuff to sell and lots of eager buyers.

This was the big plan, then. It wasn't rocket science, but at least they were on the same page. They also had smaller plans to support the big one. For example, for the stuff they were going to sell, like music and merchandise, they needed a product plan. To build fans and followers, they needed a marketing plan. To manage the money, they needed a finance plan, and to make it all happen, they needed an operations plan. All of this was Terry's responsibility.

The first thing Terry did was activate the touring plan. It was long with lots of shows. Small and bigger venues. He was careful in his planning. He wanted to push them. Force them to be tight. Explore not only the music but also themselves and their relationships. He also wanted them to have plenty of time for jamming, choosing practice rooms along the route with care, hoping that the experiences might spark creativity.

In the beginning, the band approached the tour with youthful exuberance – as if they were all on holiday together. None of them considered that anything could go wrong, convinced that they were above setbacks. But even though Spyder and Honey lived together, they hadn't spent more than a couple of hours with Anton at any one time. And, of course, no one really knew Wiggy. But who cared? They were bulletproof; and now, of course, they were professional musicians.

At first, it *was* like a honeymoon – everything was new, fun, and filled with parties. But once the reality of life on the road kicked in, they started to get to know each other, started to work each other out. Musically, they played some good gigs and some not-so-good gigs. The bad ones were generally because the crowd didn't know their music. This was a learning curve because they'd never experienced an audience that didn't cheer them on. At home, even if they were supporting another act, they were new and local, and everyone was rooting for them. Now, however, they weren't on home soil, and the audiences could be fickle.

Spyder suggested that when crowds were indifferent, they should try harder to connect. Anton found this difficult because he liked to stick to his own style and was uncomfortable with having to act. On one occasion, he became so angry, shouting at the crowd to shut up during a song. The result was a barrage of abuse, so Anton threw them the bird and walked off stage. Sy had to usher them out of the back door.

Later that night, they had their first band argument. Spyder was unhappy that Anton had abandoned them. Anton said they should have followed him. Honey said that he had to learn to deal with hecklers, that she had to put up with arthros who stood in front of her, leering. Anton said she shouldn't wear provocative outfits. That got Spyder's hackles up – same old Anton, they said. Honey said to Spyder that she could fight her own battles.

"And *you're* always so impatient and short-tempered," she continued.

"And you're always so bloody perfect, Miss Goody Two-Shoes," Spyder shot back.

"Don't call her that," Wiggy replied, with a rare show of passion.

"I beg your pardon?" Spyder replied. "And when are you ever going to tidy up after yourself?"

"Well, when are you going to stop mummying me?" Wiggy grumbled back. "It's, like, embarrassing when you threaten to put me over your knee."

"That's just so *you*, isn't it, Spyder?" Anton scoffed. "Always trying to make out you're the mature one."

"Oh, my goodness, Anton!" Spyder gasped. "If only you had the slightest bit of maturity, you wouldn't be so lazy. Or late."

"They're right," Honey scolded. "I mean, I have to remind you about stuff all the time. When are you going to step up? Take an interest in what's going on around you?"

"Me – step up?" Anton fired back. "Says you who always has her nose in a book!"

The following morning, however, while having coffee, they shared a laugh about the whole conversation – and promised to work on their flaws. It was all part of the learning process.

At the start of the tour, the three original band members had made sure Wiggy was included in everything. He treated every new experience with childlike enthusiasm, asking questions and listening intently. The others began to look on him as a younger sibling. He always wanted an ice-cream: three scoops in a big cone. It was endearing, so sharing an ice cream became their pre-gig ritual.

Over time, Anton began to bond with Wiggy and even took him on a Parade of the Possible march in support of inter-species relationships. But Wiggy didn't like big crowds or the noise. He called it a sensory overload, so he chose to skip most of these events, preferring to be absorbed in his laptop. He always had some work on.

As the tour progressed, the band began generating increasingly positive reviews. Word spread that this was a band worth listening to. Fans admired their look, how they acted, and most of all, their authenticity. The non-binary spider who shouldn't be messed with, the super-talented neurodivergent earwig, the chic punk bee, and the socially conscious ant, who never ran out of things to say. Spyder, Wiggy, Honey B and Anton were *them*. Of course, this wasn't down to chance – Blake and Brie were very good at their jobs.

So, despite the odd hiccup, the band was coming on very nicely.

And then Honey received a text from her mother. Ironically, it was after they'd played their biggest show so far. As the music filled the hall and the crowd cheered, Honey had never felt more connected to the band, the crew, the audience, and her new way of life.

"I saw some pictures of you. Call me," the text had said simply. Honey was taken aback by the curt, sharp tone. Despite Honey's occasional texts to her mother, explaining where she was and what she was doing, she hadn't heard from her in ages.

Later that evening, she showed Anton. No one had spoken much about their parents or their background, but Honey knew that Anton was estranged from his family. That may have been one of the reasons they had grown closer. For his part, Anton knew that Honey's mother was distantly related to a bee queen and that she was rich (although she wasn't interested in that type of lifestyle).

So, after Spyder and Sy went clubbing and Wiggy retired to bed, Honey and Anton stayed back at the hotel. They talked quietly about why Anton's mother had never shown him any affection and what he might have done to deserve it. For Honey's mother, it was all about image. She'd always told her daughter that she loved her, but Honey felt there were always strings attached. That evening, they decided to visit their mothers together, hoping they'd find some courage in each other's support.

#

When they arrived at Anton's house, his mother greeted them at the door with a polite smile. No hugs, no excitement – just a quiet 'come in'. She led them into the sitting room, brought out tea and biscuits, and offered them around. When she sat down, her eyes were impassive, her gaze flicking between Anton and Honey, thin lips pressed together in a tight smile. Anton shifted uncomfortably; it all felt too formal, a bit surreal. The sitting room was filled with memories of Christmas and birthday teas, TV shows, first kisses, and childhood silences – a place where he and his mother had shared quiet company as he grew up. There had been no father. Anton had asked about him many times, but his mother was never forthcoming.

They exchanged small talk about the weather and the neighbours, and Anton wondered if he had done the right thing to visit.

"So," his mother said, folding her hands in her lap. "Why now?"

Anton blinked. "S-sorry. What do you mean?"

She leaned back, and the creases on her forehead furrowed. "You left. You haven't been back. You haven't been in touch." She glanced at Honey quickly. "Why come back now?"

His mother's brittle, distant smile returned. He knew she was lying when she said, "And, by the way, as you can see, I've been fine."

Honey shifted beside him and, almost imperceptibly, pressed her hand into the side of Anton's thigh. Comforting, reassuring. Urging him to continue. His pulse quickened. He'd convinced himself that he didn't need his mother's approval, that he was better off without her baggage. But now, here in this room, he felt vulnerable and guilty for leaving.

"I don't know. I wanted to show you... I mean, I wanted you to see what I had achieved," he said, his voice rougher than he intended.

For a moment, his mother was silent, her eyes searching his. "You're doing well?" she asked finally, although her voice was guarded. "The band? I just hope it's what you really want."

Something flared in Anton. Resentment? Frustration?

"It is... How would you know what I want, anyway?" The words slipped out before he could stop them. His mother flinched, and he instantly regretted what he'd said – although he saw something else in her eyes, which flickered and vanished. A softness, maybe. Or a regret hidden amongst all that disapproval.

He wanted to apologise, but he couldn't bring himself to. Instead, he thought back to his first school concert. He'd been learning the guitar for a while, playing in beginner ensembles, feeling fine. But then he was due to perform in public for the first time. Just him. On his own. In front of the school.

As the moment got closer, the nerves had built until, just before he was due to go on, to his everlasting embarrassment, he threw up. He barely had time to compose himself before his impatient music teacher shoved him onto the stage, but no one had warned him about the lights. They blinded him, obscuring most of the crowd. That helped. He spotted his mother, a friendly silhouette beyond the glow. A kind face, willing him on. He had focused on it and managed to start the song.

When the closing note drifted over the hushed audience, there had been a beat of silence. Then, the cheers had hit him. At first, he smiled meekly, but as whoops and whistles filled the air, he burst with the widest grin. Later at home, his mother, uncharacteristically, had told him how proud she was. That he had made her cry. He was pleased that he'd made her happy because he knew she wasn't happy very often. He couldn't think of another time she had expressed any support for him.

Now, as she stared out of the window, lost in a faraway thought, an awkward silence filled the neat little room. Anton felt his fingers curl into a fist, then relax as Honey placed her hand on his. All he'd ever wanted was a simple, 'how was your day, love?' It would have meant the world. But his mother's silence fuelled his rebellion: skipping classes, refusing chores, out until all hours. Tattoos, tatty clothes. *Give me a reaction* they screamed, but none was ever forthcoming. In the end, he'd asked himself, 'what's the point?' – and so had dropped out of school and left home.

"More tea," his mother murmured to herself as if it would solve everything. She retreated to the kitchen, not waiting for an answer.

Anton exhaled, a strange ache in his chest. "Maybe this was a mistake," he muttered.

Honey shook her head, her eyes steady on his. "No. Sometimes you have to try, even if it doesn't turn out how you want."

His mother returned with a tray carrying three new mugs of tea and a plate of mini cakes. She placed them on the table with careful precision. "Orange cakes. They were your favourite, weren't they?"

No one went for a cup, but Anton took a cake, the familiar taste a small comfort.

He looked up and caught his mother's eye. Did he see a flicker of pride there? *It's just me, hoping.*

He searched the floor, and whispered, "Why, mum?" Forcing himself to look at her, he continued, "Why could you never support what I did? Didn't you know I was desperate for some sign of approval?"

His mother looked shocked. "What do you mean? Of course, I did." She stood up, asking politely: "Now, Honey, more tea?" When Honey declined, she busied herself, tidying away, avoiding any more conversation on the subject.

As they said their goodbyes, Anton felt the ache of things left unsaid. Nothing had been resolved. They hugged awkwardly, and for a brief moment, her hand lingered on his shoulder. "Will you come back and see me again?"

Anton looked at his mum, surprised. "Sure, mum." He took Honey's hand. "And maybe you could come to a show?"

His mum smiled and Anton saw the faintest sparkle come into her eyes. It lifted him. He gave the small, faded house one last look and felt a strange blend of sadness and relief.

#

Honey had agreed with her mother to meet at a café. Neutral territory. She sat nervously in her fishnets, a miniskirt, and a blouse buttoned up to her neck. At least she wouldn't be accused of showing her cleavage. Beside her, Anton wore frayed black pants and a white tee-shirt with a band motif across his chest. They both wore sunglasses, a more common accessory these days.

Her mother approached, smart and stylish. Honey straightened, gripping Anton's hand a little tighter.

"Honey," her mother said a little out of breath, surveying her daughter critically. There was a note of distaste in her tone. Her eyes flicked to Anton, lingering on his attire before she turned back to her daughter. "I see you brought company."

"Mum, this is my friend Anton," Honey said firmly. Her mother acknowledged him with a curt nod.

He extended his hand, hoping a friendly grin might defuse the tension. "Nice to meet you."

She hesitated before accepting. "Likewise," she replied.

Honey's mother immediately updated her daughter on family goings-on. Mainly who had achieved what. The work that had to be done to the house. The garden. She had had to let some staff go.

"So, sweetheart," her mother said, folding her arms neatly. "I was hoping we could talk about... well, you."

Honey braced herself. "Yeah, I figured."

Her mother's gaze swept over her daughter's outfit. "You've certainly... changed," she said. "I hardly recognised you."

Honey, no longer the little girl in pretty dresses who loved riding and playing the cello, who had so much 'potential', felt her jaw tighten. "Well, I'm still here, Mum. Just... appreciating different things."

"I know, darling. I can see that. But I'm worried. *This* lifestyle." She gestured vaguely at Honey and Anton. "The pop group. It doesn't seem like something you'd choose if you were thinking clearly."

Honey took a steadying breath, fighting back her bubbling irritation. "Mum, I *am* thinking clearly. I didn't just fall into this – I chose it. I've found a life that means something to me. Friends I can count on who appreciate me for who I am."

Her mother sighed, shifting her gaze to the napkin she was carefully folding. "So, you're telling me these causes and communities... are more important than your family?"

Honey's words were soft yet resolute. "No, Mum! I love my family. I'm just asking you to try to understand and accept who I am now."

There was a long, heavy pause. Honey hoped it might bridge the gap between them. Her mother took a slow sip of water, but her expression hardened.

"What would you have me understand?" Her voice was clipped. "You've aligned yourself with..." Again, she waved her arms vaguely, unable – or unwilling – to articulate the word. "With people I just don't understand. All this rejection of decency, and respectability."

As if on cue, a young butterfly and bee approached their table shyly.

"C-c-could we get a selfie, Honey?" the little bee asked nervously.

Honey broke into a large, friendly smile. "Sure, you guys – of course." The bee held up her phone and snapped away. "Can we get one with Anton as well?" the butterfly added.

The four of them gathered for a quick shot, drawing curious glances from neighbouring tables.

"Thanks, Honey!" the butterfly squealed as she and the bee made to leave. "We love you. You too, Anton!"

As Anton returned to his seat, he addressed Honey's mum. His voice was gentle but firm. "With all due respect, that's your interpretation. But I see someone who *has* found her place... and people who respect her talent."

Honey watched her mother's expression as Anton spoke passionately about the band, the tour, and the future. Her face remained sharp, her lips pursed, and when Anton had finished, she turned her focus back to her daughter.

"Is this what you truly want, Honey?" Her voice wavered slightly, and her eyes, usually so guarded, now looked reflective. "To live this way? To be part of this world?"

Honey's heart tightened. Behind the polished exterior, she sensed her mother struggling, clinging to a daughter who no longer existed. Honey felt sad. She longed for the insect across the table to accept her new life. This mother who had raised her, who had kissed her goodnight every night.

"Yes, I do," Honey replied softly, feeling Anton's supportive hand on her arm. "But I also want you to be part of it. I'm not asking you to understand everything, just to accept that this is me now and that I'm happy."

Her mother stared at her with an unreadable expression. Then, quite abruptly, she stood, brushing down her skirt, gathering her thoughts. "I don't know if I can do that, Honey."

The words hung heavily. Not surprising; just disappointing. She gave Anton a short nod.

"I'll always love you, Honey. But I can't pretend to support... this." She gestured again, encapsulating her daughter's life in a single sweeping motion, before bending down and kissing her on both cheeks. And then, without another word, she turned and walked out of the café.

Honey listened, emotionless, as the sound of her mother's clicking heels faded away. Anton kept hold her hand.

7

The Hornets

In another territory, another child considered a parent. Queen Vespa looked at the portrait in the centre of the mantlepiece. Her mother, Velutina, stared out between two other photographs. One showed her and her seven sisters, all grinning happily. The other was the photo of her and Hal that she'd posted on Insectagram all those years ago. She smiled at her husband, then picked up the frame and gently kissed his image before carefully replacing it.

Today was her wedding anniversary. Today was the anniversary of the slaughter of her family. But today would also be her day of justice.

Vespa caught a glimpse of herself in the mirror. Her large black eyes still shone above sharply chiselled cheekbones. Her chin was a little longer, but her lips were still full and protruded handsomely from her face. The small creases at the edges of her eyes and her mouth betrayed not just advancing years but also a weight borne wearily.

Her quiet reflection was interrupted.

"Your Majesty." Her Chief Advisor bowed.

"Zir Hugh – I'm pleased to see you."

"Thank you, my dear. And may I ask how you are today?"

Only Zir Hugh referred to her in such affectionate terms, and only ever in private. Since that hideous day, he had been her pillar. It was he who had issued those haunting words – *"they've all been poisoned"* – and told her she had survived because she hadn't been drinking. It was he who had accompanied her back to the royal quarters. Then, he'd provided a shoulder to cry on as well as a wall for her anger and frustration. He had become like a dear uncle as well as an advisor. Vespa knew she could trust him with her life.

How was she feeling? How would anyone feel on such a painful day? Time had provided some medicine, but at night when she closed her eyes, she could still see the bodies of her family sprawled grotesquely around the table of death – limbs outstretched, throats clutched, eyes frozen open.

Vespa moved to the window where the white curtains fluttered softly. Outside, way beyond The Nest, in the Central Square, swarms of hornets were gathering. They were joined by a mix of species from nearby villages, employed on the many new developments happening in The Grove, the traditional home of Vespa and her ancestors. Thousands more had come from surrounding territories to watch the spectacle.

She remembered how news of that day had spread across the world almost instantly. Somehow, photos of her husband, cold and unresponsive, and her mother's grotesque poses made their way onto social media. The global reaction was one of disbelief and sorrow. Other arthro leaders were swift to offer their condolences. How could such brutality occur in this modern era? There was a strong resolve that the perpetrators be brought to justice. Yet, within a few days of the tragedy, most of the world had turned its attention to the next chapter in the global news cycle.

"I'm fine, Zir Hugh," she lied, standing straighter. "This is a day we have waited a long time for."

"It is indeed," the royal retainer replied. He knew that the complete massacre of Vespa's family would have inevitably resulted in the collapse of the Grove Hornets. Leaderless, the drones and workers would have scattered or perished. But Vespa had survived, and so did their society. Although the world eventually forgot, Vespa was determined to find the perpetrators. Who would have wanted this destruction? Someone internally? Another hornet community? Another species?

"Summon Hendrix, will you, Zir Hugh."

Her lengthy mourning period, spent alone in her quarters, had given Vespa time to reflect. When she emerged, it was with a determination to build on her mother's lifelong work to ensure that the hornets – *her* hornets – would grow and thrive and be proud. In the days following her coronation, she assembled a team of advisors, some old and some new, and instructed them to bring her a plan. They returned with strategies in four areas: infrastructure, education and innovation, defense, and law and order. Colonel Hendrix was responsible for the latter. His influence, though, also extended to the other portfolios.

Zir Hugh bowed and, without a word, slipped away.

Queen Vespa had never taken to Hendrix. She sensed a darkness behind his eyes, faint shadows rooted deeply in his past. His father had been a quiet, efficient civil servant who had risen to become Minister in the Department of Civic Harmony. His mother, by contrast, was a decorated and battle-hardened war hero. She was a stern and imposing figure, intolerant of weakness.

From an early age, Hendrix bore the weight of his mother's unrealistic expectations and constant criticisms. At home, he was continually reminded that he would never match her battlefield glories. At school, his lack of social skills made him an easy target for bullies.

The bruises he carried – emotional and physical – hardened into armour and forged in him a ruthless determination. To his mother's scorn, he joined the army, where he quickly gained a reputation for precision and control. He rose through the ranks not because of charisma or popularity, but through sheer, relentless efficiency. Most surprisingly, he discovered a talent for violence, which he was happy to nurture.

Vespa knew Hendrix was clever, ruthless, and unwaveringly patriotic. On his advice, she established the Federal Security Service with him as commanding officer. Its purpose was to safeguard the community from both internal and external threats. Disciplined, methodical, and loyal, every young hornet aspired to wear the slick dark uniform and black-and-yellow stinger insignia of the FSS.

As time wore on, however, their methods became the subject of whispered concerns. Rumours of detentions without trial, over-zealous surveillance, and the use of informants within civil society drew comparisons to some of the darker chapters in arthropod history. Queen Vespa wasn't unaware of the rumours, harbouring a faint unease about the service's methods – but she was determined to maintain unity and order at all costs.

"Your Majesty."

Vespa turned to find a hornet in immaculate uniform standing firmly at attention. When she had first met Hendrix, she was taken by his size. Instead of a strong, bulking hornet, Colonel Hendrix was slight and wiry. He spoke in quiet, precise tones, often peering over the top of his spectacles. Apart from a prominent scar on his cheek, he would have looked more at home in a university campus than on a battlefield. Still, he had a reputation as both an effective administrator and a formidable soldier.

"Colonel Hendrix," she replied, holding the back of her palm towards him. "I trust everything is in place?"

Hendrix took his Queen's hand and bowed formally, clipping his heels as he did. He then stood to attention and replied in the affirmative.

"Good. Now, please, come and join me," she indicated a chair. "Tell me about your trip to The Lowlands."

The Lowlands weren't defined by borders, nor did they have a government, a constitution, or even a permanent population. Instead, there was an understanding between swarms, collectives, kaleidoscopes, and orchestras that Lowland residents should work individually for the good of all. And in general, the region had thrived. Pollinators kept the land abundant in blossoms, so agriculture and infrastructure flourished. But the gains for primary industries and public works came at the expense of defense. Nature saw to it that Queens produced more workers but fewer soldiers, which, after a while, led to a rise in crime. The elders gathered to discuss what action to take and decided to outsource homeland security and policing. Colonel Hendrix had just returned from presenting the Grove Hornets' tender.

The Colonel smiled at his Queen. It wasn't the type of smile that engaged all facial muscles. His forehead, eyes, nostrils, lips and chin remained expressionless. Hendrix smiled only with his mouth.

"Everything went very smoothly, Your Majesty." He spoke very deliberately. "I presented our proposal and impressed on their congress our assets and our ability to activate them immediately."

Hendrix's negotiation tactics had been simple. In a show of strength, he had ordered regiments of hornets to assemble on the edge of The Lowlands for training exercises.

"I'm sure you did, Colonel," Vespa replied, knowingly. "And the terms?"

"The terms were accepted... enthusiastically." Hendrix removed his glasses and examined them carefully. Then he pulled out a handkerchief from an inside pocket and began cleaning the lenses studiously. "I explained that we had the expertise to assist in many areas of Lowlands governance and that it would therefore be our honour to serve on their most esteemed assembly." He put his spectacles back on the end of his nose, tucked his handkerchief into his pocket, and looked icily at the Queen. "They were happy to, er, acquiesce."

Vespa nodded. "Good. Good. Well, I mustn't keep you any longer. You must have some final preparations to make."

"Indeed, Your Majesty. Thank you." Hendrix bowed, then slapped a salute before turning towards the door.

"Oh. One other thing, Colonel Hendrix."

The Head of the FSS paused and turned to face the Queen. "Your Majesty?"

"The Helionix Project. The Council would appreciate an update. Tomorrow morning?"

"As you wish, my Queen." Hendrix bowed slowly and marched out of the chamber.

#

Queen Vespa entered the State Room flanked by senior members of the Royal Wingtenders. Two bodyguards from her Personal Protection Unit accompanied them.

"My Queen." Zir Hugh bowed deeply. "I hope the preparations meet your approval."

Vespa smiled at her chief advisor. "Thank you, Zir Hugh. I'm sure everything will be fine."

She swept past him, pausing at the entrance to the balcony that overlooked the Central Square. Composed herself.

Then Vespa leaned towards one of her uniformed escorts and whispered to him. He nodded and ordered another officer away.

At her signal, the balcony's curtain drew back, allowing the shuffling and chattering from the assembled masses to drift up to the Queen. Hornets filled almost the entire square, with other arthros straining to see at the back. Vespa took a measured breath and stepped forward. The reception was thunderous. Despite standing on this balcony many times before, she had never experienced a gathering of quite this scale. She paused, taking a moment to compose herself. The crowd's cheering went on: a cacophony of respect and affection for a popular princess who had become a beloved Queen.

The cameras of the assembled press clicked and flashed as Vespa stood tall, allowing the applause to ripple around her, occasionally acknowledging it with a modest wave. Finally, she held her hand up, and the cheers subsided. She pressed her palms together, the fingers held upwards in front of her thorax. She looked to each corner of the square before speaking slowly and deliberately.

"My fellow hornets. Arthropods from The Grove. My dear friends from abroad. From the bottom of my heart, I thank you for this wonderful reception." There was more applause.

"Today, on our annual day of mourning, we remember Queen Velutina, Zir Hal and my sisters, the Princesses Victoria, Valerina and Violet, Helma, Honoria, Harriet and Hildegard, and their beloved partners."

A shout of "Bless you, Queen Vespa!" rang out from the front, and a fresh wave of applause spread through the crowd.

Vespa raised a hand. "Thank you. Thank you all." She waited until the applause receded again. "The passing of a Queen is a time of great unease, and your patience and understanding at a time of great distress demonstrated not just the high regard in which you held my mother and my family, but the belief you had in our community and our species.

"Queen Velutina recognised the need to balance tradition with progress. She understood the challenges you face every day as you carry out your duties within this vast ecosystem. She aimed to foster friendship and unity with our cousins across all arthropod classes and species..."

Vespa paused, her eyes scanning the square below. "On this day, we recognise her attempt to build a new relationship between hornets and other insects. A relationship of understanding, kindness, and above all, respect."

A murmur of agreement spread through the great gathering, and in serious, lowered tones, Vespa continued. "There were those who did not share her vision. There were those who would do anything to exterminate our species." She let the words hang, her gaze once again sweeping across the sea of faces. "And there were those..." she paused, considering her words. "There *are* those who would like to see the annihilation of all hornets."

Another uneasy murmur rippled through the crowd.

Vespa raised her arms, ready to increase the intensity of the next part of her speech. "Back then, you determined not to be frightened; not to be dictated to; never again to allow our way of life to be challenged. And to leave no stone unturned in the search for the murderers, no matter how long it took!"

The crowd was growing excited, responding to each emphasis with louder claps and yells. Vespa let the crescendo rise before giving her next command, loud and clear.

"Bring in the prisoners!"

Silence fell like a guillotine. Every hornet strained forward and focused on the area to the right of the balcony. Prisoners? What prisoners? The silence magnified the rustle of the summer breeze.

Then two FSS officers appeared with a praying mantis, its legs shackled, its antennae limp and hanging low. It shuffled, unsteadily. Deathly thin, its usually shiny green exoskeleton was dull, bruised and baggy. With its head bent, the mantis stared hopelessly at the ground, its forelegs folded as if in prayer.

Behind it, two more officers brought in another prisoner – a locust. It was bruised around the face and missing a wing. But unlike the mantis, it struggled against its restraints, eyes blazing with defiance.

"My fellow hornets, these two insects have been found by our High Court to be guilty of murder, attempted murder, and high treason. Thanks to our intelligence agency, led by Colonel Hendrix, we were able to identify and extradite them..." Hendrix, standing behind and to the right of the Queen, bowed. "The punishment for their crimes is death by slice. We will show no mercy!"

A tense hush spread through the Central Square. The crowd seemed unsure. Everyone was relieved that the perpetrators had finally been captured, but death by slice?

Vespa gestured, and a hornet dressed in black stepped from the shadows behind the prisoners. Without ceremony or theatrics, her blade swept through the air, severing the mantis's head in a single stroke. It took a moment, but eventually, it rolled off its thorax. The body crumpled instantly, the head rolling dramatically across the balcony floor.

The locust no longer struggled but stared, paralysed by shock. He closed his eyes, waiting for the inevitable. Vespa's voice echoed around the square as she addressed the forlorn creature.

"One last time, tell us who sent you, and I will spare your life."

Lips curling, the locust met Vespa's gaze and hissed: "I have nothing to say."

Vespa's eyelids rose. Her signal was unmistakable. The blade struck for a second time, slicing cleanly through the locust's neck. Its head rolled awkwardly, momentum taking it towards the edge of the balcony, where it dropped over the edge.

The crowd watched, transfixed. A deathly silence fell across the square. Below the execution platform, a young worker hornet caught the head. She had simply reached out as she might to a falling fruit. In her hands, the lifeless eyes of the locust stared back at her. Dark blood oozed over her hands. Those around her staggered back, shocked. And then the worker hornet turned to the crowd behind her and held the gruesome trophy aloft. A scream, curdled deep in her abdomen, escaped – not just from her mouth but seemingly from every pore in her body.

And like the most contagious of viruses, the scream spread through the crowd of hornets. It was bloodthirsty and wild. A cry of fear, awe, horror; but also, a terrifying sense of relief. Further back, all the other insects, myriapods and arachnids, drew in a collective gasp, and then they too joined the chorus of ferocious shrieks.

Vespa let the calls rise to a crescendo, then lifted a taming hand. Slowly, the noise subsided.

"My mother, your former Queen, showed courage and foresight in reaching out to other communities in friendship. I am pleased to share that we have been invited to provide security services in The Lowlands, and we look forward to working with other regions."

She leaned forward, her voice dropping to a deliberate, foreboding hush. "My fellow hornets," she said, "I shall never shrink from the burden of duty – my duty to you, and to our kind."

Then, with her voice gathering strength, she addressed the gathering: "Let it be declared that from this day forward, hornets shall no longer hang their heads in shame, for we shall only stand tall with pride. We shall not doubt our duty to the ecosystem. And we shall never, *ever* flinch from that most earnest of responsibilities."

She flung her arms wide, drawing out the last words, inviting the crowd to celebrate with her. And they complied. The Central Square erupted into a deafening roar of approval, drunk on patriotic pride and renewed love for their Queen. In a show of community, Vespa clapped back to the four corners of the square, before turning around and sweeping back to the vestibule.

Zir Hugh was waiting for her. "Your Majesty," he said, bowing. "Such a rousing speech."

"Thank you. I hope we can count on the Council's continued support."

"Of course, your Majesty." He bowed again as the Queen disappeared with her attendants. In the quiet that followed, he couldn't help but feel the smallest pang of unease.

8

The Couple

"Gee! Hon! Have you seen this?" Anton called from the sofa. He was scrolling and tapping his phone.

"What?" Honey was doodling on a guitar on the other side of the rehearsal room.

"An execution. Literally! On Insecta! An actual execution. Two insects."

"A what? Let me see." Honey placed the instrument on a stand and slumped beside Anton, shifting his hand so she could get a better look at the screen.

"Oh my god! That's awful!"

Anton shook his head. "They were apparently executed for the murder of an old hornet queen. Do you remember – the queen and all her children poisoned at a wedding?"

"Yeah, yeah. That's right. I remember my parents' shock at the time. Gruesome." She shook her head and went back to her guitar. "I'd *hate* to be a hornet."

Anton picked up his own guitar, watched Honey's chord progression, and tried to follow it. "Thankless. You know, we learn in school how important hornets are to the balance of the ecosystem. You know, population control and all that. But, well, it must be hard..."

He struggled with his finger placement. "Show me that chord – slowly!" He laughed, then continued: "I knew a couple of hornets at school. They had no friends. Basically, everyone was scared of them. A bit sad, really."

"I know," Honey replied, not really listening.

The two band members played away, exploring different chords, finding a few new pathways. They were enjoying themselves.

"It's actually weird that we haven't done this before," Anton declared.

Them Creepy Crawlies always wrote in a specific way. Anton would bring the song, and the others would add their parts. Occasionally, they might suggest small changes, but mostly, the song belonged to Anton.

This rehearsal room was one of the better spaces Terry had hired for the band. It had a bit of character. The dark red walls and carpet exuded a cosy warmth, rather than the stark white boxes they usually practiced in. Instead of black plastic chairs, there was an old sofa tucked in the corner. That was where Anton sat, facing Honey, who was now in front of a microphone. The band had spent most of the afternoon jamming, working on some new songs and trying out different intros and endings to some old ones.

"Do we know where the others went this evening?" Honey asked, picking up a new Anton noodle.

"Exploring was all Spyder said. 'Don't wait up' was their parting shot," Anton replied with a wry smile. "Wiggy's on a date with his laptop."

Honey giggled. "What's the venue for tomorrow night?"

Anton placed his guitar on the sofa and grabbed his phone from the coffee table. Tapped and scrolled.

"TASC Performing Arts Centre." He kept tapping. "It's on a university campus. We're supporting a band called Size of a Leaf. They're a…" Anton mimed air quotes, "concept band, apparently."

In his finest newscaster accent, Anton read out the blurb.

"Fusing the boundaries between sonic innovation and performance art, Size of a Leaf weaves together rich, atmospheric soundscapes with evocative choreography and immersive theatricality. Their work transcends mere auditory experience, inviting the audience into a multidimensional narrative. Each performance is an exploration of the insect ethos, where music, movement and drama coalesce in a dynamic interplay of tension and release."

"Thank you, Terry!" Honey said dramatically. She had added a new chord to Anton's progression. "What does it say about us?"

Anton found their write-up. "Them Creepy Crawlies is a raw, honest rock 'n' roll band mixing yesterday with tomorrow. Expect gritty riffs, catchy hooks, and a passion for unbalanced guitar pop. They're carving out their place one show at a time with a high-energy, no-frills sound that connects with fans who want to feel the music as much as hear it."

"That's cool," said Honey, nodding distractedly. She'd added a second chord to Anton's noodle. "Who wrote that?"

Anton picked up his guitar and slung it around his neck. "Don't know. Terry, I suppose."

"A termite of many talents is our Terry," Honey mused.

"Mmm," murmured Anton, watching Honey's fingers as she demonstrated the chord positioning. But try as he might, he couldn't get it. "Show me that again," he asked.

Honey slowed her picking and repeated the progression while Anton explored inversions higher up the neck of his guitar, tentatively humming along.

After a while, they found separate guitar spots and grew comfortable with the chord changes and timing. Anton hummed a series of melodies as Honey layered harmonies, until they settled on something they both liked.

"That's really nice," said Anton.

"It is, isn't it?" Honey agreed. "Simple, sweet, and soulful."

"It's a piece of unbalanced pop," Anton joked, and they both giggled.

They worked on the progression a while longer as Anton tried out some lyrics. He wasn't one for love songs, but he could feel himself being pulled that way.

He opened his lyric book and started scribbling couplets while Honey strummed a fresh set of chords. Occasionally, Anton would look up from his book to suggest ideas, happy for Honey to craft the song. He watched her fingers glide smoothly along the fretboard, noticing for the first time how long and slender they were.

After a while, they had a verse and a chorus. Honey hummed out the melody for the chorus. It was repetitive, passionate, soaring – a bit clichéd, but they both loved it for that very reason.

Anton had never heard Honey sing properly before. He sensed vulnerability and loneliness in her voice. Anton understood her better now; their friendship had grown deeper after visiting their mothers, becoming more effortless – as if they'd spent countless hours discussing everything and nothing. As Honey hummed absentmindedly, he thought he was simply uncovering new layers of his friend.

"Fancy a drink?" she offered suddenly.

Honey abandoned her guitar and walked over to the service area at the end of the room. Anton had never doubted Honey's allure. She was tall for a bee. Slender. Not classically pretty, but she still turned everyone's heads. Brie was right, Anton thought: she wouldn't be out of place on a catwalk. Despite many admirers, to Anton's knowledge, Honey had never had a serious partner. He'd wondered if she and Spyder were more than friends.

Honey returned to the sofa, handing a tin to Anton.

"What?" she grinned playfully, and Anton felt a prickle in his chest. As Honey took a long sip, he picked up his guitar again and resumed playing, but found himself stealing glances at her. He noticed a strand of her hair out of place, the curve of her cheek, her elegant eyelashes, the curl of her lip. These weren't things he'd noticed before. That prickle had become an awkward flutter. He tried to ignore it, started testing different chord progressions. Words began to flow, and he hastily jotted them down.

The aching pain of love that's unreturned.

Honey shifted in her seat, and Anton sensed she might be aware of the charge coming off him. He hoped he wasn't making her uncomfortable. She glanced up from her guitar, catching Anton's gaze.

"You okay over there? Got some interesting words?"

When hopes brew quick from glances across the room...

"Yeah, sort of," Anton replied, hoping his voice sounded casual. There was a pause before Honey went back to her guitar. Anton felt unsettled. This was Honey, his bass player. Honey, his friend. Honey. Someone who knew about his failed relationships, his many faults.

...at party time. Moving you to tears. Your inscape now revealed.

"What about this?" Honey played a new section of the song, looking at him, inviting him to harmonise. Without thinking, he joined in, matching her chords and pausing occasionally to scribble down new words, phrases that would usually lie well outside his comfort zone.

Through the blackest nights, and the bitter dawn,

In the coldest seas, when all hope is gone...

Anton couldn't remember exactly when it started, this feeling. Maybe it had been building for a while, so gradual that he hadn't noticed until it was impossible to ignore. Or maybe it was something new, sprung on him tonight without warning. Either way, it was definitely here now – and Anton didn't know what to do with it.

When the engines whine, and the sailors cry,
I'll be safely in your arms, my love.

"That's it!" Honey announced. "That's the song!" As she played it through, Anton traced the words in his head. These were new emotions for him to write about – attraction, longing – and they sat uneasily.

Honey let the final chord ring around the room, before looking up at Anton, expressionless. "Are you ready to sing it?" she asked.

Anton smiled weakly. "Well, the words are still a bit raw and need a bit of refining. And they're a bit different from what I've written before."

Dare I?

Anton picked up his guitar, preparing to reveal himself. Preparing to make a fool of himself. Preparing – potentially – to really complicate things. *But it could be about anyone...*

Honey counted them in. Anton hesitated, coughed, started again, made a mistake, and apologised. *I can't believe I'm feeling so nervous.* He should stop now. Say the words weren't right. Say he needed more time.

But then he realised that they'd finished the intro, and he was singing the first verse. The second verse. Eyes closed, he couldn't look at Honey. She must know the words were for her. She joined in on the chorus. *Good sign.* Third verse. She hummed the harmony. Her accompaniment soared when she joined in again on the final chorus. He wasn't ready for that, and it brought tears to his eyes.

And then it was over.

There was a pause. Neither of them said anything. Honey dropped her guitar and stood. She walked to the middle of the room and stood there, her back to him. *I knew I shouldn't have done it.* A door had opened that could never be closed.

"What the hell, Anton?" She didn't look at him. "What the hell," she murmured.

She won't be able to dismiss it with a shrug or pretend it never happened. Anton knew he'd struggle to forget these emotions. He could bury the song, but he wouldn't be able to bury his feelings. *God, that's it – that's the end of the band.*

He sat, and she stood. He wanted to ask what she felt, but the words were stuck somewhere between his mind and his mouth. It had been too much, too soon. Once again, it was about him. Same old selfish Anton.

Then, without a word, Honey turned, strode towards him, pulled his guitar off his lap, threw it onto the sofa, leaned over staring intensely at him, wrapped her upper arms around his neck, and kissed him.

She sat down beside him and kissed him again. Anton's heart raced, his mind spun, and he came alive with sensations he hadn't felt before. Their tongues searched. Lips explored. Fingers touched. With Honey! His friend!

When she finally pulled away, breathless, the room felt different. Lighter, somehow. She held his hand. "Those words, Anton, they moved *me* to tears. Made me think that I, too, felt..."

"Felt what?" Anton asked nervously, his mouth suddenly dry, his eyes searching hers for an answer.

"I don't know. Lately, after the visits... I've just been feeling, like, something's different between us."

Anton took a deep breath, the words tumbling out before he could stop them. "I know. Me too. I think I might... like you. More than just, you know, as a friend."

For a moment, the room felt impossibly still. Honey didn't say anything right away, so Anton's heart started to sink again. But then she kissed him playfully on the cheek. And then his lips, again, giggling. She felt warm and reassuring. Maybe he hadn't ruined everything, after all.

She pressed into his neck, and they stayed like that until Honey pulled herself free and looked at Anton. "Now what? Do we tell the others?"

"Tell them what? That we kissed? I don't think so. Not yet. Let's just see where this takes us."

So, they went back to just sitting there, comfortable with each other. Saying nothing. Happy that whatever the future held, this was a moment that neither of them would ever forget.

#

They presented the song to the rest of the band at the next rehearsal. Like they had done when they first came up with it, they played on acoustic guitars. With voices locked in, their harmonies soared. It was raw, emotional, and beautiful.

"Bloody hell," Spyder blurted as the last note faded. "That was incredible. I love it – the melody, the voices, the words for goodness' sake. Bloody hell, man!"

"I'd say it, ah, needs very little," Wiggy added unemotionally, scratching his chin. "Bit of, er, piano maybe, in the verses? And some, ah, strings in the chorus?"

"Light drums in the middle to give it a bit of a lift?" Honey suggested.

"Cool, babe. That'll work. Something like…" Spyder gave the biggest, loudest, punkiest beat they could muster, smashing the cymbals and drums together. It was as inappropriate as an inappropriate thing could be. "Like that?" they suggested innocently.

"Mmm. Let me think… *No!*" laughed Honey, replacing the acoustic guitar with her bass.

"Hey, Anton man!" Spyder called from behind the kit. "This is a love song, yeah? Your first official love song! Who's it about, dude? Is it Ems? Or…" They dropped their voice to sound melodramatic: "someone you haven't told us about?"

"Yeah, A-Anton," Wiggy teased. "Tell us who it is!"

A beam of embarrassment flashed across Anton's face. He almost burst with the thought of Honey, and he would have loved to tell them all, but he held silent, happy merely to be the focus of their banter. He was determined not to meet Honey's eyes.

"What do you reckon, Hon?" Spyder asked. "I mean, you were there. Didn't you wonder who Anton was writing about?"

Honey kept her back turned. "You know Anton," she said. "An ant of mystery. Now, come on, are we gonna give this a go?" She turned with a smile and flashed a 'ready?' look at Wiggy, who sat at the piano.

At the end, when they'd all agreed on their parts, they knew they had a hit. Sy sent some footage to Terry, and Terry forwarded it to the producer he had chosen.

They named the track 'I See You', the first song Anton and Honey had composed together. And it wouldn't be the last, for as they continued touring, Honey and Anton discovered they were an exceptionally productive writing team. The others encouraged them, giving the duo space to explore their ideas. Of course, it also gave them space to explore each other.

Writing had become easy now. Similar to 'I See You', each new song often began with an Anton riff – usually something he'd held onto for ages without finishing. Honey shone a new light on them. That was the beauty of their partnership: each channelled their past, present and future, blending their memories, experiences and influences into something uniquely theirs. Sometimes it didn't work but, when it did, it erupted. For Anton and Honey, right here and now, it was their moment.

Passion drove their work – not just for each other but for everything around them. They used their music to express how they felt about themselves, their families, their friends, and the world around them. They used their energy to fuel a verse or a chorus, whether at a practice, on a beach, or in a hotel room.

The secrecy of their budding relationship only added to their creative charge. Surreptitious glances, hidden touches, and stolen kisses in corridors became part of their ritual. Owning something no one knew about made them feel special; made them feel that, together, they could conquer the world.

A consequence of their newfound creativity was that the band became closer. There was no jealousy because, for Wiggy and Spyder, it was a thrill to ride the journey. There were no more questions and no more teasing, only mutual respect. Everyone understood that if Wiggy and Spyder had just been any old guitarist/keyboardist and drummer, the songs wouldn't be as good as they were. The understanding gave everyone confidence and a mutual sense of ownership.

Before long, the band began incorporating one or two new songs into their sets, and by the end of the tour, a quarter of the set consisted of new Anton/Honey compositions. Terry even pushed Brie and Blake to spend more time with the band, capturing not just the shows but personal moments as well.

Everyone wanted to know what had driven the new material, so Anton and Honey sat down in a hotel lobby with Brie and Blake for their first in-depth interview.

"So, Anton, Honey, darlings. Thanks *so* much for your time," Brie began. "You both look gorgeous. How has the tour been?"

"It's been great fun, thanks," Anton replied, glancing at Honey. "We've loved every minute of it, haven't we?"

"Well, nearly every minute," Honey corrected. "There was a gig when Anton stormed off stage, leaving us to cope with a baying swarm of wasps."

Anton nodded, somewhat embarrassed at the memory. "And the time Honey ate too much ice cream and was sick just before going on stage."

"Oh, Anton, you promised you'd keep that a secret," Honey said with a nervous giggle.

"Haha! Dear me," Brie laughed, "it sounds as if the tour has brought you two closer together."

"I think it has," Honey said. "And I think it shows when we play."

Blake leaned in. "Honey, we never knew you were a songwriter. How did this collaboration come about?"

"It was luck, really," Honey said with a smile. "The others had taken off for the night and Anton and I were just messing around with our guitars. That's when we came up with 'I See You'."

"It's such a moving song. It sounds so intimate and personal. Has something changed in your creative process?" asked Brie.

Honey's smile widened. She ignored Anton's barely perceptible shake of the head. "Well," she started, her voice relaxed but with a hint of excitement, "I reckon it's all about chemistry. I've always admired Anton's work, but lately, well, everything's just clicked."

Anton shifted in his seat, his posture stiffening. He picked up the thread, trying to steer the conversation away from dangerous territory.

"We're both in a place where we can really bring out the best in each other. Chemistry is one thing, but it's more about timing. We've both grown a lot in the past year."

Honey's eyes danced mischievously. "You know, Brie, I think there's more to it than that. When you work closely with someone, you start to understand them better. It turns the writing process into something more intimate, wouldn't you say, Anton?" She stroked his shoulder, impishly.

Anton's fingers tightened slightly on the edge of his seat. He knew Honey was enjoying the thrill of taking risks. He also found it exhilarating, but at that moment, he felt nervous. It was one thing risking it with Wiggy and Spyder, but in front of a camera?

Their relationship was still new. Growing more secure, for sure, and Anton knew at some stage they'd reveal their affair – but not now. They needed to agree about coming out. The world was still adapting to cross-species relationships, so despite the disappointment of their recent visits, their mothers should hear it from them, not the press.

Blake felt the tension. He couldn't help himself. "Intimate? Oh, Honey, sweetie! Do please elaborate. Fans have speculated that these songs come from a very personal place, haven't they, Brie?"

"They certainly have," Brie replied, turning to Anton, pressing. "The words in 'I See You' are so gorgeous! So emotive! Come on, Anton," she teased, "who are they for?"

Honey looked at Anton, eyes flirty and challenging. "Yeah, Anton. Come on, tell us who they're for!"

Anton grinned. "That would be telling. Look, I reckon we've all learned to share more of ourselves in our writing. Allowed ourselves to be a bit more vulnerable, to explore our past, wonder about the future – and I think that makes the music feel more genuine."

Honey gave a little chuckle. "We definitely have."

Blake raised an eyebrow. "So, you're saying your relationship has influenced the songs?"

The butterflies exchanged glances, thinking they might have a scoop. But Honey and Anton hesitated.

"What I would say, Blake," Honey finally replied evenly, "is that we're professionals. The work comes first, and we've always maintained that."

"Yeah, absolutely," Anton agreed. "The work always comes first."

"Well, darlings," Brie concluded with a warm smile, "whatever the catalyst for these songs may be..."

"... long may it last!" added Blake.

"Absolutely! Honey. Anton. Thank you." Blake and Brie turned to the camera. "And thank you for tuning into The Social Butterflies."

After the camera was off, Honey leaned over and whispered in Anton's ear: "You almost gave it away."

Anton could feel her breath warm on his cheek. "Me? You practically shouted it from the rooftops."

Honey grinned. "Relax. We make a good team. On and off the record." Anton nudged her gently, and Honey chuckled softly, stood up, kissed Brie and Blake, suggested they catch up for a few drinks after the show, then followed Anton out of the room, pushing him playfully.

Brie turned to Blake. "Oh. My. God. Did. You. Feel. That. Heat."

Blake shook his head. "They're like *so* together."

#

The video went viral. Of course it did! Everyone loves to gossip about who might be with whom, especially if it's one species with another, and Anton and Honey's interview had stoked the rumour mill. For many arthros, particularly the older ones, the idea of ants being with bees, or earwigs with spiders, was unthinkable. Not long ago, even intra-species coupling had been forbidden by law. But liberalisation and tolerance had swept through the world, upending long-held norms and views. Males now enjoyed the same rights as females, and there was even a campaign to allow male insects to establish colonies.

Young arthropods led the social revolution, and Terry knew that Them Creepy Crawlies could be at the centre of the zeitgeist. He saw it as an opportunity, whereas Anton, Honey, Spyder and Wiggy saw it as a responsibility. Proudly multi-species, they felt it was their duty to promote equality. Of course, they recognised that bees and spiders possessed different skills and thus tended towards different positions in society, but, well, why shouldn't the workforce building a nest for ants include earwigs and spiders? And if a bee wanted to couple with an ant... well, who was to tell them they couldn't? There was no chance of procreation – so it wasn't like mutants were going to terrorise the world!

The interview with the Social Butterflies and the ensuing speculation prompted Anton and Honey to discuss coming out. Honey was all for it. For the first time in her life, she felt liberated and a little out of control. It was both scary and exciting. She wanted to be a role model for other arthros that felt constrained by their species, gender, or position in the ecosystem. She wanted to show them it was possible to take your own path in life, not just the one you were born into.

Surprisingly, Anton was more reserved. He wanted the world to see them as partners – he adored Honey and stood by all the marginalised groups she supported. However, he was worried about their relationship being used as a symbol of liberal change and social justice. He didn't want them to become a rallying point for others.

It was quite an about-turn. Honey, quiet, contained and demure, shielded by her bass guitar, was finding a voice, while Anton, performer and proclaimer, had become camera-shy.

But first, they had to tell their bandmates.

On the final afternoon of the tour, Honey and Spyder sat on a bench at a deserted esplanade overlooking the beach, the tide miles out beyond acres of cold, wet sand.

"I knew it! I knew it!" Spyder exclaimed, the news bringing warmth to a grey day. "I mean, you can't write those lyrics, that music, without something going on, yeah?"

They turned, serious. "But are you sure? I mean, Anton can still be Anton."

Despite everything, Honey felt melancholic. She held one of Spyder's hand in hers, leaning her head against their shoulder. "Everything's going to be okay, isn't it?"

"Of course, it is, Hon... Why do you say that?"

"Oh, I don't know. It just feels like things are changing. We're changing. I'm changing."

"But isn't that a good thing? The band's in a great place. The tour was totally cool. The four of us have become closer friends. The new songs... I mean, hang on, girl!"

"But don't you feel you've lost something?"

"No! Well, yes, I suppose. But nothing I'm sorry about. Look babe, don't get me wrong, I love the shop and I love the community. But, well, look at me." Spyder stood up. On this dreary day, their sunnies and hair looked bigger than ever. Split black jeans, low-hanging black tee shirt under a long leather jacket. As they gave an awkward spin, their menagerie of bangles and bracelets and necklaces clattered like a dozen wind-chimes.

"I was born to be in a band!" they joked.

Honey began to weep.

"Sweetie. What is it? Come on." Spyder sat back down and held Honey. "Why the tears?"

"Everything's happening so quickly," Honey sobbed. "Anton. The music. The band. I feel I'm discovering a new me, and I'm frightened of who that might be."

Spyder broke their embrace, gently holding their friend by the shoulder. "It's alright to be scared, Honey."

Honey's words were tangled. "It's like, I've left everything behind. My old life, my family, money, privilege. A few months ago, I was in school! I'm here now, not knowing whether the band will make it, how I'll make a living, figuring things out with Anton."

She swallowed, looking meekly at her friend. "It's scary. What if I've made a mistake? What if leaving all that behind was stupid? My mother thinks I'm throwing my life away. What if she's right?"

The words spilled out. Spyder had never heard their friend speak so openly. She was the sensible one – the one who appeared to have her life sorted.

Spyder looked their mate straight in the eyes. "Honey, listen. You didn't leave that life behind because it was easy. You did it because you wanted more than what your parents were offering. You wanted to live your own life, not the one they'd plotted for you."

Honey nodded. She knew Spyder was right, yet she couldn't shake her gnawing anxiety. "But what if I don't know how to do this new me? What if I mess it all up?"

"Babe, you can't help who you are. I should know! You just gotta trust yourself." They switched to a playful gangster accent. "A bit of vulnerability never hurt no one, schweetheart!"

A giggle forced its way through Honey's tears.

"So, you're okay with leaving the shop and your brood?"

"The shop? Sure. It's boring if I'm honest. But it's in good hands. The community will look after it."

"But the brood?" Honey pressed.

Spyder looked thoughtful. "Yeah. That's tougher. But, you know, I can't play mummy and daddy forever. There's strong leadership now, so they'll be fine. Anyway, I can see them when I'm home."

The two friends sat silently for a while, staring out across the sand, listening to the sound of the distant sea. Honey pulled her knees up to her chest, resting her chin on them as she glanced sideways at Spyder, who was leaning back against the bench, head tilted toward the sky.

Honey loved their wild energy and rebellious, free spirit, and how it was so different from her own placid introspection.

"Spyder?" Her voice was soft, almost drowned by the wind.

"Hmm?"

"I've been thinking..." She paused, choosing her words carefully. "I wanted to ask you something."

Spyder turned their head slightly, catching Honey's gaze. "Go on then," they encouraged, a playful smile tugging a corner of their lips. "You know you can ask me anything."

"It's just... I've noticed you've been acting a little different lately. I mean, you've always been you – but there's something else. Like, maybe something's been on your mind?"

"What do you mean by 'different'?"

"I don't know," Honey admitted. "Maybe not different, but more thoughtful, I guess. And I was wondering... if it has anything to do with, you know, how you've been figuring things out. About yourself."

Spyder raised an eyebrow and sat up a bit straighter. "Ah, right. I see where this is going. You mean, because I don't really fit into the whole 'boy or girl' thing, yeah?"

Honey nodded, relieved that Spyder wasn't shutting down the conversation.

"Yeah, that's part of it. I know you're comfortable with who you are. But I've been wanting to ask how you're really doing with it. Does it ever... get to you?"

Spyder let out a long sigh, leaning forward with their elbows on their knees, their hands clasped together. "Oh, sweetie! Thanks for asking. There's no simple answer. You know, I'm not uncomfortable with myself. Like, on the street, growing up, it wasn't as if I had a mother giving me dolls or action figures, trying to shape my gender. And clothes? It wasn't my body that told me what to wear – it was my soul."

Honey listened intently. She'd always admired how bold Spyder was about their identity. How unafraid they seemed, living outside the expectations of others.

"But," Spyder continued, frowning slightly, "it's not always easy, yeah? Arthros want to put us in one box or another. They want life to be simple. But it isn't, is it?"

Honey reached out and placed a hand on Spyder's arm, offering a comforting squeeze.

Spyder smiled. "I guess it's tiring sometimes, you know – always being the one standing out."

Honey lightened the conversation. "You guess?"

They both giggled before Spyder carried on. "Seriously, though, there are days I just want to blend in."

Honey nodded. "That makes sense," she said softly. "But I hope you know that the people who really care about you –

me, Anton, Wiggy, Sy, even Terry – we love you for who you are."

Spyder leaned across and hugged their friend. "Thanks, Honey. That means a lot."

"There's... one other thing I wanted to ask. It's a bit more personal."

Spyder groaned. "Oh, bloody hell! What now?"

"Well," Honey began, "I was wondering... if there's anyone you fancy?"

Spyder let out a sudden laugh, clearly caught off guard. "Fancy! What are we in, some romantic novel now?"

Honey blushed, rolling her eyes. "Okay, fine. Is there anyone you... like?"

Spyder's expression softened, and they looked down at their hands for a moment. When they finally spoke, their voice was quieter, more thoughtful. "I don't know, honestly. I mean, I have crushes. There was a stage I wondered if we might, you know, get it together." Spyder nudged Honey teasingly.

"But it's not really about gender for me. I just like people who make me feel, ah... seen, I guess. People who accept me for who I am, without trying to change me or fit me into their idea of who I should be."

A sense of understanding settled between them. "It's not about labels, is it?" Honey said.

"Exactly!" Spyder agreed. "And right now, I'm not really looking for anyone. But... if someone comes along who gets me, well, I guess I'll know."

Honey nodded, and the two returned to contemplating the view.

Anton's conversation with Wiggy was much simpler. They were at the venue, setting things up on the stage. "Cool," Wiggy said when Anton broke the news to him, not even looking up as he fiddled with connections. "I'm happy for you. I like Honey. She's pretty. *And* she plays good bass." And that was that.

When Spyder and Honey arrived, Spyder went straight up to Anton and gave him a smothering hug, whispering something serious in his ear. Kissed him full on the lips. Wiggy, of course, was much more reserved, offering Honey a shy smile and an awkward thumbs-up. But she appreciated this gentle show of support just as much as Anton appreciated Spyder's grandiose one.

9

The Record That Broke Them

The space was too small for nine arthros, yet they all managed to cram into the black-walled room. A single window looked into the studio, set up with drums, amplifiers and speakers. In front of the window was a control panel of confusing knobs and sliders, with two screens above it crowded with cryptic codes and colourful graphs. Sitting in front of it all was a grasshopper.

Behind her, pressed against the back wall, was a settee designed for two people. On it sat Wiggy and Anton, with Honey perched on his knee. Sy balanced on the arm beside Spyder, who stood, back to the wall. On the other side of the door was Terry. Blake and Brie tiptoed around the room, their cameras occasionally flashing.

No one talked. They were all waiting for the grasshopper.

It was the third time the inner circle of Them Creepy Crawlies had come together since the final gig of the tour. The very next day, the band had met in this same room when Terry had introduced them to George. Terry had explained that George's role was to help the band produce the very best record. Help, not dictate, George emphasised. Later, they'd looked up George's credentials and discovered she had a fine reputation for producing young bands.

George had a feline face with a slim, pointed chin and a small, pert nose. Her eyes, shaped like an alien's, were yellow with a tiny black dot in the middle. She was dressed casually in a bodysuit, with two sets of pretty wings neatly tucked behind her. She had a calm and composed posture, and came across as very friendly, saying things like "What do you think if..." or "Give me a sense of..."

George had started out making music in her bedroom on her laptop. She became hooked and, determined to build a career in music, talked her way into studios. No one made coffee like George! She watched how bands set up, how engineers prepared their equipment. The first band she produced reached number one in the charts. The second did too. Suddenly, George was in the spotlight.

She was very knowledgeable, and the band appreciated that. Because she could discuss deep-tech with Wiggy, she managed to coax him out of his comfort zone. She understood Spyder's competitiveness and drive and challenged them to explore the possibilities of drum machines and sampling – which in turn made Honey consider complementary bass sounds and techniques. With Anton, she encouraged him to take more control in his guitar playing, but to be less controlling over his vocal delivery.

They all soaked it up. In truth, they loved spending time at the studio – it was all new and exciting, and they were literally living the dream. Meanwhile, Anton and Honey were growing closer as a couple. Once they'd told their bandmates, the news had quickly spread. Not everyone was thrilled because Anton was a divisive character. What was Honey doing with him? Wasn't she far too nice, mature, pretty, polite, funny and intelligent for him? It didn't faze Honey. She knew Anton, knew what she was getting herself into; and anyway, it was *her* chemistry that had been rocked, not anyone else's. They were spending more time together – out and about, just the two of them, visiting museums, going to a gig, or exploring record shops. They became more recognisable, which they found fun – posing for photos, making new friends, getting invited to new parties. They started to feel like pop stars!

When it was time for Honey and Anton to record the vocals for 'I See You', everyone came to listen. Wiggy and Spyder sat on the control room couch, joking. Terry sat beside George at the mixer as she made last-minute adjustments. In the studio, Sy made sure the microphone stands were in the right place. It was the moment they'd all been waiting for.

Honey and Anton arrived in the studio like two gladiators entering the ring. They were dressed down in sloppy casuals, each carrying a bottle of water. Brie and Blair floated after them, like seconds, but instead of towels, they had cameras. Everyone stopped what they were doing as an air of excited expectancy spread across the bleachers. Anton stretched out his arms, circled his abdomen, and his neck too, trying to release tension. Honey placed her song-sheet on a music stand, ran through some vocal exercises, sipped from her bottle. They both placed headphones over their heads.

"Ready?" George asked into her intercom and received a thumbs-up from the two singers. The tape rolled. Anton sang. Honey sang. They listened back.

"Another take?" George asked, leaning into the desk microphone. Anton and Honey exchanged nods, and they sang again.

They listened back. "Better," George suggested, "but let's give it another go."

They nodded. Honey took a drink of water, Anton stretched his neck again, and they recorded again... and again. After ten takes, it still wasn't clicking. "Really close, guys," George encouraged, remaining positive. "I reckon the next one will be good."

But it wasn't.

For the umpteenth time, Anton fiddled with the positioning of his mic. "Hon, are you feeling okay? You seem to be having a problem finding those harmonies today."

"No, I'm good," she replied, reassuringly.

After another take, Anton stepped back from the mic and coughed. "Yeah, I reckon it's the harmony right at the start. Can we try it together without the backing track?"

"Sure," Honey replied. She took another drink of water before singing her part.

"No, no. Together, yeah?" Anton insisted.

Honey smiled at her partner. "Oh, okay. Do you want to count us in?"

They both took their positions. Anton said one, two, then mouthed three, four, but that caused him to miss his opening note. Honey continued with her part. Anton tried to find his, but he couldn't.

"Wait, wait, wait!" he called out sharply. "Can you wait for me, please? Thank you."

In the control booth, Spyder and Wiggy shifted uncomfortably.

Honey kept her friendly smile. "Sorry, Anton. Come on then. Let's have another go. How do you want to do it?"

They tried again and again, but Anton was losing focus. He was increasingly snappy with Honey as she batted away his frustrations. After another unsatisfactory take, he turned his attention to Brie and Blake, roughing up his hair. "Look, can you guys stop taking photos for a minute? It's putting us off. In fact, can you just delete everything you've taken so far?"

As compliant and gushing as ever, Brie said, "Of course, darling!", and the two butterflies retreated to the back of the room where Sy was on his phone.

"Dude, what are you even doing?" Anton grumped, his mood worsening by the minute.

At first, Sy didn't know Anton was talking to him. "Stay cool, man, yeah? I'm just here to help."

"Stay cool, man, yeah?" Anton parroted sarcastically. "Maybe make yourself useful, then. Like, put the kettle on. Or go get us some drinks."

"No worries, man." Brie gave Sy a comforting touch of the arm as he stood. "You alright, girl?" he murmured to Honey as he passed her.

Anton saw Honey give Sy a reassuring smile. "What do you mean, is she alright?" he called after him, challenging.

Sy turned to face Anton. "I mean, you ain't treating her good, man. Chill man, yeah?"

"Don't tell me to 'chill, man.'" And then he looked away from Sy, arrogantly deciding he didn't matter. "And don't come back," he barked. "It's not like you do anything, anyway."

He turned back to Honey, oblivious to her shocked look. "Let's go again," Anton ordered.

Honey stared at Anton, stunned. She didn't recognise the ant in front of her. As Anton resumed his position at the mic, Sy mouthed "it's okay" to her and left the room, trailed by an embarrassed Blake and Brie muttering apologies. Anton ignored them all.

"Okay, that's it," called George. "I think it's time for a break."

"No," Anton corrected in an oddly calm tone. "I said let's go again. Honey's close to getting it, aren't you Hon?"

Honey didn't reply. She picked up her water bottle, grabbed her jacket, and made for the door, waving slightly at a sympathetic George through the window.

"Honey! Where are you going? Come on, you're almost there!"

But Honey didn't pause, and Anton watched as she made for the door.

"HONEY!"

Honey shuddered, momentarily frightened, then quickly recovered and slipped out of the studio. Outside, Spyder, Sy, Brie and Blake waited, while Terry and Wiggy emerged from the control room behind them.

Honey hugged Sy. "I'm so sorry."

"Bloody Anton," Spyder muttered, putting a comforting arm around Honey's waist. "Come on. Let's get outta here." They led Honey down the corridor.

The others weren't quite sure what to do next, until Brie exclaimed: "I know! Let's go to our place! Blake, darling, we can just hang out, can't we? We have lots of wine!"

Blake smiled back. "Splendid idea, darling. Come on, everyone, follow me!"

#

Anton sat on a stool at the back of the studio, strumming a guitar, locked in a world of indignation. He was angry at Honey for not nailing the harmonies. Angry at Brie and Blake for getting in the way. Angry at Sy for being Sy. Angry at George for cueing at the wrong places. Angry at Terry for not managing the situation. Angry at Wiggy for... he didn't even know why he was angry at Wiggy, but he was.

He put the guitar down and sat behind the kit, drumming out a simple 4 x 4 beat. *Can I really be bothered with all this?* The band. None of them understood what it was like being Anton. Singer. Guitarist. Writer. *Maybe I should make a solo album?* Did he really need the others? He picked up the beat, but he wasn't a drummer. He tried some different rolls but couldn't carry them, which made him more frustrated. He tried again but still couldn't get it. Growing increasingly frustrated, he gave up all attempts to keep time and just smashed the drums. Repeatedly. Chaotically. Chiming the cymbals. Hammering the toms. Faster and faster. Harder and harder. His arm muscles started to tense. No timing in his feet. Faster and faster. Harder and harder. Eyes closed, head down, determined to keep going. The chaos intensified until tears welled up, and finally, arms aching, he flung the drumsticks across the room.

He held his head in his hands, squeezing his eyes shut as tightly as he could, desperate to make it all go away. But he knew it wouldn't. He knew he'd been a dick – just the same old Anton. This time, his apology might not count for anything, and they probably wouldn't forgive him. *There must be something wrong with me.* He sighed. *I just don't seem to be able to grow up.* He scratched his head, roughing his hair.

George came into the room to tidy away the leads and microphones. Anton looked at her with a mix of apology and embarrassment, like a naughty schoolkid who'd been caught red-handed. She looked at him, the end of her lips raised, and her eyes narrowed. It wasn't the first time she'd experienced a musician behaving badly.

Anton slumped back into a seat, his legs stretched out in front, slouching and gloomy. He expected George to say something, but she didn't. She just tidied up around him. Without turning to her, he said as she busied, "I don't know where that came from." She didn't answer, but it didn't matter because, really, he was talking to himself.

He blew out a long breath and stared at his feet. "I should apologise. But do I say sorry to everyone together, or should I go round and apologise to each one?"

After a pause, Anton added: "I have a reputation for hollow apologies." He looked up at George, who was looping up a mic lead. "Do you know where they all went?"

"Blake's and Brie's." It was Terry. He spoke into the control room mic. "But listen – can I give you some advice?"

Anton's heart sank further. "You're still here," he said quietly.

A moment later, Terry stood in front of Anton, arms behind his back, legs apart like a sergeant major about to dress down a conscript.

"Seek out each person, my boy. Tell them you're sorry and explain why you reacted as you did."

"And why did I react the way I did, Terry?" Anton asked, his voice full of hopelessness.

"Isn't it obvious?"

Anton looked at Terry quizzically. He changed position, straightening up a bit as Terry pulled up a chair in front of him. He sat in his usual way, two top hands on the white stick out in front of him. From behind his thick black glasses, he searched Anton's face.

"Pressure, Anton. You felt pressure," the termite growled. "Think about it for a moment."

Anton looked around the large, white-lit, soulless room. The big window. He'd been on display, like an animal in a zoo, where everyone was armed not with cameras, but with expectation. Everyone wanted to be there because they wanted to share the final, critical part of the production, together. In this most expectant arena, Anton had tried to sing the most sensitive and beautiful of songs – a song that was to take the band to a whole new level.

"As did Honey," George added.

Of course she did! He had been thinking only of himself, and that made him despise himself even more. He ran his hands over his face, cursing himself. *She'll have felt it way more than me. She needed my reassurance and support.*

"And all I did was blame her." He sat there for a while, shaking his head, coming to terms with his actions. Then he pulled a phone out of his pocket and started frantically texting, organising to meet each member of the gang. He told them he had something he needed to say. He said something clever about another apology.

"Can you do me a favour?" he asked George. She nodded, understanding immediately. And with that, Anton dashed out of the studio, phone in hand, determined to be on time.

#

Anton paced up and down the now-transformed studio. Gone were the banks of amps and speakers, the snakes of cables, the mess of drums, the black plastic chairs. Gone, too, were the white walls, because in their place were black curtains, pulled in to form a smaller, intimate space. After his final apology, he had rushed to buy as many flowers as he could afford, which now decorated the room.

Anton had spoken with everyone, and they had all accepted his apology, acknowledging the pressure he was under. He admitted that it was no excuse for his behaviour, which he deeply regretted. He loved Honey. He loved all of them. He said he was a better ant now than he had ever been – although he still had a way to go.

George had found a spread of rugs that now covered the floor. Two comfortable stools stood behind one microphone. The mic was the centrepiece of the room, sleek and cylindrical, a metal grille on top of a polished solid body. Between each stool was a table covered with a red velvet throw holding some drinks and another vase. Shaded lamps around the floor added to the warmth of the space.

The only problem was he hadn't spoken to Honey yet. It had been Terry who'd asked her to come back, so while Spyder was off getting ready to go to the butterflies' place, Honey made her way through the evening's half-light to the studio. She was realistic enough to know that the record needed to be finished and it was probably best that she and Anton recorded their parts separately. Anton's outburst had shocked and scared her. Back at home, Spyder insisted she end the relationship, saying he wasn't to be trusted and would always let her down. Relationships were never simple, she had countered, wanting to give Anton some benefit of the doubt, but as she approached the studio door, she was definitely less sure how she felt about Anton. Anyway, she would do her vocal track, meet up with the gang later, and see how she stood tomorrow.

She was still wrestling with her feelings when she knocked at the control room door. George motioned her into the studio, turning off the coms and drawing the curtain between the two areas.

Inside, Anton was sitting on a stool. She was surprised – she hadn't expected him to be there. He looked somehow different. Still attractive, though, and this made her feel angry with herself. She looked around the transformed space and then turned to leave.

Anton quickly stood up, his eyes crinkled with emotion. "I know I've said this before, Honey, but imagine all my other apologies added together. Double it. Triple it. That's how sorry I am."

She reached for the door. "Please, don't go," Anton pleaded. "Can we talk... just for a moment."

Honey paused.

"Please forgive me. I couldn't bear falling out with you," he whispered, lowering his head. "Or not being with you... I behaved appallingly."

Without turning, Honey replied: "You did, Anton. Not just to me. To Sy. To Brie and Blake."

"I know. I've spoken to them. Explained."

"Explained?" She turned to face him, worry etched across her face. "Maybe you can explain it to me then, as well."

He couldn't help thinking how great she looked. Natural. No makeup. Hair shiny and up in a pony. "I shouldn't have acted the way I did. It was pressure – I just didn't recognise it, or cope with it; I took it out on everyone else."

"Anton," she said flatly, shaking her head, "it's not an apology if you put yourself at the centre of it."

"Sorry! I know. I know!" Anton insisted. "What I mean is that I should have been there for you. Not thinking about myself. I know you felt more pressure than me. All I'm saying is that I was blinded by what was going on inside me. But I know that doesn't excuse the way I acted."

Honey finally moved into the room. She looked around. "This is nice," she murmured, reaching out to touch Anton's forearm.

"Can you forgive me?" he asked, taking her hand in his. Honey met his eyes. "But you scared me, Anton. And the others. I saw something in you I hadn't seen before. A ruthlessness…"

She sat on one of the stools. "Look, we were both under pressure. I get it. Everyone was watching. But please, Anton, never treat me like that again."

She stretched out her hand. He took it, and she pulled him close. He held her tightly, desperately. It took a moment for her to respond, but when she finally did, relief washed over him. She let him rest his head against her thorax, feeling his lips there. She leaned her head back and closed her eyes, enjoying his attention, enjoying the high of making up. Anton promised himself, there and then, that he'd never let Honey down again.

As they kissed, George's voice came over the speaker.

"Right then. Are you guys ready?"

"Absolutely," they both said in unison.

#

So, here they all were in the little control room. All nine of them gathered to hear the final version of 'I See You'. George swivelled her chair slowly through 360 degrees, looking at each member of the band in turn. She pressed the play button, and for the next three minutes and forty-five seconds, no one spoke, no one touched their phones, and no one moved.

When the song ended, they all sat in stunned silence – even George, who just stared through the studio as if remembering the other evening. She knew it was good, perhaps the best thing she had ever produced. But what did the others think? She was unusually apprehensive. Finally, she spun around to face the band.

"Well?"

"Oh, my *God*," Spyder whispered, hardly able to contain their excitement. "It's totally amazing, George. I mean: totally." They lifted their sunnies and rubbed their eyes, before turning to Anton and Honey.

"What the hell, you guys? What the actual *hell!*"

"It sounds great, George," said Anton, leaning forward with a beaming smile on his face. "Really great. What do you think, Hon?"

It hadn't taken long to lay down the track, which, in a way, Honey regretted. The session had been special. They hadn't had to make up the emotion. It had come from deep inside them – all the relief, renewed respect, the overcome anger, the real love. Now everyone could hear it.

"I love it. Thank you," she said, hugging George and kissing her on the cheek.

"Right," said Terry, returning to his managerial tone. "I'll put it up for release straight away. Well done everyone – I'm sure it's going to be a hit." Terry bowed slightly, turned and left, leaving the young ones to their excitement.

Over the next three weeks, Brie and Blake took charge of the band's future, leading a social media campaign to boost interest in the upcoming release. It began with them wearing headphones, bobbing to a silent beat with the caption 'listening to our new obsession!' They did this in various settings: out walking, having dinner, at a club, even in the bath. Interest soared.

Next, the butterflies posted a series of behind-the-scenes footage – no faces, just hands setting up in the studio. 'Get ready for something awesome!' Of course, most of their followers knew they were working with Them Creepy Crawlies, and could guess what hand belonged to what species, but it didn't stop the questions flowing.

Finally, a 15-second snippet of the song's soaring chorus was released alongside striking visuals. The clip went viral as fans started using it in their own videos, dancing and lip-syncing to the track.

On release day, they all gathered at The Basement, where the band was hosting a virtual listening party. Anton, Honey, Spyder and Wiggy squeezed onto the couch while their friends filled the rest of the room, being interviewed and sharing stories about the band. For those watching on the livestream, it looked like a gathering of the coolest, grungiest, most exotic-looking mix of arthropods ever. Ants and spiders, butterflies and centipedes, beetles and ticks.

Five minutes before the song dropped, Brie invited all their subscribers to put on their headphones. Immediately, they felt like they were part of the band's inner circle. They heard the band chat about how they made the song, and then, five minutes before the general release, the song came through their headphones. Everyone was encouraged to film their reactions and share them. Within moments, 'I See You' was trending globally.

After the general release dropped, and their friends headed home feeling elated to have been there, only the inner circle remained. Wiggy sat at his piano, plinking absent-mindedly, while Sy and Spyder tidied up, washed, and put everything away. Anton and Honey fidgeted on the sofa, exchanging small talk as Brie and Blake curated the continuing online commentary.

Meanwhile, Terry and George stood at the workbench with a laptop open, the band's artist page open on the most popular streaming channel.

They watched.

The band had talked about what numbers the new release might generate. George had suggested that a new indie punk band like Them Creepy Crawlies might expect a few thousand streams on the days following a release.

They watched.

Terry was more optimistic. His contacts had suggested ten or twenty thousand streams in the week following the release. That had excited the band.

They watched.

George refreshed the page to get an up-to-date report. She turned to Terry, frowning. He looked back at her, expressionless. She refreshed again, and Terry nodded. He cleared his throat. "May I have your attention."

Everyone stopped what they were doing and looked at the termite. This was the moment they'd all been waiting for.

George refreshed again.

"According to this," Terry said deliberately, straining at the screen, "the number of listeners right now is… twenty-two thousand, three hundred and forty-four."

No one really knew what that meant. Spyder and Sy peered over Terry's shoulder. "Now it's twenty-two thousand, nine hundred and eighty-three," Spyder said. "No, it's twenty-five thousand, two hundred and twenty-two. Wait! Twenty-six thousand and seven."

"What does it mean?" Sy asked.

"It means," said George, wrapping her arm around Spyder and pulling them close, "that we're on the way to having a seriously major hit!"

Everyone surged to the table, squeezing excitedly around the little laptop, eyes glued to the screen as if it were the best film ever. For the next hour, they watched the counter, celebrating when the number climbed, willing it back up if it fell.

In the end, on the first day of release, 'I See You' was streamed precisely two million, thirty-four thousand, one hundred and thirteen times, and by the end of the first week, the song had been streamed eighteen million, six hundred and six thousand, nine hundred and thirty-two times. 'I See You' was the most streamed track in the world that week.

The *whole* world.

Anton, Honey, Spyder and Wiggy instantly became famous.

None of the band had expected this level of success, and no one was ready for it. Well, you wouldn't be, would you? You might dream about it, like what you'd do if you won the lottery. But imagine it actually happening!

Luckily, they had Terry. And Terry had a 'just in case' plan.

10

The Fame Game

The first sign that things had changed came the next morning, when Blake logged into the band's socials and found thousands of DMs. Most were complimentary, some were intimidating, and a couple were downright frightening. Blake had to report a threatening message to the police.

The second sign came when the band met up at The Bee's Knees. Although they'd all received a message to gather later at Terry's office, they agreed first on coffee. Very soon, after they sat down, the café filled up. Everybody was taking photos, and a constant stream of insects, arachnids and myriapods approached their table. Some came to say how much they loved the record, but many just took selfies and left. Word had spread that Them Creepy Crawlies was at the Central Market, and the café and adjacent walkways were soon packed.

For the band, it was great fun – a bit weird, but super-exciting. They happily signed autographs and posed for photos.

In the end, however, the café couldn't cope with the crowds. The manager appeared, looking frazzled, apologising profusely. They understood. The band slipped out from behind their table, still posing as they weaved through the crowd, amid shouts of "Anton! Honeeeey! Spyder! Wigster! Please don't go! Sign this! I love you!"

They followed the manager through the bustling kitchen and out of a side door into an empty street. They were high on the first taste of fame, and no one could have a normal conversation. There was a lot of playful gabbling and giggling, adrenalin firing on all cylinders. At the top of the alley, at the main road, they turned in the direction of Terry's office. Suddenly, someone outside the main entrance to the Central Market spotted them, shouted their names and pointed. A group of enthusiastic fans started to hurry towards them. Anton, Honey, Spyder and Wiggy didn't need to discuss what to do. They turned and made for Terry's at the double, with Anton frantically calling ahead for help. As their pace quickened, so did the fans', until everyone was flat out.

They burst through the doors of the office block, and the security – two beefy dung beetles – bolted the doors behind them. Out of breath, they collapsed onto the lobby chairs and, looking back out of the building, watched in disbelief as a crowd quickly formed. Then a very secretarial-looking bee with horn-rimmed glasses, hair pulled back severely, and a spotless suit, invited them to follow her to a meeting room.

Terry, the butterflies and George stood at the far end of the room, in deep conversation with two beetles, one smartly dressed in business attire, the other distinctly bohemian. They all looked up at the band, as they entered the room giggling and gambolling.

"How are you feeling?" George asked kindly when they'd all taken a seat at the big table.

"A bit under-prepared," Anton admitted good-naturedly, rocking on his chair as he perched a leg on the table in front of him. The others nodded in agreement.

"Now," Terry began, calling everyone to order. "This is Belle. She's going to be your..." Terry paused, searching for the correct designation.

"Personal organiser," Belle suggested, flashing a big, friendly smile around the table. "I'm the one you call if you need something," she added, sweeping a light, transparent fabric over her shoulder. Under her multi-coloured head-dress, large green eyes sparkled with warmth.

"Like sex, drugs or rock 'n' roll?" Spyder laughed, twirling their chair.

"Anything," Belle repeated with a mischievous wink.

Terry cleared his throat. "And this is Beaumont. He'll be your security advisor."

"Good morning, everyone." Beaumont stood up, bowing slightly in no particular direction. There was no warmth in his demeanour, merely efficiency. "I'm looking forward to working with you."

Anton shifted uncomfortably. "Terry," he grimaced. "Security advisors? Personal organisers? Is this all necessary?"

Beaumont cut in sharply. "You're going to find that your lives have changed. People will be talking about you. Watching you. Wanting to meet you."

"That's right," Blake added sympathetically. "We've already had to flag some abusive messages to the authorities."

"Really?" Anton replied sceptically.

"Really," Beaumont repeated solemnly. "If any of you want to go somewhere, you need to let me know. There are some weird arthros out there."

"Now, to business." Terry called the meeting back to order, handing each band member a bright red folder. The first page was an agenda, with ten items listed. Anton winced as he started to read: No. 1 'Appearances'; No. 2 'Financial Update'; No. 3 'Security'. He chucked the page back onto the table.

"Don't worry, I'm not going through this one by one," Terry said. "That'll be Belle's job. But I do want to talk about the last item."

Anton picked the sheet back up. "Number 10, 'Tour'. But we've just come off a tour. Spent weeks in the studio. Are you suggesting we go out again?" Anton's tone was defiant. "I don't know about you lot, but I was hoping for a bit of R and R."

The others murmured their assent.

"It's not a suggestion, Anton," Terry said.

The two insects stared at each other from opposite ends of the table.

George intervened. "Guys, we've just had an incredible launch. The song is trending. Downloads are amazing. Followers. Appearance requests. This morning should have given you some idea of what's going on, yeah? They love you! If you want to build on your success, you need to go out again. It'll be a bit different this time, though, won't it, Terry?"

Terry shook another sheet of paper at the band. They rummaged through their folder and found the relevant section. Anton nodded as he read. He couldn't argue with any of it. He considered doing it anyway – just for badness – but thought he should probably give it a break this time.

Anton smiled at Terry. "Fair enough." He addressed the others. "What do you think?" There was a second round of nodding. They then discussed venues, sound, hotels, appearances, and travel. Beaumont briefed them about security. Belle about calendars. Honey held Anton's hand and said he wasn't good with calendars. Spyder asked about clothes. Wiggy didn't ask anything.

At the end, Beaumont announced that a vehicle was waiting at the back entrance to take them home. As they left, Anton threw an arm around Honey's neck and pulled her close. Spyder, likewise, threw one of theirs around a surprised Wiggy, kissing him on the cheek. Wiggy beamed. Everyone was in high spirits. They had entered the building as newcomers but were leaving as pop stars.

#

Someone with a headset and mic appeared at the green room door and told Belle it was time. Relief washed over the band – they were moments away from playing the biggest gig of their lives.

Since the release of 'I See You', it had been a whirlwind of interviews, radio appearances, practice sessions, meetings, shopping, fittings, and even media training. The single had notched up over thirty million streams now, and their Insectagram had over two million followers.

On their first tour, they made their own way to the venues. Now they were whisked everywhere by chauffeurs in blacked-out SUVs. No more doing make-up in public toilets. Although they each had their own changing room, they liked to prepare in their hotel room and come ready. Just final touches at the venue – tonight, it was hair and make-up by a chatty and effervescent cricket.

Wiggy's stage outfits remained simple: jeans, a tee, some gel to keep his hair in place. Spyder, forever glamorous, was in a silver flared jumpsuit, big silver earrings and boots, and their trademark bubble sunnies. Honey wore a red patterned mini kilt over black tights with an armless black turtleneck blouse. Her severe fringe hung just above her eyes, across which she'd painted a strip of black makeup. Anton was in black leather pants and a leather jacket. Though initially tense about baring his chest, Honey and the butterflies had convinced him to embrace the look. Tousled, spiky hair now added to his raw, edgy frontman persona.

They followed the headset, Beaumont at the front, Belle at the rear. They passed a lot of familiar faces, portraits behind glass, hanging from the corridor walls. The excitement grew as Spyder tapped out rhythms on their thigh, Honey slapped her midriff with a thumb, and Anton gazed, transfixed by the legacy of the legendary artistes passing by. Only Wiggy seemed calm, absorbed as usual in his phone.

They reached the backstage area. It was a soulless, transient place, full of boxes, crates, unused lights, and pieces of scaffolding. You could hear noise, though – the structureless cackling of a big crowd mixed with pre-concert playlist booming from the PA.

Anton stood apart, locked in his thoughts. No one tried to speak to him, and he didn't try to engage anyone. He felt as if he was underwater, a place where the noise seemed both miles away and locked inside his head. He watched Honey and Spyder laugh and joke. Terry and Wiggy were talking in muted undertones. Belle and the headgear looked at run sheets.

Despite all their recent success, Anton's crippling nerves remained. Instead of reflecting on the journey that brought him to this point, all he could think about was not being sick. He shifted his weight from one foot to the other. Shook out his fingers. Twisted his neck. Bent his knees. Someone patted him on the back. He looked around to see someone he didn't know wish him luck. He smiled. Shook out his fingers again. Imagined a chord progression. Recited some tricky words.

Stand. I'm getting all dizzy,
Stand. I'm spinning in circles,
Close your eyes, pick a point, deep breaths,
Close your eyes, pick a point, deep breaths, breaths, breaths,
breaths.

Tonight, being their most significant show, only added to his anxiety. He'd had to deal with a who's who of musicians coming and going all evening, wanting to meet him. He'd had to shake hands with a slew of suits introduced by Terry – something he really disliked.

Panic churned inside him. *Here I am, resplendent, in black leather and bare chest, and all I want to do is lie down in the foetal position.* Taking the advice from his song 'Panic Attack', he closed his eyes, trying to control the waves of nausea. Deep breaths. Breaths. Breaths. In, out. In, out. He untwisted the top of his water bottle, sipped, spilled a bit, sipped again. *Let's get going, for goodness' sake.*

His nerves had nothing to do with forgetting words or playing the wrong chords – he knew he was word-perfect, chord-perfect. They had become highly competent, professional performers. He knew the crowd would adore the band. Him. No one made fun of his lyrics.

Finally!

The headset nodded to Belle, who told Spyder and Honey. Terry shook Wiggy's hand. Then the other three musicians grouped around Anton. They knew how he was feeling, but there was nothing they could say to make him feel better. Everyone put their arms around each other like a basketball team did before taking the court. They leaned in, heads touching. Nothing needed to be said as they felt the energy pass from antennae to antennae.

As always, Anton broke away first. He felt some comfort in the huddle, but the nausea always got the better of him, and he had to stand up straight. They made their way to the bottom of the heavy steps that led to the stage. Headset stood on guard, fiddling with her mic. Above them, on stage, someone was saying something. The words boomed out across the arena. There was a cheer, and the headset pulled her hand away, clearing the way for the band.

The house lights dimmed and the stage lights went from red to green, as spots crisscrossed the stage and audience.

"They're gonna bloody love us!" Spyder shouted excitedly. "Come on!"

They bounded up the steps, and as they emerged into the lights, a great roar went up from the crowd. Spyder leapt up onto their riser, smacked the drums a few times, and shuffled the seat into a better position. They flexed their four drumming arms as someone set bottles of water beside them.

Ready.

Wiggy lurched to the far side of the stage, gave an awkward wave, picked up the guitar waiting for him, and slung it over his shoulder. He checked the dials before making sure his various computers and keyboards were on. All good, he turned to smile at Spyder.

Ready.

On the near side, Honey switched on her bass amp, played a quick run, and walked to the front of the stage. She checked her microphone stand and fiddled with the height before looking out and smiling. Then she retreated to stand in front of her amp.

Ready.

And that left Anton.

Once the others were ready, Anton walked onto the stage. If the welcome for Spyder, Honey and Wiggy was like a warm wave lapping onto a tropical beach, for Anton it was like a tsunami, crashing over the stage. The singer, the man in the middle, the focus of thousands of eyes. It would be him that the cameras would focus on – sure, they'd capture Honey's performance, Spyder's and Wiggy's. But Anton was the centre of attention. That was his blessing, and his burden.

He checked his amplifier, adjusting a knob from six to seven and then back to six, before picking up his guitar and carefully placing it around his neck. He kept his eyes fixed on the amp as his heart pounded. He stummed. *Graaannng.* The crowd cheered. Finally, he turned, face to the floor, and walked to the front of the stage. For a moment, he focused on the mic stand, adjusting it, and then, with his heart thumping, he turned to Honey, hoping for some medicine. She gave him a smile and a reassuring nod.

"Good evening!" he shouted. The crowd roared back at him.

He strummed again, top to bottom – *Graaannng* – and the crowd roared once more. Surprised by the volume, he beamed with excitement.

"Thanks for coming out tonight!" *Graaannng.* With the next roar, he could feel the pain in his chest subsiding. His heart hadn't split his ribcage. He wasn't going to be sick. It was going to be okay.

That was their cue. No one needed to look as they knew what was coming. Spyder banged their drumsticks together: one, two, three, four.

Them Creepy Crawlies was on their way.

11

The Festival (1)

"**A**nton! Honey! This way! Come on! One together! Hey!"

Head down, Anton pushed wearily through the scrum of arthros gathered outside the restaurant. Thanks to his insistence on another bottle of wine, he and Honey were already late for a band meeting, and this was going to hold them back further. Despite his dark glasses, the flashes blinded him, and he stumbled into the throng of paparazzi.

"Sorry," he offered with a strained smile, trying to keep his humour intact.

"Been drinking again then, Anton?" the cockroach smirked. Anton sighed with frustrated resignation. Yes, he'd had a few drinks, but no more than usual. With no gig that night, he and Honey had enjoyed a pleasant evening with friends – but it seemed they couldn't go anywhere these days without attracting a posse of fans and photographers. What had once been new and fun was beginning to grate.

"Guys! Over here! That's it! Hey!" the calls continued.

Anton found Honey's hand and together they waved, smiling, scanning the crowd, trying to give everyone that perfect Insectagram shot.

"You look hot tonight, Honey!" called a horsefly, leering above the din. "Give us one of those flirty smiles, yeah?"

Honey ignored him. A month or two back, she might have played along, but now the advances felt tiresome and unnerving. Instead, she accepted a phone from a young moth, turned, grinned, and snapped a few selfies with the thrilled fan.

"C'mon, sweetheart. What about a selfie with me?" the horsefly insisted, shoving his way to the front. He was old, sweaty, and repulsive.

"Hey, dude, back off!" Anton slurred, extending his hand and searching for Beaumont, who was trying to carve a path through the crowd.

The horsefly sniggered. "Worried you'll lose that pretty little bee of yours? Hey, Honey, what you doing later?" he taunted.

Even as Honey tried to lead him away, Anton, fuelled by an evening of wine, felt his anger mounting. He pulled Honey aside. "I said back off," he growled, grabbing the horsefly by the neck and knocking his camera to the ground. The horsefly retaliated by pushing Anton hard in the chest and, for the second time in a minute, Anton stumbled backwards.

"Anton! Honey! This way! Come on! One together! Hey!"

Anton lost it. He lunged at the horsefly, tackling him around the abdomen, and the two crashed to the ground. In the ensuing thunder of clicking cameras, Beaumont and Honey dragged a still seething Anton away towards the waiting vehicle.

"What they hell were you thinking, Anton?" Honey fumed, as they sped off, dodging onlookers desperate for one last photo.

"What do you mean?" Anton replied innocently, stretching out, feeling rather pleased with himself.

"That horsefly?"

"Yeah! I showed him, didn't I?" He lurched towards Honey, searching for a congratulatory kiss, but she recoiled immediately.

"I don't need anyone to stand up for me," Honey snapped, pushing·him back angrily. "You know, Anton, maybe you shouldn't drink so much."

Anton ignored her. She was right, though – alcohol didn't suit him. This wasn't the first time he'd become aggressive after drinking, although he liked how wine temporarily eased the pressure he felt almost every day. Not on stage – he felt in control then; but all the other demands success placed on him: appearances, public scrutiny, recognition. He hated it all, and he knew it brought out the worst in him – the very traits he'd promised his bandmates he would leave behind.

Sitting in the back of the car, peering out the window as the streets flashed by, he felt flat. He'd been feeling unfulfilled for a while now. *This isn't how it's supposed to be.*

On the other side of the back seat, Honey also stared out of the window. She feared that she and Anton were growing apart, and it worried her. While he increasingly struggled to cope with success, Honey had blossomed. At first, she'd maintained a low profile, finding the attention overwhelming. But, determined to use her newfound fame to promote the issues she felt passionately about, she had gradually increased her outreach on social media. It had been Anton who'd encouraged her to make selected appearances, and he had joined her, enjoying the limelight and the platform. But when he had failed to show up for one event, she was forced to lie, telling everyone he was sick. He had arrived worse for wear at another, making inappropriate comments to senior advocates for inter-species coupling. Eventually, Honey stopped asking him.

Spyder, however, often accompanied Honey, and they soon became the darlings of the liberal, progressive community – a bee dating an ant and a gender-neutral spider were perfect role models! But they were also, of course, regular targets for the conservative media. As the buildings rushed past, Honey smiled at the memory of one particular interview with a disapproving elderly host who'd questioned whether their relationship challenged traditional values.

"How do you justify what some call an 'unnatural' way of living?" he had asked.

"Our relationship is founded on love, respect, and mutual support," she had replied. "Anton and I aren't defying tradition; we're broadening our understanding of what love can be."

"But isn't it true that many believe such relationships go against the natural order?" the interviewer pressed. "There are those who argue that by promoting this lifestyle, you're undermining the very foundation of the ecosystem."

Honey was about to say something about how love, in any form, can strengthen the world, when Spyder cut in. "Oh, come on, man! When did arthros ever stick to one way of doing things? History is about change, isn't it? We're loud and proud of who we are!"

The interviewer, smiling uncertainly, refocused on Honey. "Critics also say that your relationship with Anton is just a passing phase, a youthful rebellion against traditional values. How do you respond to concerns that this could break down societal norms – or negatively impact children's upbringing?"

Honey remained calm and measured. "There's no evidence to suggest that our relationship disrupts family or societal values. Stability and love can take many forms, and we're focused on living authentically."

"Exactly!" Spyder interjected. "And let's be honest," they added, squeezing the interviewer's thigh playfully, "if a little bit of extra flavour means we get to challenge outdated notions, then why not? I say, if love makes people smile or think twice, that's a win!"

The thigh squeeze and the interviewer's awkward reaction became memes and, naturally, went viral.

"We're here," Beaumont announced as a valet opened Honey's door. She nudged Anton awake and led him up the steps into the lounge. In the corner, Spyder and Wiggy were already waiting. Terry made a point of looking at his watch.

"Terry. How's it going, man?" Anton mumbled as Honey apologised for being late. Although they owed just about everything to the termite, Anton still couldn't warm to him.

Anton shimmied along the sofa and high-fived Wiggy, who was delighted to see the singer. The two had grown close: Wiggy sort of hero-worshipped Anton, while Anton saw Wiggy as the little brother he'd never had. Of all the band members, Wiggy had changed the least. He'd found himself a new set of friends, for whom a good night out was a superhero movie or a ghost hunt; and as ever, he was never far from his laptop.

Terry sat as taut as ever, letting the bandmates catch up. He was happy to listen to the gossip and stories, proud of his young charges and the team he'd put around them. If he was honest, he was also proud of his own achievement. Bar the odd incident, things were going surprisingly smoothly.

After a pause, Terry said in his customary laconic tone, "I have some news." He had a knack for cutting through the chatter – a quality Anton found infuriating.

Once he had everyone's attention, he added: "We have been asked to play at a festival."

He paused, letting the suspense build. Every band dreamed of playing at a festival. There was something mystical about these great, sweeping communes of musicians and fans. And there was always a chance that the one you played at, or attended, would be the one that was remembered for years afterwards – the one where people would forever say, "I was there, you know..."

"Alright, Terry," Anton said impatiently. "Tell us... what festival?"

"I thought you'd never ask." Terry smiled. He and Anton knew how to wind each other up.

"Well, come on, Terry. What festival is it?" asked Honey, tension creeping into her voice. All eyes were now firmly fixed on the manager.

"You really want to know?" he teased, clearly enjoying himself.

"YES!" the insects shouted in unison.

"Flutterbury. The headline has pulled out, so we're closing the Second Stage at Flutterbury."

There was stunned silence. Jaws visibly dropped and antennae quivered as the news slowly sunk in. Then, like a volcano that can't hold back the pressure that's been building at its core, the four friends erupted in an exuberant stream of molten joy.

Ask any band what festival they dreamed of playing at, and nine out of ten would say Flutterbury. It was the coolest, most iconic, most magical music festival of them all. There was something otherworldly about Flutterbury. Hundreds of thousands of arthropods coming together for three days in an ancient part of the countryside to celebrate the harmonious rhythm of music, dance and life.

#

The site was nestled in meadows surrounded by gently rolling hills. As they drove in, the band marvelled at the small city of multicoloured tents that spread out before them like a giant quilt haphazardly stitched together. They threw their bags inside the entrances of their eco-tents and headed out to explore.

Later, seated on a rug far up the hill in front of the Second Stage, surrounded by a teeming mass of arthros young and old, plain and exotic, doing the same, Them Creepy Crawlies watched the sun dip below the hive-shaped structure and the horizon beyond.

"Can't believe we're going to be playing there in two days' time," Honey said, sitting with one elbow on a raised knee, another thrown casually around Anton.

Wiggy lay on his back, eyes fixed on the sky. "A dream come true," he mumbled.

"Hey," Anton teased, wriggling free of Honey's embrace, placing his drink to one side to tickle Wiggy gently. "Did you hear that? Did Wiggy actually *say* something?"

"Come on!" Spyder jumped up. "It's the perfect time to explore." They playfully kicked at Anton, who grabbed their foot and wrestled them to the ground. He started tickling them, too.

"Ah! Ah! Get off! Watch my hair! Honey – help!" came the high-pitched remonstrations.

Honey giggled before leaping into the playful fray. "Wiggyyyyy!" Anton hollered as he pulled the guitarist into the mix.

If anyone in the crowd realised that one of the headline acts was now tumbling on the rug in joyful exuberance, they wouldn't have been surprised. That was the magic of Flutterbury. No one cared whether you were a band member or a fan – if you were there, you belonged.

Eventually, the band picked themselves up, brushed off the grass, and set off. In the fading light, the way was lit by glowworms and lightning bugs. The growing hum of cicadas and crickets felt reassuring and homely in this fantastical new world. The four friends wandered aimlessly. It was hard not to stare. Music filled the air, and they stopped regularly to listen to a pick-up performance: the cascading tones of butterfly flautists, the rhythmic tapping of beetle percussionists, angelic honeybee harpists, a haunting siku-playing centipede.

"What a perfect way to end the beginning," Anton mused, puffing on a hookah. They'd discovered a small shisha café and, relaxing on large cushions, they took turns to partake of the heady vapours.

"That's profound," teased Honey.

Anton nodded sagely.

Wiggy spluttered after inhaling too much smoke. "W-w-what's next?"

"Wiggy!" Spyder exclaimed. "This place is really bringing you out of yourself, man!"

Wiggy gave Spyder a deadpan stare. "Shut up, Spyder. Idiot."

"Sorry dude. You know I love you," they replied, planting a soppy kiss on his cheek. Wiggy scrunched up his face like a child might do to an overly affectionate aunt.

"I don't know, man." Anton drew on the pipe and blew the steam thoughtfully into the air. "Maybe a visit to the punk tent? Remind ourselves of our roots?" He cracked open another drink. He was feeling nicely loose now.

"No, Anton. For the band," Wiggy clarified. "What's next for the band?"

They had all been wondering the same thing. After two tours, two top-ten streamed songs of the year, and overwhelming attention, everyone was feeling the strain.

"A holiday," declared Honey. "A long, relaxing holiday." She kissed Anton hard on the lips. "Right?"

"Definitely," Anton agreed. "I think a bit of time off is definitely on the cards. What do you think, Wigster?"

"Yes. That would be very good. I have lots of work to catch up on."

"Holiday, Wiggy, means holiday, yeah?" mocked Spyder. "Like, not working?" There was no reply from Wiggy. His mind had drifted off somewhere.

Honey noticed that Spyder seemed nervous and fidgety. "Come on, Spyds, spit it out. What's up?" Spyder made to say something and then stopped. Shifted uncomfortably before blurting out: "I think I've met someone!"

Honey and Anton sat up.

"Really?" said Honey, unable to hide the excitement in her voice.

"Yup, really," Spyder replied matter-of-factly, making Honey blush. "I met her online. We've been chatting. She's nice, I think. We've got things in common. She's gonna come to our performance."

Honey leaned across and gave her friend a hug. "That's fantastic, Spyder. Truly."

"Does she have a name?" Anton asked.

"Sally."

"So, she's a spider?" Honey asked cautiously.

"Well, she'd hardly be a slug," Anton replied, thinking he was being funny.

Spyder and Honey looked at Anton with surprise. He held up his hands in defence. "Sorry, sorry! I know I'm being sluggist." Honey knew he wasn't sorry and rolled her eyes.

"That's cool, Spyder," Honey continued. "Exciting! I'm looking forward to meeting her."

"Thanks, Hon. I'm just a bit nervous."

The conversation paused as they contemplated meeting Sally, whether she'd get a backstage pass, and whether it would be awkward meeting her all together.

"Punk tent?" Wiggy suggested, not having heard a word of the conversation.

"Punk tent!" agreed Spyder. "Come on. Let's go, you guys."

So, just as the evening's stage performers were due to kick off, the gang trooped out of the shisha café towards the punk stage. From the back, they listened to a group of fire ants unleash a set of loud energy, while semi-deranged fans pogoed in the mosh pit.

As they kept moving between stages, passing through folk, jazz, rock, new wave, and trance tents, some insects welcomed them warmly, while others just nodded in recognition. A few forward bugs asked for a selfie, but for the most part, everyone was immersed in their own exciting adventure.

"Right," Spyder announced after they'd watched The Beetles, "Honey and I are off to catch Alan and the Ants."

"Who?" Anton asked.

Honey read from the program. "'A flamboyant new wave band. Driving bass lines and tribal-like drumming'. It seems that the singer likes to dress up!"

"Fair enough," Anton agreed. "I'm quite keen to see the Spiders from Mars. They've also got a theatrical singer. Wanna come, Wiggy?" Wiggy nodded vigorously.

"Hey," Honey called after Anton. "Maybe go easy on the..." she pointed to the tin in his hand.

Anton ignored her and turned his attention to Wiggy, slapping him on the back. "Lead the way, then, Edward," he said with mock formality.

#

The route to the Glam Rock stage teemed with sideshow entertainments, and Anton and Wiggy soon paused to marvel at a display of aerial aerobatics by a cluster of dragonflies. They then followed a small colony of praying mantis dancers, weaving robotically.

Suddenly, all the butterflies around them lifted into the air together. Without a cue or a signal, they simultaneously took off at precisely the same time. "It's a spontaneous release," Wiggy marvelled excitedly. "I've read about it. Watch, Anton. It's amazing."

Hundreds of multi-coloured insects climbed together in a flair-like column. Reaching their apex, one by one they dived downwards until, just above the heads of the crowd, they turned inwards, before rising again in a mesmerising swirl of colour.

They eventually settled down to enjoy the set by the Spiders. Wiggy grumbled about the number of costume changes and the overblown theatricality of it all. Sharing a plate of mixed petals sprinkled with pollen, they wandered, chatting about nothing in particular, until they reached an art installation area where they stood examining a large sculpture of three pyramids made from twigs, grass and leaves with a body of mud made up of different species lying beside it.

"Definitely the abdomen of a beetle," Anton reckoned, squinting.

"Eight limbs. There's a spider in it as well," added Wiggy.

They debated whether the thorax and head were those of an ant or an earwig.

"Gotta be an earwig, surely?" came a friendly voice beside them. They turned to see another earwig admiring the sculpture.

"Wow! You're Wiggy from Them Creepy Crawlies, aren't you?" said the young earwig, slightly starstruck. "Cool!"

He turned and said: "Hey guys, look. It's Wiggy and Anton from Them Creepy Crawlies." Two ants, a spider and a hornet edged closer, shyly waving hands in greetings.

"We're all massive Them Creepy Crawlies fans, aren't we?" The other insects nodded enthusiastically, garbling various greetings to Anton and Wiggy.

"Yay!" said Anton, hand-slapping each insect. He was definitely a bit worse for wear now.

The earwig, however, wanted to talk to Wiggy. "Your guitar and synthesiser have made such a difference to the sound," he enthused. "There's more depth and texture to the songs now."

"Sorry, Anton. Man, we love your songs," one of the ants said.

"Thanks, guys. But s'all good," Anton slurred, wrapping an arm around Wiggy. "His sound has made a real difference."

"Dude, the BSR1000 gives you a real warmth. But when you kick in the C230, you manage to achieve... what did you call it, Harry... cosmic contusion," one of the ants teased. The older hornet nodded.

"Yeah, but don't forget the old 3X3Z processor he uses gives that earthy analogue overlay," the other ant added. They all agreed.

Wiggy beamed. "You guys know your stuff."

The hornet continued. "May I ask where you picked up the original Orange TT10? Weren't there only twenty made before they went into mass production."

"Twelve," replied Wiggy.

"Really! Only Twelve. Must have been expensive," the hornet exclaimed.

"Dunno," Wiggy shrugged. "Our manager found it."

Anton loved it when his friend became animated. No one could discuss equipment with such passion as Wiggy.

"Hey, Wigs," Anton interjected as Wiggy joined his circle of new mates and programming experts. "I'm knackered, mate, and a little tipsy, so I'm heading off. You gonna be alright?"

Wiggy jumped up, hugged Anton and assured him he'd be fine, promising to return later. After exchanging goodbyes, Anton set off back through the throng to the camping area, where he found Honey and Spyder sitting around a campfire, chatting with the drummer and bass player from Alan and the Ants. Anton lingered for a moment, mumbled his apologies, and stumbled off to his tent.

Later, lying on his bed, listening to the late-night sounds of the festival, he felt content for the first time in a while. *Maybe it's all going to be okay, after all.*

12

The Confession

Anton awoke to the chirps and trills of grasshoppers busying themselves somewhere in the artist camping area. Beams of morning sun streamed through the tent window as he lay on his back, head cradled between his upper arms, watching, sleepily, as the light chased shadows around the floor and walls. Dust particles caught in the light's path twinkled, and he remembered watching the same thing in his childhood bed. Remembered how it added a mystical quality to the room and took him away from the reality of his disappointing life. But today, he was looking forward eagerly to what the day might hold.

He yawned, stretched, and dragged himself out of bed. Feeling a little heady, he threw on some clothes and set off for the food court, finding Honey and Spyder there with coffee and algae toast, arthro watching.

"I'm gonna need some of that," Anton groaned.

Arthro watching was one of their favourite pastimes. Many pleasant hours had been wasted at The Bee's Knees, watching the world go by, offering critical commentary on clothes or haircuts. Guessing ages and who did what. Today, however, they weren't just watching any arthros. They were observing some of the biggest music stars alive.

"I'm not sure if 'guessing the profession' poses much of a challenge this morning," Honey remarked. The three of them sat and gawped at the musicians who had recently risen from bed.

"Look," Spyder whispered from behind a hand. Anton and Honey followed Spyder's gaze. "It's The Chameleon!"

"Don't look!" hissed Spyder. Anton and Honey quickly averted their eyes, staring directly at their drummer. Honey surreptitiously dropped a fork and, on her way to retrieve it, stole a sneaky peek.

Honey put the fork back on the table. "Doesn't he look so normal without make-up?"

"Is he a he or a she?" asked Anton.

"Actually, I think a they," Spyder corrected.

Almost on cue, The Chameleon, thin and delicate, in a lime, yellow and tan one-piece, looked straight at them and nodded hello. With straight faces, they nodded back. The Chameleon moved off towards the buffet, and the trio leaned in to share large, childish grins.

"They're probably thinking," Anton drawled in a mock accent, "well, now I know what Spyder from Them Creepy Crawlies looks like in the morning." He winced as Spyder playfully kicked him under the table.

After some more stargazing, Honey came up with a new game. What-they'd-do-if-they-weren't-a-popstar. "Or what they wouldn't do," Spyder suggested mischievously.

"Yeah, yeah! Let's do that! I'll start," Honey said enthusiastically. "The Chameleon wouldn't be a check-out attendant."

"Or a gym attendant," giggled Spyder. They all laughed.

They watched the lead singer of The Crickets, famous for his heavy, dark-rimmed glasses, sit down with a plate at a nearby table. He also nodded at them, so Anton waved back. "Weird to think that these arthros seem to know who we are. Maybe they're playing the same game as us."

Quick as a flash, Honey replied: "Like Spyder would never be a customer service representative."

"Or a counsellor," mocked Anton as he pretended to pick up a phone. "Hello, is that Spyder? I'm looking for someone patient, calm, and non-judgemental..."

"Hello, is that Anton?" Spyder retorted. "I'm looking for someone unreliable, unpunctual, and up his own arse."

"Oh, you mean the one that writes those great songs?" Anton quipped.

"Now, now, children!" Honey intervened, playing the adult in the room. She made to get up from the table. "Right, I'm off to look at the vintage clothes shops. Anyone coming?"

The other two declined. Spyder was going to find a yoga class, and Anton was going to lie down. They agreed to meet at the rehearsal stage at the nominated time.

"Maybe wake up Wiggy, Anton," Honey called as she left. "And bring a setlist with you." Anton shot a tired look upwards. As if he'd forget to write out the setlist!

He wandered back to the camping area and Wiggy's tent. He shook the door and called out, but there was no reply. Increasingly louder calls and vigorous shakes failed to provoke a response, so Anton unzipped the tent and went in. Wiggy's bed hadn't been slept in. *He must've stayed with that group of insects from last night. I'll see him at rehearsal.*

#

Anton arrived a little late, feeling edgy. Everyone else was there and ready. Spyder behind their drum kit, hair pulled up high above a bandana, scrolling through their phone. Honey on a chair in front of her amplifier, head down, as she practised her lines. She threw Anton a 'you're late' look and returned to her practice, which only made Anton even more tetchy.

Brie and Blake fluttered around, snapping photos and video clips. Sy fiddled with cables and checked microphones. Further back, George and Terry sat behind a mixing desk while Belle scrolled furiously through her phone. Beaumont stood to attention at the door.

"Sorry, I'm late," Anton said without any conviction, grabbing his guitar, flicking his foot-switch to check his tuning. Spyder put their phone in their breast pocket and gave the drums a roll. "Set-list?"

Anton turned to Spyder. "Sorry. Forgot. Give us a minute." He took out his phone and started noting down songs. Spyder shook their head.

"And did you wake up Wiggy?" Honey asked.

Anton glanced around. "He wasn't there. And his bed hadn't been slept in. Maybe he hooked up," Anton remarked, smiling, unconcerned, sipping from his bottle of water.

Spyder tapped their phone a few times and held it to their ear. "He's not picking up," they said after a while. "Weird. He's usually the first to arrive."

"Hey! Terry," Spyder called. "You heard from Wiggy?"

Terry shook his head, so they returned to what they were doing, assuming he'd turn up any minute. After a while, there was still no sign of Wiggy, so Terry made his way to the stage. "No one has seen or heard from him. No texts or anything?" They all shook their heads.

"Hey!" Terry called to the others. "Anyone heard from Wiggy? Belle? Beaumont?" They shook their heads as well. Terry took out his phone and tried to call him.

"So, who was with him last?" Terry asked when there was no answer.

"It would have been me, I suppose," Anton said.

"Okay, good," said Terry. "When was that?"

Anton recounted the previous evening, which culminated in him and Wiggy discovering the art installations, hanging out with the nerdy arthros, and discussing music and equipment.

"So, you left him with strangers?" Terry asked.

Anton looked up, surprised at Terry's tone. "I did, Terry," Anton replied curtly. His head had started to throb a little.

Terry raised his eyebrows. "Okay. What species were they? Ants? Spiders?"

Anton reeled off the ones he could remember.

"You said a hornet?" Terry interrupted. "You're sure it wasn't a bee?"

"Terry, mate, I think I know the difference between a hornet and a bee. But yeah, definitely a hornet. He was the one asking most of the questions. He seemed super up on stuff."

Terry's expression hardened. He switched to his serious, fatherly voice. "I want you to think very carefully, Anton. Was there anything particular that you remember about that hornet?"

It was his condescending tone that wound Anton up. Sensing something was up, Honey and Spyder stopped what they were doing.

"No, nothing. There was nothing in particular," Anton replied, mimicking Terry's accent. "He just looked like any other hornet. Friendly, though."

"So, no defining features? Think Anton!" Terry pressed.

Anton felt his irritation rise, but he did think harder. Terry seemed concerned. Was there anything about that hornet that stood out? He closed his eyes, trying to picture the face. The side of its face. *That's right, there was something! But just to annoy him, maybe I won't tell.*

"There was, wasn't there? Anton? Anton!" Terry was becoming exasperated. "Stop being a child. THIS IS SERIOUS!"

Anton hadn't considered it might be serious. "Actually, now that I think about it, there was something. He had a scar." Anton drew a finger down the side of his face. "It ran down his right side."

Terry swore under his breath and strode to the back of the room, stick clicking in one hand, while with the other, he took out his phone. Anton, Honey and Spyder exchanged glances as they watched their manager tap twice and speak animatedly into his phone.

"You can be such a dick," Honey told Anton. He shrugged.

Although his back was turned, they could tell Terry was listening intently. Occasionally, he would turn to face them, speaking quietly to whoever was on the end of the line. There was urgency in Terry's conversation as he made another, quicker call and then asked everyone to gather round. He told them not to worry, that Wiggy had taken sick, the rehearsal was cancelled, and he'd let them know the rearranged time. He asked the band to stay.

Anton, Honey and Spyder watched their crew file out of the room before bursting with questions. How did he find Wiggy? Where was he? Was he going to be okay? Can we go to see him?

Terry said nothing. They could tell he was distracted. Some of the colour had drained from his face and his brow seemed more furrowed. The gang, now silent, watched Terry walk back and forwards across the rehearsal room. He looked at them, as if he was trying to get something straight in his head. Then he turned away. Anton, Honey and Spyder had never seen Terry act so weirdly. It worried them.

"What is it, Terry?" Anton asked sympathetically. "What's wrong?"

Terry turned to face his charges. He stood ramrod straight and his stick was planted firmly in front of him.

"Sit down, everyone, and I'll explain." He waited for them to settle before clearing his throat. "The hornet with the scar? His name is Hendrix. He's a colonel in the FSS."

"The what?" Spyder asked. "Sounds like some secret service."

"It is," Terry replied. He had their attention now. "FSS stands for Federal Security Service. It's a special unit created by the hornet queen, Vespa. Have any of you heard of her?"

"Oh my God," Honey replied, glancing at Anton. "She's been in the news recently. The Grove Hornets. You showed me, Anton... the public executions."

Anton nodded. "That's right. The insects who murdered her family. Terrible."

"Since becoming queen, Vespa has slowly and quietly been extending her influence." Terry lowered his voice. "Abroad, they've been appointed to run the internal security for several regions. At home, they've started a big infrastructure build."

"Yeah," Anton nodded. "Seemingly, the worker villages don't meet many basic standards. There was a demo to raise awareness the other week."

Spyder frowned. "Okay. So, what has this all got to do with Wiggy being sick?"

Terry turned towards Spyder. "It is my belief, and that of my superiors, that Wiggy has been kidnapped by Colonel Hendrix and is being held at The Nest."

"Kidnapped?" Anton spluttered, "Why? For what?" He stood, hands on his hips. "For goodness' sake! Who would want to kidnap Wiggy?"

Terry raised his eyebrows over the top of his dark glasses and said in a calm but firm tone: "Sit down, please, Anton."

Anton remained standing.

"We've been keeping a close watch on Vespa, Hendrix, and the FSS," Terry continued. But Anton was agitated now.

"'We', Terry? You keep saying 'we'. Who is 'we'?"

"And who are your 'superiors', Terry? I don't understand," Honey added.

From the moment he had met them, this was the moment Terry had hoped would never come. But now, given the circumstance, he was forced to tell the truth.

"'We' is Insecterpol. Insecterpol is a secret police force."

Anton was unimpressed. "Never heard of you."

Terry raised his eyebrows at Anton, but chose not to respond. Instead, very deliberately, he balanced his stick on the side of the chair, leaned forward and lifted off his glasses to reveal two black, ugly and lifeless eyes. "Hendrix did this," he grimaced.

"Insecterpol is an ancient organisation tasked with defending all arthropods against those who would upset our delicate way of life."

Anton sat down and looked at his friends. The disclosure had shaken them. Outside, day two of the festival was underway, and music filtered into their rehearsal space. But unbeknownst to the thousands of fans moving around the festival site, the manager of Them Creepy Crawlies was, in fact, a secret agent and their lead guitarist had been kidnapped by a tyrannical hornet.

"Seriously, man? You're, like, a spy?" Spyder asked incredulously.

"Strictly speaking, I'm a senior case officer, Spyder," Terry corrected, replacing his glasses and regaining his authority. "I run missions of appropriate action and I recruit and train agents..." He paused. "Like Edward. I'm his contact and handler."

"Wait, wait, wait," Spyder stuttered, shaking their head. "Wiggy's a spy? I don't believe you. Wiggy? Our Wiggy? Gentle, kind, slightly weird Wiggy?"

Terry smiled at Spyder. "Well, again, strictly speaking, he's an asset. A very valuable one. He's the best security software developer, and hacker, in the arthro kingdom. That's why he's been kidnapped."

"Because they want him to design a software program for them?"

"Or break into one," Terry replied.

Having stayed very quiet while Terry was talking, Anton now began to pace. "Okay, so let me get this straight." He pointed at Terry. "You're a secret agent. You recruited Wiggy. Wiggy joined Them Creepy Crawlies and then you joined Them Creepy Crawlies. That's not a coincidence, is it?"

"You're right, Anton. Now, please sit down and I'll explain."

Honey could see Anton bristle, so she reached out, her eyes guiding him back to the chair beside her.

"It was Edward's plan," Terry continued. "And a bloody clever one at that. The usual cover of diplomats, journalists and aid workers no longer works, but a band makes the perfect cover for travelling around the world."

"You could book gigs anywhere you were needed," Honey suggested.

"Correct. No one would suspect that a rock star and his manager were secret agents."

Spyder pursed their lips and nodded in mild appreciation. "Sure, I can buy that. But why us?" They gestured to Honey and Anton. "Why Them Creepy Crawlies?"

"The right music," Terry said, "And the right people. Our intelligence told us that fans were growing tired of poptomistic singer-songwriters and craved something real, raw and authentic. Edward loved your music so much that he suggested we run it through our algos. Our AI confirmed his theory. Your music needed a little refinement, which he provided, and I found a team to push it to the right curators."

Spyder's eyes widened as it all became clear. "So, you used us."

Honey and Anton stared at Terry, who shifted with rare discomfort.

"We saw it as a win-win. We get cover. You become stars. And look what you have achieved."

Anton's gaze hardened. "But you lied to us, Terry."

A heavy silence fell. Thoughts whirled around Anton's mind. *I was right about you, Terry.* Anton knew they should have gone with Phillip. He'd have seen them right, seen them to where they were now. *Used! How embarrassing. Someone's project, manipulated for ulterior outcomes. Now what?* The touring, the fans, the success – how much of it was truly theirs? And what about Wiggy? He remembered their first meeting at The Cave. *You set me up.* Anton shook his head and smiled. *Who'd have thought! It goes to show you can never judge a book by its cover.*

"The most important thing right now is Wiggy," Honey chimed. "I assume Interpol, or whatever you're called, has a plan to rescue him?"

"That's the thing," Terry replied. "All our agents have just been stood down. We recently discovered a security breach in our HR system. Edward has been working on a new protocol. It's being tested as we speak, but won't be ready for another 24 hours. Until then, we can't contact any of our agents."

"O-kay," Spyder said slowly. "But in 24 hours, it might be too late?"

Terry shifted uneasily. "As soon as our agents come back online, we will send the very best assets, I promise you that. Now, the best thing you can do is try to enjoy the festival. I'll update you later in the day."

And with that, Terry rose and marched from the room, leaving the three remaining bandmates staring at each other in helpless disbelief.

Spyder flicked some irritating hairs off their face. "Secret agents, kidnappers, assassins, despotic hornets. Our guitarist is a spy, and our manager is his contact." They shook their head. "You couldn't make this stuff up."

Honey remained seated, smiling benignly, watching her friend struggle with their fringe. Anton now stood behind her, his top arms pushing down on the back of her chair, antennae pulsing lightly. He was furious with Terry. *What now for the band? Success at what cost? Friendships? Relationships? Morals? Who told me success wasn't everything? It was the only thing! Wiggy...*

Anton shook his head. He started pacing. The others watched him. He set off and stopped. Started again and then stopped. His head tilted one way, then the other. He put his top arms on his hips and turned around.

"It has to be us," he said cryptically.

"What has to be us?" Honey replied.

"To rescue him."

Honey stared hard at her partner. His eyes were fixed firmly on her; she knew he was being deadly serious. He walked up to her and kissed her on the cheek. "We can't just leave him – wait for Terry's agents. They might be too late. Who knows what these hornets might do to him. No. Sorry, but I can't sit and wait. It's as simple as that."

"Oh, for God's sake!" Spyder exclaimed. "You can't be serious. Like, we're musicians, not bloody ninjas. What are we going to do, sing them into submission?"

"Spyder's right, Anton. What chance do we have against a swarm of highly trained, ruthless hornets? We know nothing about The Grove, The Nest, or wherever they're holding Wiggy. I mean, how do we even get there?"

"Okay, listen," said Anton calmly. "We can hitch a ride on one of those complimentary dragonflies."

"Ride a dragonfly?" Spyder exclaimed. "Absolutely not!"

Anton ignored them. "To the edge of The Grove, yeah? Then, what's the chance we have fans living in some of the workers' villages around The Nest? What if someone there could help us? You know, give us some inside info."

"Yeah, but what are they going to think when we pitch up on their doorstep?"

Anton thought for a moment. "We'll tell them they've won a private show from us. But they have to keep it a secret... sneak us in. Find us a way into The Nest... that's it! We're gonna give, like, a pop-up gig at The Nest and we need their help."

Spyder laughed. "You really have a vivid imagination. We obviously have to leave this to the professionals..."

Honey stared at Anton before pulling out her phone and calling up their Insectagram account.

"Wait, wait, wait. Honey! Really? What are you doing, girl?"

After a few moments of filtering, Honey looked up. "There are quite a few."

Honey and Anton scrolled through the profiles. "There! Him!"

Spyder joined them and, crowding around Honey's phone, they read his profile. "Naw," Spyder muttered. "Anyone else?"

They read a few more bios that weren't quite right, until they scrolled to a beetle called Bo. Honey clicked her profile.

"Perfect!" nodded Anton.

"So, should I call her?" Honey looked first at Anton, then at Spyder.

"This is crazy. Seriously crazy," Spyder giggled, exchanging looks with their two friends. Then their tone changed, as they spoke with a hushed, uncharacteristic seriousness. "You know there's a significant chance we'll fail? That we'll get caught? End up in some prison. Then what? Are you guys absolutely ready to do this?"

Anton's eyes burned with determination. For the first time in his life, he felt a purpose, a willingness to take responsibility.

"Yes," he said flatly. "Look, it'll be fine. Trust me."

Spyder turned to Honey. "Babe? Are you ready for this?"

Honey grinned. "I was born ready, babe."

She tapped the phone icon at the top left of the profile and put it on speaker. After a few rings, a voice on the end said: "Hey, Bo here, what's up?"

"Hi, Bo! This is Honey from Them Creepy Crawlies…"

13

The Hornets' Nest

Three giant passenger dragonflies waited at the airstrip, their long, slender bodies glimmered emerald and sapphire in the late morning sun. Delicate wings vibrated with a gentle hum of anticipation.

Anton, Honey and Spyder ducked under the pulsing wings. Moments earlier, they had hurried out of the rehearsal room, back to their tents, and grabbed a jacket and a bag of whatever they could find. At the artist information booth, they'd booked their flights that, luckily, were available straight away. They sprinted to the airstrip, agreeing not to tell Terry.

The three bandmates cautiously mounted the dragonflies' abdomens, shuffling just beyond the wings and thorax to their seats behind the heads, before belting themselves in.

"Mui Mavu, please," Anton said.

"Roger that," the lead dragonfly replied.

Anton scanned the surrounding woods, imagining a hornet spy hidden in the shadows, relaying details of their flight to some secret authority. He smiled at Honey to his right, who sat composed. Of course she did – she was a flyer. Her support gave him a huge amount of confidence, and he prayed her decision to come was driven by Wiggy's predicament rather than her love for him.

He could see, on the other side, Spyder shifting uncomfortably, all legs, attitude and swearwords. Anton could tell they were super-excited. What a story to tell the brood, assuming they got back in one piece!

Had they made the right decision to set off on this adventure to rescue Wiggy? The weight of it gnawed at him. *What if something happened to Honey or Spyder?* It would be his fault, and he'd never be able to live with himself.

Anton set his anxiety aside as the dragonflies introduced themselves as DF1, 2 and 3. DF1 briefed them on distance, time, altitude, weather, and emergency procedures. Once everyone responded with a thumbs-up, the dragonflies increased the rotation of their wings until they all rose vertically to their cruising altitude.

The formation rotated in a circle, the dragonflies scanning the skies. Way below, Anton could see a couple of insects looking up, shading their eyes from the sun. Beyond the trees, Flutterbury stretched out serenely.

"DF1 to DF2 and DF3: all clear. On my count: three, two, one…"

The passengers were caught unawares by the force of the acceleration. Gripping their reins as tightly as they could while their bodies were pushed backwards, they struggled to breathe against the rushing wind. Anton felt his muscles tense and sinews strain as his senses adjusted to the new experience. Gradually, the pressure eased, and the three passengers could settle back to enjoy the rhythm of the ride: the hum of the wings, the flow of the wind, the feeling of weightlessness.

The view was breathtaking. The summer sun bathed the land below in a silvery haze. Cloud shadows lazed across the fields. Occasionally, the silhouettes of the dragonflies darted over the patchwork of greens and browns. Anton surfed his hand outside the slipstream, enjoying the sharp rise and fall from the smallest of movements. As the dragonflies navigated smoothly through the invisible streams of air, everyone settled into their comfortable reflections.

It was DF2 who picked up on it first, a tiny pulse on an antenna. Her internal sensory system alerted her to a large mass far off to the right. She immediately reported her concerns to her colleagues. "It feels large," she said. "Really large."

"Talk to me, 2," DF1 asked. "What else do you feel?"

DF2 closed her eyes in concentration. "It seems to be moving directly towards us. Moving quickly."

Anton could sense the faintest hint of agitation in the dragonfly's tone. He stood high in his stirrups but could see only clouds. Then, one cloud appeared to move. Slowly at first, but definitely shifting, and expanding. As it drew nearer, it started to snake, slithering downwards and then stretching upwards, with the front dragging the back along the same path. It began to sparkle with countless lights.

"Locusts!" DF1 yelled.

The air began to vibrate with the clicking and popping of a million wings and legs. The dragonflies looked at each other. There was no time to land or fly above the swarm.

"Lock in everyone," said DF1 with composed authority. "Low as you can against our bodies. Flyers, deactivate your autopilot. Stay calm and good luck!"

"Here they come!" called DF3. "Heads down!"

The noise was deafening as the swarm surrounded them. The three passengers buried their heads into the thoraxes of the dragonflies and held on desperately, digging their legs in, and squeezing their eyes shut.

The dragonflies weaved and curved, twisted and turned, avoiding the locusts. To Anton, the clattering noise seemed to go on and on and on. He hung on hard as he was thrown from side to side like a passenger in some out-of-control bobsleigh. He could just pick out a scream from Spyder as he, too, grunted with the strain of holding on.

And then it was over. Like the final stretch of a roller-coaster, everything was suddenly calm as clarity was regained. Anton, Honey and Spyder opened their eyes. They stared at each other, exhaling and grinning with relief. Spyder whooped wildly.

They all turned to watch the whiplash of locusts undulate away into the distance.

"Great work, team," announced DF1, as the dragonflies resumed their connected flight modes and reset their course.

Below, they could see the locust-devastated land stretching for miles on either side.

"This is what happens when locusts swarm," Honey said. "I remember learning it at school. Individuals gather when their habitat collapses."

"I wonder why it happened here?" Anton thought out loud.

Honey shrugged.

Beneath them, the land soon returned to a patchwork quilt of greens and yellows and browns. Rectangles separated by dark borders of hedgerows. The wispy shadows of clouds sweeping across rich farmlands. They were flying east now, and although Anton couldn't tell, the ground was gathering height that would ultimately rise to the top of an escarpment. On the other side was a rift valley – the home of the Grove Hornets.

DF1 interrupted his thoughts. "We're only a few minutes out from Mui Mavu, so please prepare to land." The mini squadron circled lower, slowing until they touched down in a small clearing. As Anton, Honey and Spyder dismounted and stretched, the sound of pings went off from each of their phones.

"It's Terry," Honey said, looking up from her screen. "Should we tell him what we're doing?"

"Nah," replied Anton. "Let him worry about us for a bit. We'll call him later."

"Everyone got everything?" DF1 called. After checking their packs and pockets, they nodded. "Good. Well, this is where we say goodbye."

The passengers thanked their dragonflies and waved as they took off, climbed vertically, hovered momentarily, and then vanished into the western sky at top speed.

The gang adjusted their simple disguises of hats and sunglasses and headed towards the plumes of smoke that rose beyond the trees. Emerging from the woods, they made their way through the quaint streets of Mui Mavu until they reached the main gathering grounds. It was market day, so the noisy plaza was crammed with stalls offering goods from local farmers and market gardeners. The influx of out-of-towners made it easy for three rock stars to blend in, and they found a free table at one of the many cafés scattered through the market. A waiter scurried over, wiped down their table, and handed out menus before darting off to another table.

This marketplace was quite different from the Central Market they knew so well. The merchants here were farmers, earthy and good-humoured, their faces weathered by the land and the sun. Customers didn't follow city trends but wore practical, workworn clothes. The stalls were simple – rickety and tatty from years of use – and there wasn't a robot in sight. There were hardly any smartphones around, for that matter.

Suddenly, a beetle dropped into the spare seat at their table. "Oh! My! God!" she whispered excitedly, taking in each band member. "It's actually you. Them Creepy Crawlies. Sick!"

"Shhh!" Anton held a finger to his mouth, looking around surreptitiously. "Sorry. Hi," he apologised hurriedly. "It's just that we don't want to be recognised."

"Sorry, sorry," the beetle blushed, chasing two hands to her mouth. "Of course." She sat, offering her hand, just about managing to contain her excitement: "I'm Bo. Massive fan. But, what the hell? Like, what is this?" she whispered dramatically.

It was Spyder who replied. "You know, music can get so boring, so we thought we'd do something a bit different. Something a bit raw and real."

"Valid!" Bo exclaimed. "Like, totally!"

"We want to video as much as we can. It'll be awesome content," Honey said, taking up the narrative. It felt like a band jam, each member taking turns to solo while staying on the theme. "That's why we haven't told *anyone* about what we're doing. They all think we're at the festival."

"Yeah, even our manager," sniggered Spyder.

"Total!" Bo said. "But, hey, no faces, yeah? I don't want those officers coming after me. I'm here to earn some money and then get home and get on with my thing. I don't need any hassle."

"Absolutely," Anton agreed.

"Cool, thanks." Bo looked around. "By the way, where's Wiggy?"

"Oh, er, he's sick," Honey replied, quite quickly.

"Aww. Love that earwig. Will he be OK for your Flutter-bury show?" Bo asked sympathetically.

Anton had completely forgotten about the show they were meant to perform tomorrow evening. It now seemed so trivial. He grinned at his friends. "I certainly hope so," he said. "We need to get going though. What's the plan, Bo? You said you'd be able to get us into the camp without being seen?"

Bo smiled and handed each person a lanyard. Attached to the ribbon was a piece of plastic, and on the plastic was a photo of each of the band members, scraped from their Insectagram page.

"Normally, it takes days to get a camp pass. But, as I said, I know someone. You've come for my birthday party, by the way... Simone, Alex and Hyacinth."

"Hyacinth! Really?" Honey shook her head, and the others just laughed. Except Bo, who looked embarrassed.

"Ha! Beautiful." Anton kissed Honey square on the lips. "I still love ya!"

"Best we get you some different clothes, yeah?" Bo suggested. "You all look a bit, er, rockstarish." She smiled apologetically.

A visit to some second-hand stalls later, they were on the road. Just another group of Grove workers. Bo explained that she was employed by a construction company as a labourer on a fixed-term contract at The Nest. The pay wasn't great, but there was little to spend it on. She was saving up to travel.

"And the security guards?" Spyder asked. "We heard those guys were, like, serious."

"The Feds," confirmed Bo. "Nah. Their snap is worse than their sting. So long as you stay on the right side of them, they're cool."

Bo, Spyder and Honey chattered away while Anton wondered how they were actually going to get into The Nest and find Wiggy. They knew nothing about the place. *Still,* he told himself, *we're good at improvising. We'll figure it out.* As the midday sun warmed his face, he relaxed to their new situation. Life was weird. Six months ago, they were playing pub gigs. Now Flutterbury. And in between, they were off to spring Wiggy from some hornet captors. *Serious adventure!*

Up ahead, a bottleneck had formed on the road. As they got closer to the tailback, they could see they were approaching a checkpoint. The road they were on merged with a bigger one, where hornets were checking IDs.

"Nothing to be nervous about, guys," Bo reassured them. "You've all got your passes. Hornets aren't brought up to appreciate music, so they won't recognise you... and if they do, well, remember, you're coming to celebrate my birthday."

Solid crowd control barriers now flanked the approach to the checkpoint, making it impossible to slip through unnoticed. Anton reasoned that it would have been easy to duck into the undergrowth further back up the road and reappear somewhere down the main road.

As if on cue, two hornet police officers, dressed in severe black uniforms, emerged from the forest, one of them dragging a dazed and bruised ant by a leash. The ant's hands were tied, and she was dressed in little more than rags. Fluttering above the hornets were two Winged Aerial Surveillance Projectiles, which snapped and growled at the ant.

Everyone approaching the checkpoint stopped to watch. The ant was pulled roughly over the verge and onto the road, where she stumbled and fell to her knees. As she found her feet, the tether attached to her shackles broke, and the ant found herself free. Shocked at her fortune, she looked first at her hands, then at the officers, unsure what to do.

All the onlookers, including Anton, Honey and Spyder, held their breath, sensing something bad was about to happen. The ant took off, running drunkenly down the road. After a short distance, she darted into the bush beyond. As she did, the two WASPs shrieked overhead, wings whining as they picked up speed. The hornets tore after them, shouting for the ant to stop.

For a while, there was an ominous silence that was finally broken by desperate, bloodcurdling screams. The three friends jumped with shock. Again, there was an eerie silence, before the officers reappeared, dragging the ant towards an official building. There was no resistance, just a limp dead-weight.

No one spoke as the arthros on the road tried to process what had just happened. Gradually, the crowd resumed its slow shuffle towards the checkpoint, and a wave of tense chatter washed over them.

Only then did Anton realise that Honey was tightly gripping his upper arm. She had held on to him as the drama unfolded, and he, instinctively, had kept her protectively close.

She released her grip. "Why?" she shivered. "They must have known she had no chance. Th-th-they killed her. Why?"

Anton's throat felt tight. He had no reply.

The travellers funnelled into one of eight separate corrals, at the end of which stood two hornets. The one checking ID cards was dressed in the uniform of the Federal Security Services. The second, however, was much more unsettling. Dark glasses. A stiff, plain dark suit. A small brooch of a hornet stinger on his lapel. A band with a similar logo wrapped around the bicep of his upper right arm. While the FSS officer matched ID photos to faces, they scanned the queues, watchful, intense, as if they were hunting.

Spyder was the first to reach the checkpoint. They thrust their card at the security officer defiantly, determined not to be intimidated. The hornet ignored the glare, looking at Spyder's photo and then back at Spyder, holding their gaze a beat longer than was comfortable, then back to the photo. Without a comment, he handed the card back to Spyder, who continued forward and into the mass of recently checked arthros. They watched Anton and Honey clear the check without issue, and the three bandmates regrouped to wait for Bo.

No one talked as they relived the hideous scene on the other side of the security gates. A minute passed. Two minutes. Three. There was no sign of Bo.

"Look guys, I'm scared," Honey whispered to her friends. "I mean, these hornets. They're ruthless. Totally. What if they catch us? And Bo. Like, where is she? I don't like this at all. She was just there, behind me."

Despite his own concern, Anton forced himself to appear calm. "Okay. Let's not get too apprehensive. I'm sure she'll turn up. We'll give her a few more minutes, yeah?" Spyder and Honey nodded.

Anton watched the checkpoint, willing Bo to appear. *Honey's right. Maybe we should have stayed at home. Waited for Insecterpol. Perhaps I was too impetuous. I mean, what are we doing? Seriously! And Bo. We don't know anything about her.* Anton looked at his phone. *What if the hornets are looking for her? Intercepted our texts? Looking for us as well? If she doesn't turn up, we should give up and go home.*

"You're still here! Great! Let's get going." They whirled around to see Bo smiling at them. "Come on then, let's go," she insisted, marching off with the rest of the crowd.

"Hey, man! Wait! We were worried. What happened to you?" Spyder demanded as they fell into step.

She grinned and explained that as they had approached the security funnels, she realised she didn't have her ID. That would mean a long interview with the FSS and an even longer time to replace it.

"I couldn't risk missing the chance to hang out with you guys, so I, er, took an alternative route." She had gone in through the exit.

"How?" Spyder asked. "Surely someone would have noticed you going the wrong way."

Bo winked. "That's why I walked backwards." Bo turned around and walked backwards. But she looked as if she was going forward.

Anton grinned in disbelief. "Ha! So, all they would have seen is the back of your head. Brilliant! I've literally never seen anyone walk like that before. Can you teach us? Maybe later, at your place?" He looked at Honey and Spyder. "We could incorporate it into our act?"

"Cool!" Spyder said, trying it. The others giggled at their hopeless attempt, then high-fived each other.

The road was now crowded with arthros of multiple species, all heading towards The Grove. Anton, Spyder and Honey recognised most of the creatures, but some they had only seen in books or documentaries. Bo explained that they came from all over the world, all here to earn money. Anton said he'd heard that The Grove's facilities were of a poor standard. Bo told him that for many, it was their very first experience of running water and sanitation, so that – despite the protests – the conditions were actually much better than those they were used to at home.

"Which doesn't make it right," Honey reminded them firmly.

Bo shrugged. "Yeah, but we're not here for a holiday, are we?"

They caught their first sight of The Grove at the top of the escarpment. Emerging from the highland forest, the land suddenly dropped away, revealing a vast valley stretching north and south as far as the eye could see. On the other side, interlocking hills painted in shades of grey faded into the eastern sky. To the southern end of the valley was an old volcano that had erupted and then gone quiet thousands of years ago. Its rim was worn and jagged, with a single lonely cloud hovering eerily above. The southern slopes dipped down to a lake, which, once full, had now all but evaporated. With little rain to refill it, the resident crustaceans had left for richer waters, and only weeds covered the shallow remains.

North of the volcano, however, stretched over the floor of the valley, were dozens of ancient baobab trees. The Grove. These giant trees stood like guardians of the valley, solid and proud. Above their immense trunks, a network of branches stretched out and up like bodybuilders flexing their arms. A canopy of leaves flourished at each crown, casting deep shade over the ground.

At the centre of The Grove stood a tree that was clearly thicker, taller and stronger than the others. Where its trunk split into branches, a giant hive sat – larger than the other hives that Anton, Honey and Spyder now noticed in the other trees around it. This central hive seemed to consume the boughs of the baobab, leaving just smaller ones pushing through. This was The Nest – the capital hive of the Grove Hornets.

Approaching it, from the four corners of the compass, were four great thoroughfares throbbing with arthropods. And winding through the valley was a river that flowed so close to The Nest, it was like a great vein feeding the heart of The Grove.

Around the baobabs were sprawling workers' camps. Occasionally, the sun would catch something reflective from them – a tin roof, a piece of plastic, a scrap of metal – making the valley floor sparkle and pulse with life.

Anton felt a surge of awe and dread as the three friends took in the sheer scale of the place.

As the road wound down the side of the valley, The Grove played hide-and-seek, with sections dipping beneath a hill or ducking behind the undergrowth. But from every new vantage point, the size of The Nest grew. Closer now, it looked rougher, as if the mighty trunk had erupted with fast-drying lava that bubbled and solidified around the lower branches.

Only as they neared the mighty tree did they begin to grasp The Nest's enormous scale. It was by far the biggest structure any of them had ever seen. Beneath the hive itself, hinged to the top of the trunk, was a platform that encircled the entire tree.

Anton swore silently to himself. The scale of their challenge was becoming more apparent.

They passed the outer edges of the dormitory camps. The buildings were simple but solid enough. Down alleyways and snickets were glimpses of daily life. Arthros washed clothes and hung them on makeshift lines stretched between the huts. A constant mist of cooking smoke rose from thousands of little portable stoves.

All of the bandmates' eyes were drawn irresistibly to The Nest, which now hung heavy and bulbous above them, cradled like some grotesque offering by its supporting branches, their twisted arms gnarled by centuries of wind and rain.

Their march had slowed to a shuffle as they shared the route with workers who had just finished their shifts and were heading home. Anton caught snippets of exotic species-specific languages along with the more familiar universal tongue. The smell of hard work hung in the air like heavy perfume, and the labourers bore the smudges and stains of their efforts. There was a sense of camaraderie, so even in their tiredness, the chatter was lively – some laughs, shared stories, plans for later. He could feel their ambition and determination. No one cared about geopolitics, especially when their conditions never made the news. And they certainly wouldn't have cared about an earwig being held captive deep within The Nest.

"Here we are," Bo called outside a gate with the letter 'H' above it. "Just show the guard your ID."

For the second time that afternoon, Anton, Honey and Spyder passed through security. Anton reached behind him and found Honey's hand. She squeezed him back in mutual reassurance until the gentle push made her release it. Around them, most had gone through the check-in process many times and greeted the guards with a casual familiarity.

When it was Anton's turn, he showed his ID. The guard barely glanced at Anton before wearily tapping a screen, and the barrier swung open with a bang, letting Anton into the village.

This time, Bo was waiting for them, smiling. "I know the guard," she reassured them, and the four arthros set off through the maze of simple houses.

14

The Break In

It was late now. The remaining arthros sat around the big table that dominated Bo's living room. There had been much talking, laughter, and music. Lots of it! Anton, Spyder and Honey hadn't been the only musicians at Bo's that evening, and many of the friends she had invited brought instruments. Those who didn't were happy to tell a story or a joke or just sing along.

They had arrived in ones and twos, and Bo had sworn each of them to secrecy. Until Anton, Honey and Spyder entered the room, no one had any idea that Them Creepy Crawlies were in the house. The three bandmates started to perform an acoustic set with borrowed instruments, but it only took two songs for Bo's friends to join in – guitars, fiddles, a mandolin, a flute, even a bodhran – and it quickly became quite a session. It was one of the reasons they had chosen Bo – her Insta wall was covered in images of her and her friends doing just this.

For a few hours, the stress of the day and what was to come evaporated, and Anton, Honey and Spyder were just musicians again. Anton, aided by the local brew, was particularly keen to enjoy himself. He told stories and jokes, and for a while, he was the funniest, coolest person in the room. When he got a bit loud and lairy, he sensed Honey looking at him disapprovingly – but he didn't care. Besides, he'd met an equally boisterous beetle, and they were both set on outdoing each other. It was Spyder that followed him outside when he needed some air.

"What the hell, Anton! What are you doing, man? We're not here to have a party," they chided him.

"Chill out, Spyds," Anton mumbled back at them. "Let's enjoy ourselves while we have a chance." He chuckled. "Who knows if we'll ever be able to again."

"Mate, you're going to have to step up," Spyder told him angrily. "Wiggy's life is at stake."

"Don't you think I know that!" Anton snapped back.

The stars were out in force, and, lingering outside, he leaned against the wall, staring up at them. Since they'd left Flutterbury, the shadow of Wiggy had rarely left Anton's mind. Of course, Spyder was right. He knew he was drinking too much. He had been for a while now. Tonight, like other nights, it had dulled the reality of his topsy-turvy life. Tonight, it helped him forget the huge challenge they now faced – the situation he had put Spyder and Honey in. The horrible scene at the checkpoint returned to his mind. It was dawning on him, on all of them, that they weren't on some childhood quest, a comic book story where you always know that, in the end, the good guys will prevail. This was real. He'd seen somebody killed for the first time today. They all had. He needed to remember that. He needed to take responsibility. Anton squeezed his eyes shut and rubbed his head vigorously with his upper hands, as if trying to shake some sense into himself. How the hell were they going to get into The Nest? How were they going to find Wiggy? How were they going to get home?

His phone beeped with an incoming call. It was Terry again. He let it ring off. Saw this was the sixth missed call. The three of them had texted him earlier: 'We're good. Couldn't leave Wiggy. Talk soon x.' Terry had texted back: 'Call me urgently.' They hadn't. Because they were scared at what Terry would say, and they didn't need that. *Bloody Terry! If it wasn't for him…*

Emboldened, Anton tapped Recent then T. After one ring, Terry answered, but before he could say anything, Anton spent a minute hurling accusations and recriminations at him, after which the line went silent.

"Well?" Anton spat.

On the other end of the line, Terry cleared his throat before speaking calmly and clearly: "Access to The Nest is by retinula scan. You'll need to find an alternative way in. Don't try to fly over the fence. Try the river. Once inside, join a workforce line. You'll carry material to a receiving platform. Close to the main entrance, look for a service access point. That'll be your best chance of getting in. When you find Wiggy, get to the surface. Call. We'll send transport. Have you got all that?"

Anton had been completely wrong-footed.

"Have you got that, Anton?" Terry repeated.

"Y-yes," Anton replied.

"Right. No more communication. Good luck." And that was that. Terry rang off, leaving a dazed Anton examining his phone. He put it in his pocket and went inside.

When all the guests had gone, Anton pulled up a chair and joined Spyder, Honey and Bo at the table.

"Thank you, guys," Bo said wearily. "That was a super-sick evening."

"No, Bo. Thank *you*. We loved meeting your friends," Honey replied. "What a talented bunch."

"Aw. Thanks! They're alright, aren't they? So," Bo continued, "what's the plan for tomorrow? You'll want to get back to the festival, I presume. I can take you back up the escarpment if you want – I don't start work until the afternoon." She stretched, yawned and stood up. "But for now, well, if there's nothing else... I'm going to bed."

"Actually, there is something else," Anton said, looking a bit disoriented.

Bo sat back down. "Sure. What is it?"

"The river. Where does it go to? Like, at The Nest."

The question surprised Bo. "Oh. It flows under the Exclusion Zone fence. Why?"

Anton looked hard at Honey and Spyder. "We need to get into the Exclusion Zone."

"Ha! You don't get into the Exclusion Zone. That's why it's called the Exclusion Zone!"

"I know, I know," said Anton, keeping his gaze on Honey and Spyder. "Still, we need to get into the Exclusion Zone. I understand the river might be the way."

Bo laughed. "Look, there's zero chance. Forget footage in there. Listen, man, if you get caught... Well, you saw what happened to that ant."

The three band members continued to look at each other. It was time to come clean.

Honey turned to Bo with a look that told the beetle they were going to trust her with something important. "You know we said that Wiggy was sick?"

Bo nodded.

"Well, he's not," said Spyder, taking up the narrative. "You see, he's been kidnapped. He's being held in The Nest." They proceeded to tell Bo everything. She just sat there, perfectly still, not saying anything, listening with her mouth slightly open, her eyes darting between her three favourite musicians. Once Honey had finished explaining, there was silence.

And then Bo swore. She shook her head. She sucked in a mass of air through her nose and let it bubble slowly out of her mouth. She shook her head again, then swore once more.

"Okay. I get it," Bo finally said. After another pause, she continued. "The Exclusion Zone fence?"

The three band members listened carefully.

"Well, it doesn't like water. It's okay with rain, but in solid water, it doesn't work. That's why there's an arch. It runs over the river like a bridge."

"Okay," Anton said. "So, what security system is used under this arch?"

"Sorry, I don't know."

Anton's initial excitement was tempered. He leaned back in his chair and looked at his friends. "What do you think?"

Spyder shrugged. "Could be anything. Like an ultrasonic barrier or a pressure-sensing net. No idea!"

"The good thing is," Bo added, "there'll be no FSS. If there's a guard, it'll be a Yellow Jacket. And those guys are lazy. And stupid."

Silence returned as Bo, Spyder, Honey and Anton put on their thinking-caps. They thought about what the barrier might be and how they might break in. They also thought about water. Spyder could swim, just barely, but Honey couldn't, and neither could Anton.

"I guess all we can do is go and take a look. And then decide." Anton paused, looking at each of his friends, eyebrows raised. Spyder and Honey nodded in agreement.

"How did you know about the Exclusion Zone, Anton?" Honey asked. Anton told them all about his call with Terry. He was completely clear-headed now.

#

No one slept well that night, so it was something of a relief when Bo popped her head around the door to say it was time to go. Outside, it was still dark. Clouds hid the remaining stars and, off to the east, silent sheets of lightning flickered on the horizon. They moved in silence, the only noise the tickle of drizzle on roofs, an occasional trill of a cicada, or a cough behind a closed door.

And then, suddenly, there it was – the river. Black and cold, it was hard to see the other side. A bank of sandbags separated the water from a line of shacks, and the water gurgled and slapped against them. A narrow track wound along the bank, supporting a handful of simple decks made from repurposed timber. They jutted over the water, and it wouldn't be long before a posse of clothes washers turned up there with baskets of laundry.

"Watch your step," whispered Bo, turning on a torch and pointing it at the ground. The dull light helped her see just in front of her, and the others followed in single file: Honey, Spyder, Anton bringing up the rear.

Looming in the distance was the massive bulk of The Nest. Slits of light emanated from various points up the trunk. The underside of The Nest was lit by dull channels of moving light fired from spotlights secured to the platform. Further up were a number of what must have been flood-lights, casting a dull, dirty red sheen over the structure. It made it look ghostly and foreboding. Anton wondered how many hornets there were inside. He shivered.

Their attention shifted from The Nest to a series of glis-tening, shifting colours spreading to both sides of them. The security fence. It appeared to rise gently up ahead, before dropping back to run parallel to the ground.

Bo held up her hand, and the party stopped. Hunkering down behind the last house, she peeked around the corner of the building. There was a dead zone between them and the arch.

The dull sheen of the fence cast just enough light to reveal that the arch was surprisingly old-fashioned. Above adjacent walls of wedge-shaped blocks sat a central keystone, locked in place like the final piece of a puzzle. Attached to it was a black box with a single green LED. The crescent was low, but there was a fair gap between the surface and the roof of the arch, through which the inky water disappeared.

"Yellow Jackets," she whispered. "Two. One on either side of the river."

"Any ideas?" Anton murmured, rubbing the drizzle from his brow.

No one spoke. Trying to think, they watched, almost hypnotised, as a raft of flotsam bobbed past them and into the black hole beneath the arch. There was a brief flash of light and a slight hiss.

"Can you smell that?" Anton asked, sniffing the air.

"Burning?" wondered Bo. "A laser or something movement sensitive?"

"Must be," said Anton. "That box, on the keystone. The green LED?"

"I could shimmy onto the arch and take a look," Spyder whispered, "but you'd need to distract the Yellow Jackets."

Honey suggested she could fly to the other side and make some noise further up the fence. Bo could do the same on this side. That would give Spyder the time they needed. Moments later, Anton watched the two Yellow Jackets stiffen to attention, pull up their collars against the wind, and move off, torches shining through the rain, away from the river. "Anyone there?" Anton heard them call.

As they did, Spyder darted across the buffer zone and up the arch. Hanging over the keystone, they came across a button and flicked it off. The LED turned red. They attached a piece of thread to the switch and dropped it into the river with a drumstick attached. They'd switch it back on when they were safely on the other side.

A minute later, they regrouped. Spyder spun another thread and attached their pack to it, then cast it into the river. They all watched it float silently downstream on the rain-dotted water, but they lost sight of it before it reached the arch. There was no flash and no smell of burning. When they thought it must have gone through, Spyder pulled the bag back, and it seemed untouched. They took off their shoes and outer clothes and stashed them in their bag. "I'm the best swimmer. I'll go first."

"Really?" Honey looked nervously at her friend.

"Yup," replied Spyder firmly. "Hold this. When I reach the other side, I'll tie it off. Wait for my tugs, then secure it tightly, yeah? The next one can abseil down the current." They handed the end of a new thread to Anton and tiptoed into the water, swearing at the cold.

The current was running faster now. As the waves buried Spyder from sight, Anton let out the thread, keeping a firm hold. Bo and Honey kept a close eye on the Yellow Jackets, who, after their brief excursion, had returned to lean against the side of the arch, trying to hide from the worsening conditions. Anton felt four tugs. The line was set.

"Spyder made it?" Honey called to the others quietly. "Great. Anton, you go next."

He grabbed a guitar strap from his pack and threw an end around the line, catching it with his other hand to make a belay. He waded into the river, pushing himself off towards the black hole. The waves felt bigger, the level a little higher, and Anton maintained a firm grip on the thread. Safely under the bridge, Spyder helped him ashore, where he gave another four tugs on the line.

Honey turned to Bo and hugged her. "I guess this is it. Thanks for all your help."

"Ha! Don't mention it," Bo whispered. "It's not every day I get to play music with my favourite band. And help them break into a hornet's nest. Good luck!"

The little beetle paused for a moment to watch Honey hook herself around the line with her own guitar strap, letting the current guide her towards the arch. That's when Bo felt a sharp breeze on her back, followed by a violent gust. She wasn't sure if it was the rain or the river, but a wave of spray hit her hard on the side of the face, and she was suddenly up to her knees in a vicious swell. She moved backwards quickly, losing her balance before crawling, soaked, to the tree to which the thread was tethered. It had gone.

The flash flood instantly swallowed Honey. Taken completely by surprise, her senses scrambled as she spun helplessly in the water, struggling to understand what was happening. Instinctively, she managed to grab the flailing thread and loop it around her wrist. Water stung her eyes, so she automatically shut them. Her ears rang with a loud, cacophonous roar. She pulled on the thread, expecting it to slow her down. Nothing. Her legs kicked wildly, searching for solid ground. She wanted to breathe, but something in her mind kept telling her she must not try.

Honey tugged on the thread again. More desperately this time. Still nothing. She swore. Now completely disoriented, she started to panic. In doing so, she wasted the little air she had in her lungs. She desperately wanted to stop tumbling so she could work things out. "I really need to breathe," she told herself.

And then she felt an inevitability wash over her as she gave up trying, finding it easier to roll with the river. She terribly needed to breathe.

But she didn't. Honey couldn't feel the cold any longer. She opened her eyes and, even though she couldn't see anything, there was no watery sting. Her legs had given up searching for something solid, her wings were useless, and her arms had stopped pulling, which was a relief because her muscles ached. She had to breathe.

The discord in her ears had become a soothing, bass-driven moan, as if someone had turned down the treble button in her head. She realised she was drowning, but she felt calm. The moaning noise brought her some comfort. It was a strange sound. Her ever-quietening heartbeat gave it a slow rhythm, and she imagined her blood washing through it.

She saw her mother, who begged her to breathe.

The melody was almost silent now. That annoyed Honey, so she strained even more to hear it. And then everything went silent.

On the bank, Anton had felt the line go slack and quickly realised something was wrong. He heard the flooding river and howling wind before they broke through and over the arch. Spyder and Anton raised their hands to their faces, trying to hold back the now horizontal spray, as they leaned into the gale.

"Can you see her?" Anton shouted, squinting into the rain.

"There!" Spyder pointed to a shape that floundered uselessly.

Anton swore loudly.

"Web!" he yelled, but Spyder had already begun spinning one. Anton grabbed the end of it, ran along the bank, and dived headlong into the water, thrashing his way through the torrent towards Honey.

From her last functioning nerve, Honey's brain picked up resistance. The line had jerked her to a brutal stop, and she was being battered by the waves. Other nerves fired up, insisting that they too be heard. Honey regained consciousness. Before she thought about it, her brain made her take a breath of air. She was angry. She had tried so hard not to breathe. She waited for water to fill her lungs, wondering what it would feel like. But the drowning didn't come because, as well as water, she sucked in air. She desperately needed more air, so she coughed violently and gasped hopefully, taking in more water which made her cough again. And again.

Breathe. Cough. Breathe. Cough.

She could feel herself being dragged sideways, and she rolled onto her back, searching for more air. She managed to grab something solid with another hand and pulled. Another hand and another pull. Upwards, now, out of the water.

Her hearing returned. Not the dull drone of moments ago, but an unfeasibly loud roaring of white noise. Beyond the chaos of water, she could make out a hand that wasn't hers. It grabbed the back of her head.

"Honey!" Anton called. "Hang on! I've got you!"

With every ounce of remaining strength, Honey kicked furiously, desperate to keep her head above water. It was becoming easier now. Her feet were finally connecting with solid ground.

With one arm around her abdomen, Anton dragged Honey towards the shore, where Spyder, now up to their neck, helped them stumble onto the bank. The three of them collapsed, exhausted, and lay there for a minute, coughing and spluttering.

"I thought I'd lost you," Anton sniffled, sitting up, as reality hit home. He clung to Honey, and she kissed him fiercely. For a moment, they all sat there, close together, gazing out over the river to the escarpment beyond. The storm clouds had dispersed, and the first hints of a new day broke hazily over the horizon. The orange light washed across The Nest, outlining its ribs and ridges with shadow, until the whole fortress glowed like a metallic furnace.

Back on the other side of the bridge, the LED had returned to green, and the two Yellow Jackets shivered on either side of the river. They huddled against the base of the arch, completely unaware that three famous musicians had just become the first unauthorised arthros to break into the Exclusion Zone.

15

The Challenge

Anton stood close behind the ant in front, matching his steps as the line shuffled towards the access gate at the base of the trunk. FSS officers were posted everywhere. It was the first time Anton had really looked at them. They wore prominent dark glasses and patrol caps, which made them seem emotionless. Their thoraxes were dark brown, while their abdomens were a distinctive, almost shiny jet-black. The sharp, crisply lined uniforms were highlighted by the familiar stinger symbol on the upper lapels of their jackets. They looked much more intimidating than the woolly Yellow Jackets.

Anton, Spyder and Honey had spent the morning hidden in the long grass, recovering from their ordeal at the river. From their hideout, they watched arthros enter the Exclusion Zone and spread out around the trunk, finding a staging area to load construction materials onto their backs, forming head-to-tail lines along well-trodden paths. As they approached the trunk, it became clear that there were separate terminals for different arthropod classes, so they had to split up. The plan was to find a way onto the branches that cupped The Nest. They'd meet up there. So, Anton lined up with insects at the first terminal, Spyder joined a team of arachnids at another, while Honey joined a flight of bees at a launchpad beyond that.

It was a highly efficient operation – everyone knew their roles, and no one complained. Occasionally, fatigue caught up with older arthros, and a line guard would escort them away to some unseen place. The other workers hardly noticed; each remained focused solely on their task.

And the noise. A continuous, unremitting chorus of clicking, scraping, and scuffing. No rest, no beginning or end, no change in timing. It maintained a steady beat, foot against bark, like a kick drum, drum, drum, drum. Beneath it, sometimes another instrument drifted on the breeze: the zzzz of bees, high-pitched on take-off, lower on landing.

Anton's route wove in and out of the 'tree of life'. He knew baobab trunks could support millions of bodies. As they aged and their trunks split, insects built networks of tunnels, caves and crevices. On his way up, he passed living quarters, kitchens, and larders storing leaves, fruit, even water. He hadn't realised how much the hornets used these trunks.

Anton often had to use his bottom arms to push against his thighs for extra leverage, as the weight of his load of building materials pressed down on his abdomen. He concentrated on breathing as he drove himself upwards, maintaining a constant distance from the insect in front of him. He wasn't used to this amount of physical activity. Still, there was no question of giving up, although he barely had time to admire the spectacular caverns or give in to nerves as he crossed precarious bridges.

The final push to the platform was almost vertical through a narrow tunnel and time-worn steps. As he pushed upwards, Anton would catch an occasional chink of light as it sparkled through the column of insects above him. He was panting hard now.

He finally breached the platform. Stepping through the opening, he instinctively glanced upwards at the vast underside of The Nest. Knobbly and rough, it loomed massively overhead, almost otherworldly in its scale. The trunk split into three large primary branches which formed the base on which the hive sat. Over the years, extensions had been added to various points all over The Nest, causing these branches and other offshoots to be amalgamated into the hive itself.

Anton could make out insects climbing each of the three boughs. They served as bridges from the platform to the outer surface of The Nest, and Anton understood that he would need to get onto them. His gaze drifted back to the bottom of The Nest, where he could clearly see the lips of the main entrance. A constant flow of hornets came and went. He scanned the areas on either side of this mouth. Straining, he spotted a drone land about halfway between a branch and the entrance hole and then disappear. *A service entry! Terry said to look out for service entries.*

Anton bumped into a beetle in front of him, who reacted with weary resignation. Anton apologised and helped the beetle adjust his load, humping it back up his abdomen.

"Hey man, any idea how you join the insects over there?" He indicated the branch.

"From the bottom of the trunk," came the reply. "There are separate tunnels to access The Nest. Hey, do I know you? You look familiar."

"Maybe we met in the village," Anton replied nervously. "We should keep going."

The beetle turned and hurried after the insect in front. "Yeah, must have. What village are you in?"

Before Anton had a chance to worry about the answer, a Yellow Jacket barked at him to hurry up and stop talking. Anton raised his top arms in a gesture of apology. The last thing he wanted was to draw attention to himself.

As his line shuffled forward, Anton took in the platform around him. It was crawling with queues of arthros that had emerged from different openings. Everybody was heading towards a central area that wrapped around the three foundation branches. A tall, opaque fence restricted access from the platform to the branch area. Each queue led to a ramp that climbed to the top of the barrier. From here, the raw material they carried was dropped into large receiving vats where it was mixed with nectar brought up by the bees to make the final construction resin.

He watched the spot where he'd seen the drone disappear. There was nothing there. For a moment, he thought he'd imagined it, but then he saw a hornet appear. It hung there briefly, then fluttered its wings before flying off with a lump of something. As it did, another one landed and disappeared through the same hole. He mentally mapped the area. There might just be enough cover to reach it unnoticed.

Anton had a plan.

For the first time in a while, he thought about the others. He scanned the crowds, hoping he might catch a glimpse of them and wondered if they'd seen the same camouflaged entrance he had. Down below, he'd seen Honey glide to a vast garden that bloomed with exotic flowers. Watched her suck up nectar with the other bees and then take off. He hadn't seen her land at a platform terminal, which was where she was now, regurgitating the nectar into a reciprocal pool, where it was blended with water. The mixture oozed along a culvert, fanned by another team of bees, before continuing under the security fence and dripping into a vat.

"Change, please," Honey heard a bee call five places in front of her. The carrier bee proceeded to swap places with a fanner bee.

Having deposited her nectar, Honey flew back down to the gardens to refill. As she drank her fill of nectar, she asked about shifting position with a fanner. "Just swap when you need a rest," someone told her. "All positions are equally important."

Honey had a plan.

Spyder, meanwhile, was in awe of the sheer number of arthros on the platform. They paused to take it all in and were promptly bumped from behind. They spun around angrily.

"Don't look at me like that," the spider behind them snapped, her upper arms on her hips in readiness for an argument. "You were the one who stopped suddenly."

This was no time for a confrontation, Spyder told themself, so they just gave the spider a stare, turned around, and continued forward. They examined the secure area ahead, as well as the ramps and vats, and the nearby bees. Reaching the end of the ramp, they noticed that slugs mixed the material inside the vats, then guided the paste through an outlet into a tubular lean-to. On the other side of the lean-to, more arthros were loading the finished product onto their backs and marching up a branch and onto The Nest.

Spyder had a plan.

#

Anton was three ants away from the edge of the vat when a swirl of nervous excitement hit him. It was risky, but he couldn't see another way to get past the fence and reach the inner area. The ant in front of him released his load. Anton was next. He backed up to the edge and then pointed to something behind the line.

"What's that?" he called. As the curious insects glanced around, Anton dropped over the edge.

He landed on his back, slightly winded, and immediately started to sink through the sludge. Flailing, he pushed upwards, half swimming, half grabbing until he was able to take a breath. His hand hit something solid, and he clung on, feeling himself being dragged through the mix. Luckily, the blind slug couldn't tell the difference between a chunk of building material and an ant.

Anton slithered unceremoniously through a spigot and onto a conveyor belt carrying blocks of hardening goo. A shower immediately washed him down. Scrubbing the slurry from his eyes, he had just enough time to leap off before he passed through an opening where a long line of arthros were loading up the construction material to transport onto The Nest.

The annex was nearly dark, lit only by a faint glow at the end of the escalator. He spotted a small exit door, low to his right, presumably for service access. He opened the door slightly and peered outside. To the right was the security fence; to the left, the queue of insects hauling the newly processed paste onto their backs as it emerged from the annex.

Anton slipped through the door and into the nearest line. The ant behind him seemed not to care. Having grabbed a load of material, Anton followed the line to the branch. His line was one of five sets, each with a lane moving up and down. As he started climbing, he realised he was heading up the middle of the branch and he needed to be in the one that would pass closest to The Nest. He looked around for Yellow Jackets. No one was paying any attention, so he simply skipped across each lane until he was in the right one.

"Man, these insects are stupid," rang a familiar voice. Anton grinned, just stopping himself from turning around and hugging Spyder. "I saw you a while ago. The goo really smells, doesn't it. No one saw me leap and no arthro's paying any attention to anything. Worker or Yellow Jacket. I literally jumped the queue, and no one cared."

"Any sign of Honey?" Anton whispered.

"Up ahead, two lanes to your left," Spyder replied.

Anton blew a sigh of relief. She was walking towards them. On her second trip to the platform, she'd asked for a change of role and, when no one was looking, glided over the fence. She'd been walking up and down the branch, hoping she wasn't the only one to make it, that it was the right one, and wondering what to do if it wasn't. She passed them without any acknowledgment, but she wore the biggest smile. A little further on, she slipped across into Anton and Spyder's line.

Anton was the first to reach the spot where the branch fused with The Nest. In a flash, he leapt off the branch and onto the muddy exterior of The Nest, hiding in the shadows of the branch. Spyder and Honey followed. Reunited, they hugged quickly, then moved gingerly towards the service entrance, ensuring their path stayed hidden among the criss-crossing twigs, leaves and undergrowth hanging beneath The Nest.

Just before the service entrance, Anton set out across a twig with Spyder close behind. Halfway across, it twitched. It was the tiniest tremor, but Anton's antennae immediately sensed danger, and swiftly swept the surface. It wasn't bark. Wasn't wood. Anton's eyes widened as he realised they'd stepped onto a stick insect. The creature groaned under the weight, her long limbs digging deeper into her anchoring leaves. She turned angrily to see an ant and a spider on her back and started to shake, hoping to dislodge her unwelcome guests. But this put more pressure on her grip, and she was forced to let go of her hind legs. As she swung, Anton managed to scramble forward, over her head and onto the safety of the leaf beyond. Spyder tried to follow, but this made the stick insect more frustrated and more determined to rid her back of its load. The increased shaking eventually made her rip the leaf she was holding, and the two creatures fell in a flurry of limbs.

The stick insect set her wings and, cursing, flew away. Spyder's legs clawed frantically at the empty air. There was nothing to hold on to. As they fell, back-first, they caught Anton's look of horror. In desperation, they shot out a silk thread which snared on a stalk, jerking Spyder to a halt. But the energy was too great for the anchor to hold, and they fell again, slamming into something with a crash that rang painfully in their ears. Every last drop of air was driven from their body. Spyder imagined that this was what happened when you died – the moment before your body crumbled into a heap of bones. They waited for the end.

Spyder managed to roll onto their side. "Moving's good," they thought. "There must be some working bones, nerves and joints."

They concluded that the fall hadn't killed them. They had a flash of another street spider telling them she knew something like this would happen. Spyder remembered holding her hand when they had fallen, winded, on their back as a child. They had slipped off something. She'd told them not to panic, to trust her, that they'd be alright, as long as they kept breathing. So Spyder concentrated on staying calm. They closed their eyes and tried to take some long breaths. Slowly, their diaphragm began to resume its normal function, and they managed to suck in some air. But that made her slide. Anxiously, Spyder stabbed a claw into the surface. They scrambled for purchase, but there was none. They tried to shoot a thread, but their spinnerets had been disabled by the impact. They had landed on the only leaf hanging from a skinny branch that jutted out defiantly from the back of one of the big branches. The leaf was new and shiny and flat. The half closest to the stalk stuck out horizontally, but the bottom half, to which Spyder currently hung, bent perilously toward the ground. Spyder remained perfectly still, wondering what to do.

Anton and Honey had watched, frozen, as their friend fell. Honey screamed when they hit the leaf before diving down and hovering in front of them. The thread that had momentarily held Spyder was floating uselessly. Honey grabbed it and flew up to Anton, who tied it off, and then swung down to where Spyder clung helplessly to their life-saving leaf.

"It's okay, Spyder," Anton reassured his friend. "We've got you."

Anton tentatively held out an arm. "Spyder, very slowly, I want you to reach out and grab my arm."

"I-I can't. I just c-can't."

"You have to try," Honey called. "Come on, lift your arm. Yes! That's it."

With their face pressed hard against the leaf and their body completely still, Spyder slowly lifted their arm until they felt Anton's.

"That's it," Anton said calmly. He looked at Honey. "Can you secure the guitar-strap around both of our arms?

"That's great... Now, Spyder, you need to let go of the leaf so I can swing you onto my back."

Spyder pressed their forehead into the leaf one last time. They swallowed, squeezed their eyes hard shut, unclenched their claw, and let go. They felt themselves being swung through the air in an arc before slapping hard onto Anton's back.

"Cool," Anton grunted. "Loosen your grip around my neck a bit so I can breathe and pull us up."

Safely back on the flat section of the leaf, the three bandmates embraced. "This is becoming a bit of a habit," Honey said, not really joking.

"Thank you, guys," Spyder whispered, resting their head briefly on Honey's shoulder.

"No worries," Anton replied, freeing Spyder from their thread. He wrapped the end around the stalk and helped Spyder onto it, holding the bottom tight as they shimmied towards Honey, who was waiting in the foliage beneath The Nest. When Spyder had reached safety, Anton started to climb up.

But as he climbed, he failed to notice the Yellow Jacket. A member of the Entrance Patrol Unit, AC Wairimu was a recent recruit. At the morning briefing, she had learned that the frequency of flights was to be increased. Everyone was ordered to maintain a higher-than-usual Level 3 alert. That afternoon, the AC's superior had asked her to concentrate on the outer reaches of the Entrance Patrol Zone, maintaining close attention to the surface. It was by chance that, at the time Anton was climbing back up the thread, AC Wairimu's flight path brought her into the same area.

At first, Wairimu thought it was a bit of pollen or a stray dandelion seed, but as it seemed to be rising in a straight line, she went to investigate. She was shocked to see an ant. Wairimu drew her weapon while hovering at a safe distance.

"Attention!" she called. "You are in a restricted zone. Stop climbing immediately and return to the leaf below!"

Anton's first thought was for the safety of his friends. He glanced upwards to see an alarmed Spyder and Honey, who had also spotted the Yellow Jacket. He had no option but to carry out the AC's command, so he carefully descended back to the leaf as ordered.

Wairimu landed a safe distance away. She'd been taught to shoot first and ask questions later, so she switched her weapon to stun and, to Anton's complete shock, fired. Instantly, Anton felt his muscles weaken and completely incapacitated, he slowly slumped to the surface of the leaf. The AC took off. She had seen Anton's surreptitious glance at Honey and Spyder; now, her weapon still drawn, she went to investigate.

Spyder and Honey had had just enough time to find cover in a small crevice surrounded by foliage. They huddled together, anxiously listening to the approaching buzz of the Yellow Jacket. They didn't know, though, that the inexperienced AC had made two critical mistakes. First, she had forgotten to call in her find to control. Second, she had shot Anton in the more protected thorax rather than the softer abdomen. This meant that the stun serum hadn't penetrated deeply, and Anton had already managed to retrieve the thread and was now frantically climbing back up towards The Nest.

"Come out now!" the Yellow Jacket ordered, hovering just in front of Spyder's and Honey's hiding hole. Remembering this time to report the security breach, she reached for her temple.

As he clambered onto the leaf, Anton prayed he wasn't too late. He could see the Yellow Jacket, so, still holding the end of the thread, he sprinted up the stem, sprung onto a leaf, and launched himself. All thoughts of calling in to control were forgotten as AC Wairimu strained to see what had hit her. Struggling to maintain a stable hover, she kicked out with her legs, trying to dislodge Anton, who had managed to scramble onto the AC's abdomen and haul himself towards her thorax. There, he wedged himself between her wing bases and, gripping the membranes, began rocking his weight from side to side, not really sure what he was trying to achieve. The Yellow Jacket held her weapon in her bottom arms, and while her legs tried to kick Anton, her top arms acted as flight stabilisers – which meant that every time she reached for her temple, she lost her balance.

AC Wairimu did manage to fire a few rounds, but with all the pushing and pulling, they flew harmlessly into the void. Now desperate to contact control, she decided to stop trying to counter Anton's movements and let herself fall.

"May...!" she cried against the roar of the wind and grinding wings. "Inful..."

She never finished the sentence. When Anton had landed on the Yellow Jacket, he'd secured the thread around the base of her abdomen, just above her stinger. Now, at the end of the slack, the two insects lurched to a sudden stop. Anton clawed at her upper wings, ripping and leaving them useless. He leapt back onto the thread and started shimmying upwards, feeling it twisting and vibrating as the Yellow Jacket tried to shake herself free.

"Cut the thread!" he called to Honey, who was now hovering beside him. "Cut the thread!"

Untethered, the Yellow Jacket fell silently to Earth.

Back on a twig, Anton crumpled to his knees, exhausted.

"Bloody hell!" Spyder exclaimed. "What... was... THAT!" They shook their head incredulously. "I mean, who are you, man? Some sort of ninja commando?" They chuckled in disbelief.

But Anton wasn't laughing. He gazed out into the empty air. From their panoramic vantage point, he could see half the platform with countless lines of tiny insects marching back and forth to the ramps, four separate elevators of bees, lifting off from the colourful gardens and floating up and over the platform's edge to the dryers. He saw the residential camps cut through by the winding river and then, beyond, the dormant volcano and the edge of the dying lake.

He rubbed his face hard and blew out a blast of air. He started to shiver as the trauma of his death-defying actions kicked in. He felt Honey beside him, her arms wrapped around him. But he felt numb. His mind was full of bouncing images. *What's going on? What are we doing? We're musicians, for goodness' sake! I could have died. We should be at Flutterbury, with other musicians. We could have DIED. Every one of us... What have I got us into? Wiggy. TERRY!*

"This is crazy," he whispered. "Seriously. In the last few hours, each of us should have died. This is not who we are. We need to be at home. We need to be safe." Anton looked at Honey and then Spyder. "We're musicians, not... Seriously! What are we doing?"

Tears welled in Anton's eyes. He reached out and took Honey's hands in his. "You nearly died at the river." He turned to Spyder, extending a hand to them as well. "And you... just now." Anton shook his head and stared morosely into the distance, shoulders slumped, lost in thought.

"But we didn't die, did we?" Honey replied softly. "You saved me. And Spyder. Twice."

"You don't get it, do you? We should never have put ourselves in this position in the first place. I shouldn't have." Anton shook his head. "It's all my fault."

"Oh my God, Anton," Spyder said tersely. "It's not about you. Stop feeling sorry for yourself. We didn't follow you blindly. We made our own decisions, yeah? When are you going to realise that we're a team, man? A bloody good one at that. Each of us brings our own skills and talents. That's why the band's successful. Not because of you. Or Honey. Or me.

It's because of all of us. And Wiggy's a part of that. We're stronger together."

"They're right, Anton," Honey said calmly. "Back at Flutterbury, you did the right thing. We couldn't leave Wiggy. He's one of us. We had to try. Look, we know you hate taking responsibility. But – here's the thing – sometimes you just *do*. Like, instinctively. You have to accept who you are."

And then Honey fired the killer blow. She had to say it. "You're not your father, Anton."

It hit him right between the eyes. Even though he heard what she said clearly and was looking straight at her when she said it, it took him a moment to absorb it. His first reaction was to shout something like 'what do you know about my father?' or 'my father's got nothing to do with this!' or 'who are you to tell me I'm not like my father!' but he didn't. Because it dawned on him, as he sat under the biggest hornets' hive in the world, that he had longed to hear those words from someone. The ghost of the father he never knew had haunted him all his life, warping his relationship with his mother, shaping his distrust of anyone in authority. His father was the spirit of his mother's depression, and she had let it consume her. For the first time, he realised that her embarrassment, mixed with his confusion, built layers and layers of misunderstanding between them. Ultimately, it made him distrustful of responsibility and potential role models – people like Terry. Drove him to tempt failure. To gamble with his friendships. With any relationship that really mattered. It drove him away.

Anton had read somewhere that great leaders find comfort in uncertainty. As he sat there between his two friends, knowing that a swarm of killer hornets was only moments away and that the simple world he had known yesterday was gone forever, he felt strangely calm. In fact, he realised with surprise, he'd never felt so calm.

Anton stood up and offered his hands to his friends, helping them to their feet. "Thank you," he said. "Now, let's go and save Wiggy."

<h1 style="text-align:center">16</h1>

The Interrogation

Deep within The Nest, Wiggy sat strapped to a large white operating bed. Strangely enough, he wasn't uncomfortable. The manacles around his wrists allowed some movement, and the belt around his abdomen didn't restrict his breathing. He could easily wiggle his toes and jiggle both of his ankles.

Wiggy could see that he was back in the small, sterile room that resembled a dentist's surgery. It was bright, but there were no visible light sources. Instead, the perfectly aligned, hexagonal wall panels glowed from within. A long white cabinet stood against the opposite wall, with three black boxes stacked on top. They were sleek and shiny and looked ominous. The only other piece of furniture was a small white stool.

He'd been led into the room by two FSS guards, who had secured him and left without a word. Wiggy hadn't asked any questions. The first time he'd come to the room, he'd rambled frantically, pleading for answers. The guards' silence had terrified him. He had struggled desperately when they forced him to lie down on the bed. He wasn't a brave earwig, so he had sobbed and pleaded. Wiggy had watched a lot of old spy movies, so he imagined them drilling into his teeth, pulling out his pincers, or whipping his feet.

He was completely unprepared for this. The night before, he vaguely remembered having a friendly chat about music gear with a bunch of insects he quite liked. The next thing he knew, he was waking in darkness on a cold, hard floor with a pounding head. Where was he? Was this some kind of joke?

He had found the door, but it was locked. He had shouted for help, but no one came. He had rattled the handle, yelled some more, and finally – hoarse – had given up. His phone had gone, so he had no idea of the time, but he desperately didn't want to be late for rehearsal. He had tried the door again, shouted a bit more. Still nothing. What was going on?

When Wiggy heard a key rattle in the lock, he had breathed a sigh of relief. He stood up, expecting to see Anton or Spyder, grinning with an explanation. He'd kill them! But when the door opened, it wasn't his bandmates; it was two hornets dressed in imposing black uniforms. They looked frightening. He simply said, "About time," and made to leave. He'd had no idea why they held him so roughly, and had struggled angrily and asked about Anton and the gig. But they force-marched him to the little room and shackled him to the bed.

When a hornet wearing white personal protection gear arrived, Wiggy's fear had spiked. The hornet reached into the first black box and withdrew a syringe. He filled it with liquid from the second box, and squirted some of it out to ensure the correct dosage, all the while smiling at Wiggy with sadistic sympathy. Wiggy had strained with terror as the hornet injected him, but almost immediately the drug took effect, replacing his panic with a soporific calm. He'd drifted off to sleep, later waking up groggy and disorientated but still high. He passed in and out of consciousness until, eventually, they escorted him back to the room in which he now lay.

The same hornet in protective gear administered a dose from the third box. Fuzzily happy, Wiggy thanked him. He lay there for some time before another hornet came in and pulled up the stool beside his bed. Wiggy recognised the scar down the right side of his face.

Hendrix was courteous, almost gentle. He explained that he had been drugged and taken to the hornet hive known as The Nest. He told Wiggy that his work was innovative, that he was a big fan, but now they needed access to The Cloud. Hendrix apologised for any distress they may have caused, and assured Wiggy he could leave as soon as he'd helped them.

"You know about The Cloud?" Wiggy slurred, a grin spreading across his face. "That's nice. You know, no one's supposed to know about it." He held a finger to his lips and blew a shush, beaming at Hendrix like a naughty schoolboy.

Wiggy remembered Terry had warned him that something like this might happen someday. Of course, Wiggy hadn't believed him. Terry had sighed and reminded him that what he was doing wasn't a game. But if he ever found himself caught, he should try to stay calm. He had a duty to stay strong and not give away any information. Someone would come to rescue him.

Despite himself, Wiggy felt strangely happy. He liked that this hornet admired his work. And so he should, thought Wiggy, because it was brilliant. He had longed to tell Anton, Honey and Spyder about his other, secret life. He wondered if they were getting ready to do the show without him.

Wiggy looked at Hendrix, mischief in his eyes. "You know that access to The Cloud is password protected, right? And I don't know the passwords. So, even if you torture me," he giggled at the thought, "I still won't be able to give you them." He added as a defiant afterthought: "And even if I did, I wouldn't tell you."

He remembered how much fun he'd had coming up with the security protocols. It felt ages ago, now. Four passwords in four different levels of his subconscious: memory, dreams, emotions, and imagination. Each of them reset every time. Hot and cold. And of course, they'd need a neural resonator – and you can't just go down to the store and buy one of those.

It was Hendrix's turn to giggle. "But we have our own neural resonator. I would love to show you."

"That's weird," said Wiggy. "I was just thinking about that."

"I know, my dear boy. I know. Look."

Hendrix tapped a button, and the back of the bed rose slowly. Wiggy watched in confusion as a hologram of himself lying on the bed appeared, with Hendrix sitting beside him. Above him, images and words materialised. They seemed to drift out of his head into the air and float for a bit before gradually disintegrating.

They were his recent thoughts.

For the first time, Wiggy realised that sensors were attached to his temples and the back of his head, precisely where his central nervous system connected with his brain. He would have been horrified if it weren't for the drugs. How clever, he thought. Brilliant technology!

"Thank you," Hendrix replied wryly, as Wiggy's latest thought drifted and popped into nothingness. "So, you see, I now know that there are four passwords, and they are all in your subconscious."

Wiggy shook his head. "Yes, but only I can get into my subconscious using a resonator. Only I can find the passwords. Only I can access The Cloud."

Hendrix grinned. "Not exactly, my young earwig. Not exactly."

He pressed a button, and the hornet with the white protective suit returned, giving Hendrix a nod after checking Wiggy's vitals on screens behind him. A series of panels opened to the left and right, revealing another small room.

Hendrix released Wiggy's binds and motioned for him to follow.

"Come," he said politely.

Wiggy swung his legs off the bed and followed Hendrix into the next room. It was also hexagonal and bare, apart from a chair where a technician sat. He tapped a switch, and a control panel slid from the wall to form a semicircular, unsupported workstation. Another tap, and two rectangular chambers emerged from the opposite wall. Wiggy saw that they were about the size of coffins, but almost completely transparent. The technician tapped again, and each chamber opened lengthwise with a whoosh and a puff of gas. Steps automatically folded down.

"You see, Edward," Hendrix said, speaking very slowly and deliberately, "we have developed a dual neural resonator. This means that we can enter your subconscious together."

Hendrix climbed into one of the chambers and lay down, gesturing for Wiggy to enter the second one. As Wiggy lay back and shifted his weight, invisible padding adjusted around him, moulding gently to his body. As he moved, the support shifted with him, as if he were lying on a waterbed. He felt perfectly at ease and unexpectedly calm. He'd spent most of his life in a state of mild anxiety, but right now, he felt totally composed. He was actually enjoying it! He knew that he was under the influence of some chemical and that he should be terrified, but he wasn't.

Someone else was going to be in his subconscious at the same time. This is going to be fun, Wiggy thought to himself. Weird, but fun. He had only been in his subconscious twice. The first time was when he used his own resonator. Terry had been furious and made him destroy it.

The second time was in a secure Insecterpol facility. The interface with The Cloud had been a large helmet. Terry and other officials had watched from behind a glass window. The Cloud's neural resonator was set to '10', meaning that the new passwords would be the toughest possible. When he'd reached the final password, Terry told him the data had been downloaded onto a hidden drive and immediately destroyed. The technicians had been pleased. Wiggy remembered nothing.

This time, though, it would be different. Hendrix would be there with him. Wiggy felt both excited and nervous. He'd never explored his subconscious with someone else... er, obviously.

When the side of the chamber closed, Wiggy felt a wave of nausea, followed by mild panic as the coffins slid back into the wall. For a moment, he couldn't see anything. He could hear his breathing quicken. Then, suddenly, he found himself in a school playground. He saw himself as a child, standing in the middle of a group of other children holding hands and skipping in a circle.

Ring-a-ring o' roses,
A pocket full of posies.
A-tishoo! A-tishoo!
We all fall down.

The words echoed hypnotically as the young arthros repeated the nursery rhyme over and over. Wiggy could feel himself looking down at the scene, sensing the sadness of the little earwig in the middle, standing with his head bowed, quietly sobbing. He could also feel Hendrix looking down beside him.

When the little earwig lay down on the ground, Wiggy felt an icy draft, so he made him get back to his feet. The child held his hands over his ears, trying to block out his bullies, but the chill remained. The child shoved his hands into his pockets, hoping to escape the cold. Now, with nothing left to lose, he looked at the chain of tormentors, searching for a weakness. He selected the link between two of the smaller arthros and charged.

The scene shifted. Now, Wiggy saw an older kid standing beneath a gallery of sepia-toned photographs, portraits of previous students who had fallen fighting for their species. His hands clutched a balcony, and he looked over a central hall where pupils hurried to class.

A new time, a new set of bullies.

"Are you a weirdo?" a fat earwig sneered.

"What's it like being a freak?" another giggled.

"Eddie's a freak! Eddie's a freak! Eddie's a freak!" the group sang.

Wiggy felt the coldness of the scene seep into him. He remembered it and how he had reacted back then. His younger self turned away, unsure how to respond, willing them to stop, wondering why someone older didn't intervene, wondering how he would escape.

Hendrix, sensing Wiggy's hesitation, spoke impatiently: "You have to do something."

Wiggy made his younger self prepare. The teenager's eyes hardened as he squeezed his fingers into fists. He was going to show them that he wasn't an earwig who could be bullied.

He turned to face them. "You know," he said confidently, "I'm glad I'm not like the rest of you. I'm glad I'm different. Why don't you just grow up?"

The young Wiggy didn't flinch when the fat one threatened to punch him. Instead, he stared him down until the intimidators dispersed, not quite sure if they'd won, laughing anyway, pretending they had. The young earwig was determined not to cower to their sort again.

Everything turned black, and Wiggy remembered he was being interrogated. His vassal slid back into the light of the room and opened. Wiggy sat up feeling unsteady, and a technician helped him from his pod.

"We'll resume in Level 2 shortly," Hendrix told him, as he climbed from his pod. "Take him back to his cell," he ordered.

#

Wiggy looked directly upwards from his neural resonator at the bright hexagonal cells of the ceiling. Hendrix lay in the pod beside him, but Wiggy didn't feel the need to acknowledge him. He felt the slightest jolt as the pod retracted, and for the fourth time, darkness took over as he prepared for the final journey into his subconscious.

He had no recollection of the previous expeditions through his memory, dreams and emotions. This was one of the beauties of his design. But he found it fascinating that the hornets had worked out a way to delay the transfer between levels once the password had been triggered. In a way, he was glad that they had. Although he had no idea of the time, in his hazy, narcotic-fuelled state, he felt exhausted and doubted he would have had the strength to go through all four levels one after the other – especially with someone else in his head.

Wiggy felt a spark of excitement. He was curious about the next level: his imagination. He hoped that his subconscious had hidden the password well, and Hendrix wouldn't be able to find it.

It was dark. Then Wiggy saw planes of colours, shifting like a kid's kaleidoscope. The tunnel of geometric shapes swirled into fractured landscapes until, all of a sudden, Wiggy and Hendrix stood on separate black stone plinths. They were two among hundreds. Wiggy was holding a guitar, attached to a simple amplifier. He looked over the edge to see that the circular platforms on which he and Hendrix stood were floating in space.

"Let's get on with it, please," Hendrix said politely, scanning the surreal surroundings.

Wiggy approached a mic that he'd only just noticed, and his voice echoed around the emptiness. "What do you suggest?"

Hendrix didn't reply, so Wiggy shrugged, took off his guitar, and stepped off his plinth and onto a shimmering gangway that appeared at the end of each step. Staring across the void at him, Hendrix copied Wiggy on a parallel path, stepping from pillar to pillar. As Wiggy stepped onto a different plinth, he found himself playing a new instrument with a different musician, and making a new sound – one he'd never heard before.

"Why do I feel so cold?" Hendrix yelled, rubbing his hands together and turning up his collar. Anton could see ice forming on Hendrix's wings and antennae. He was shivering violently.

"Make it stop, please!"

Wiggy remembered that he'd set up the system so you felt colder the further away from the password you strayed. But why wasn't he feeling cold? They were both heading in the same direction.

"Must be the wrong way," Wiggy thought to himself, unaffected by the freezing wind shearing through the space and pelting them with snow. "Let's return to the first pillar!" he shouted. Wiggy had no idea which pillar was the first one he'd landed on, but he started off as quickly as he could in the opposite direction, with Hendrix mirroring him off to his right.

Presently, the snow vanished, the wind settled, and the scene shifted to a desert. They were in a corridor of floating doors. Hendrix swung his jacket over his shoulder. "Excellent," he cooed. "One of these must contain the password."

But as he reached for the first door handle, it sprouted living vines that lashed out, grabbing his arm. He hissed in pain as a thorn jabbed the back of his hand. As he tugged desperately to free himself, the vines held on tighter, which made him madder, pulling more aggressively. The vines started to entangle the colonel's entire body, crushing him until he could hardly breathe.

"You need to be calm," Wiggy told him. "They're reacting to your anger. Concentrate."

Sure enough, when Hendrix forced himself to relax, the vines loosened, allowing him to yank himself free. He glared at Wiggy, who just shrugged.

They continued through the shifting landscape, encountering one figment of Wiggy's imagination after another. They had to swim a sea filled with green-tinted poison, pass a hideous sleeping monster without waking it, and even capture a billowing shadow.

Now, both sweating in the oppressive heat, a huge hall stretched out before them. Wiggy stepped in cautiously. The walls were lined with reflective panels, and the mirrored floor rippled with every step the two insects took, distorting their reflections and making them seem unsteady and blurred. At the very end floated a glowing sphere, softly pulsing with energy. When he approached it, Wiggy hesitated, walked around it, suspecting a new trap. Hendrix, however, couldn't resist the urge to touch it.

The moment his fingers touched its surface, the sphere vanished, leaving behind a cloud of words that dissolved in the air. Hendrix and Wiggy felt a shudder. The force intensified until the mirrored panels began to collapse around them. They started sprinting back towards the entrance, but as hard as they tried to run, the less progress they seemed to make. And then they started to fall, tumbling uncontrollably in slow-motion through space.

They landed on solid ground. Wiggy felt different. Above, the sky churned with tropical storm clouds while lightning crackled around them like an exposed wire. At the top of a far-off cliff, Wiggy could just make out a castle.

"Come on!" Hendrix shouted and set off, sweating in the humid air, battling against the howling wind and lashing rain. Having struggled up the bluff, they reached the fortress gates, heavy and wooden, guarded by hornet-shaped robot sentinels that snapped at the two insects. Wiggy drew a sword and prepared to lunge, but Hendrix held him back.

"Leave this to me!" he bellowed, shoving the earwig behind him. His charge was full-blooded, but before he reached them, the sentinels dissolved. Hendrix hauled up the portcullis and led Wiggy into the fortress, into a grand hall where tapestries hung from the walls between giant insect figures in traditional armour. At the far end of the hall stood a vault door.

Hendrix looked at Wiggy. "The key?" Wiggy shook his head.

"Think!" Hendrix shouted.

"No! *You* think!" Wiggy retorted, surprising himself at his bluntness. He waved his arms around the room. "Do you think this is about me?"

Hendrix didn't understand. "The storm, the castle, the sentinels, the soldiers. It's not my imagination, is it? It's yours!"

Hendrix turned to the tapestries and, with a flash of recognition, realised that they depicted pivotal moments in his life: his mother returning home from war, his father comforting him, being bullied in the art room at school, his graduation from military school, a brief affair with a drone, torturing civilians, his High Council appointment, and Queen Vespa. Walking around the tapestries, Hendrix's feelings swung from sadness to joy, shame to honour, love to hate. He sized some up from different angles. He frowned at his mother, smiled at his lover, scowled at the Queen. Then he spotted his father, and lovingly placed his hand on the old hornet's face. He noticed that his father wore a medal around his neck. It was his mother's Medal of Honour. He moved his hand to the medal. It felt real. To his shock, he was able to pick it out through the woven surface. He examined it, remembering his mother's taunting words all those years ago: "Only in the shadows of your imagination will such a medal ever be yours."

The key!

He brought the medal to the vault door and placed it into a hollow recess that sat just below the handle. When Hendrix set the medal in the pocket, the edges clicked in with a satisfying precision. A subtle twist engaged hidden pins, like the tumblers of a lock. Metal chimed with metal, and the mechanism stirred awake. The door swung open, revealing a chamber with a single stone pedestal. Resting on it was a scroll, glowing softly.

"So," Wiggy murmured, "the final password was in your head, not mine. My subconscious must have used the resonator to plant it there. Brilliant! You have to give it to my imagination, though. That was a pretty cool idea!" He looked at Hendrix with a lopsided smile. "You've really got some issues, haven't you? You should talk to someone."

Hendrix flexed his limbs and circled his neck. He smiled back at Wiggy and let out a chuckle that grew into an unhinged, bellowing roar. He lifted the scroll and let it unfurl. Written in elegant script was the final password:

Strength Through Unity.

A powerful silver light flooded the chamber, and the fortress started to crumble, extinguishing the light until it was completely dark.

17

The Rescue

Having squeezed unnoticed through the service entrance, Spyder and Honey stood together, gazing around the cavernous chamber. Underfoot it felt thick and robust, but halfway up the walls were more translucent, delicate and papery. As the walls rose to an apex, they could make out cracks in the membrane, with some sections peeling away. The place smelled sweetly pungent, the odour of hornet eco-trash, remnants of which were scattered across the floor.

"Our nests are different from hornets'," Honey whispered, "but I reckon we're in a silo for composting material. See the holes at the top of the roof?" Spyder nodded, looking at the very top of the chamber. "Refuse outlets – too thin for us," added Honey. "But the one in the middle? I think that might be an access passage."

"Yeah, I can see it," said Spyder. "It certainly looks bigger than the others from here."

With their neck still stretched back, Spyder eyed first Honey and then Anton and saw both were looking at them. Spyder smiled back and returned their attention to the ceiling, feeling the lingering gaze of their two friends.

"What?" Spyder said, looking at Anton. "*What?*" they repeated, before realising what the stare implied.

Spyder was by far the best climber of the three, so they set off, scaling the walls of the membrane, carefully navigating the cracks and peeling layers until they reached the middle slit. Anton and Honey watched as Spyder cautiously forced their top arms, then their head through the hole, while their bottom arms and legs dangled. The insects smiled at each other as Spyder's legs rotated slowly through three hundred and sixty degrees as the spider surveyed the space beyond, then disappeared completely through the slit.

Spyder was gone for a few minutes. But just before Anton and Honey started to worry, they reappeared and rappelled down a newly dropped silk, landing right beside the two relieved friends.

"The slit leads straight into a dormitory for baby hornets," Spyder said with a shiver. "There are thousands of them – all in a sort of honeycomb of cells."

Anton asked if they'd seen any trace of Yellow Jackets.

"None. But I did see an old nursing hornet. There are quite a few exits, though. I had a quick look through one."

"More dorms?" Honey asked.

Spyder nodded.

"It makes sense," said Honey. "There'll be layers of them circling out from the central hub where the Queen's quarters are located. I don't know, but maybe Wiggy's there as well. We need to go deeper."

"Okay," Spyder muttered. "But the hornets... how the hell do we avoid them?"

Honey picked up some of the muck from the floor, lightly recoiling at the odour. "We should rub ourselves with this rotten stuff. It's covered in hornet scent. If we bump into one and it's pitch dark, well... hopefully they'll only smell hornet." She looked at Anton.

"I don't have a better idea. Spyder?" Spyder shrugged.

"Okay. Let's do it," Anton grimaced, reaching down and brushing a handful of rotting detritus over himself. Resigned, the others followed suit.

Then Anton grabbed the silk thread and pulled himself up to the ceiling, where, hanging on with his middle arms, he stretched his top arms through the hole, and hauled himself into the dormitory.

He stood there in awe. Before him was a massive wall of hexagonal cells stretching all the way from the floor to the ceiling, from one side of the room to a central walkway, then to the wall on the other side. Inside each cell was a creamy hornet larva, facing forward, neatly packed into its tiny bedroom chamber. Little black eyes stared out like symmetrical pebbles stuck to a wall of honey.

The entire space moaned with growing life. Minute hearts beating, little mouths breathing, underdeveloped legs flickering, like one vast body waiting for its biological alarm clock to go off. Looking down the passageway, Anton could see that, to the left and right, there were dozens of similar blocks. It was like an old-fashioned library where, in place of books, there were shelves upon shelves of infant hornets.

"Jeez!" Spyder exclaimed, now standing beside Anton, scanning the chamber. "And this is just one nursery. There must be thousands."

"Hundreds of thousands," Honey corrected, pulling the silk through the hole, bundling it and hiding it in the corner. "These are new larvae, probably just hatched. The workers haven't capped the cells yet – that's why you can see them. There'll be more developed pupae deeper in," she added, matter-of-factly.

Spyder looked at Anton. They both shivered.

They tiptoed down the thin passageway that separated the chambers. The top cells were so high it was hard to make out the individual larvae. Honey took the lead, peering around each lattice to check for any nursing hornets. At the end of the chamber, she stopped and carefully poked her head out of the door. A tunnel led deeper into The Nest.

Over her shoulder, Anton glanced left and right. It was pitch black, which was a problem. He placed his pack on the ground, rummaged around, and pulled out a small rectangular object, slightly chubbier than a phone – his guitar tuner. He pressed a button, and a tiny LED started to glow: just enough to light up a passage of rough, hardened mud that twisted upwards. The three friends crept out of the dorm and began climbing the passage, their hearts pounding a little faster as they moved past chamber after chamber of transforming hornets.

"Hold it," Anton whispered suddenly, his antennae twitching. He extinguished the light. They all froze. "Someone's coming!"

They were between dorm entrances. "What do we do?" Spyder asked, looking up and down the passageway, trying to remain calm.

"We stand our ground and don't panic," Anton said calmly. "Trust the cloak of scent. Honey… at the front," he ordered. "We'll stand close behind you. That way, our outlines will be confusing." He squeezed her shoulder. "You okay to do the talking?" She nodded.

They waited as the sound of three chatting hornets approached.

"Oh! Hi there," one of the hornets said cheerfully when she sensed Honey. "How's it goin'?"

"I'm fine, thank you," Honey replied sweetly, her heart pounding as fast as it ever had. She willed the hornets to keep heading to wherever they were going.

Another asked which dormitory she was from. Honey had no idea how the nurseries were named, but she managed to stutter: "D-do you know, I'm j-just new here and am still finding my way around. M-may I ask what nursery you work at?"

The third one pointed down the passageway. "H4." She explained that the number signified the corridor, and the letter the room. "Think of it like the spokes of a wheel, with corridors stretching out from the axis of the central hub."

"You'll get the idea soon enough," the first one said light-heartedly. "Anyway, we should go, or we'll be late for our shift. Nice to meet you. Probably see you around."

"Yeah, s-see you around," Honey repeated with a small wave as the three hornets continued on their way. "Hey, let's grab a coffee sometime," one of them called back.

"Great!" Honey replied.

When the hornets disappeared around a corner, Honey, Anton and Spyder let out a collective sigh of relief. The combination of the aroma and blurred silhouette had done the trick.

But just as they were about to continue, a voice sang out. "Hey there! Hello! Are you still there? I didn't get your name or your dorm number?"

Honey's heart sank, and she wished she hadn't been so nice. One of the nurses was coming back. She could just make out the heat outline. Anton and Spyder froze as the nurse drew closer.

"Is everything alright?" the nurse asked, sounding a little confused. They were exposed, now, three separate bodies. As well as what looked like a hornet, the nursing hornet could see the heat signatures of a spider and an ant. She was just about to activate her neural alert when Honey leapt at her, jamming one hand over her mouth while slapping nectar over her alarm glands.

Shocked by Honey's completely unexpected behaviour, Anton and Spyder could only watch as the dumbfounded nurse struggled, desperately trying to grind her mandibles and call for help. But the sticky nectar kept them apart.

Finally rousing themself, Spyder grabbed a shot of web and wrapped it around the nurse's limbs. She tried to speak, but only a muffled mumble came out. When Anton tried to lift her, she managed to free one of her legs and kicked out, catching Anton in the mouth. He winced but, now with Spyder and Honey helping, managed to drag the nurse into the nearest dormitory and prop her against the wall.

Anton knelt in front of her, wiping the blood from his lip. Spyder and Honey stood behind him, staring down at their prisoner. In the dull red light of the dormitory, they could make out her features.

"She's not a hornet," Honey exclaimed. "She's a bee!"

The nurse nodded her head urgently.

"Wow!" Spyder exclaimed. "A migrant bee working inside The Nest. Like, her neuros must have been reset to an intranet."

The bee nodded again.

"We don't want to hurt you," Honey said gently, "but we're looking for our friend. He's an earwig. Been kidnapped. Brought here against his will. Have you heard about a new prisoner?"

The bee looked to each of her captors. Wide-eyed, she shook her head, willing them to believe her.

Anton moved ever so slightly closer to the bee, his voice calm but serious. "It's really important."

The bee stared back at Anton, frozen with a mixture of fear and confusion. Anton sighed impatiently. "Please... have you heard about a captured earwig?"

When the nurse grunted defiantly, trying to shake off her manacles, Anton stood up, looking back at her with frustration. The silence was broken only by the hum of growing baby hornets.

"Sting her," he said unemotionally.

Honey glared at the bee. "Are you sure about this?" she asked, her voice heavy with the weight of the question. Behind her, Spyder shifted uncomfortably. The use of force was something they hadn't considered. It would mean crossing a line that hadn't existed in their world – until now.

Honey had already shocked herself when she'd flung herself at the bee. Not what's expected from a boarding school bee. The question she posed, though, wasn't directed at the bee or Anton. It was directed at herself. How far would she go to save a friend? As Honey moved closer, the bee pushed back harder against the wall. She squeezed her eyes shut, clenched her teeth, and turned her head to the side, waiting for the sting.

Honey leaned over and gently touched the bee on her thorax. "Don't worry, I'm not going to hurt you," she said reassuringly. "But I know you know about our friend. It'll have been broadcast on your neurals."

The bee's eyes hardened, determined to keep any information she had to herself.

"Look, you of all insects know what a bee sting feels like. So, let me ask you again," Honey said edgily. "Have you heard about our friend?"

The bee hesitated. The creature opposite her looked desperate enough to use her venom. She well knew the excruciating pain that a sting could cause. She wavered, then finally relented and gave a quick, sharp nod.

"Good. Thank you. Do you know where he is?"

The bee's eyes darkened. She'd been shown the cells during her induction tour. It was a harrowing place that smelt of fear, and she had no intention of ever going back there.

Tentatively, she nodded.

Honey looked at her bandmates. They had no choice but to trust the bee, so Honey used the edge of her stinger to cut the binds. With her eyes firmly on Honey and top hands held up in submission, the bee very slowly stretched her wings once and then a second time, careful not to cause a buzz. Spyder reached around to the back of her head and released the gag. The bee stretched her jaws.

"We'll keep your glands covered up for now," Anton said. "We don't want you becoming anxious and setting off your neurals. Okay?"

The bee nodded but then started gibbering in panic. "The FSS. If they discover you, they'll kill you. They'll kill me. I've helped you. They'll find my family. Your family. Kill them all."

"Shhh," Anton interrupted, waving his hands and looking around in alarm. "Calm down! Let's start with your name, yeah?"

"Bisma," the bee replied, masking her distress. After a pause, she added: "And you're Anton. And you're Honey and Spyder. You're Them Creepy Crawlies. And the friend you're trying to rescue, it's Wiggy, isn't it?" She was calmer now.

They were caught off guard. None of them expected anyone to recognise them. Not inside the depths of The Nest. The three band members looked at each other with surprise, a silent agreement passing between them. Anton and Honey left it to Spyder to explain what had happened: Wiggy's secret life, Terry, Insecterpol, Bo, nearly drowning, the Yellow Jacket... and what they knew of Colonel Hendrix and Queen Vespa.

Like Bo before her, Bisma blew out a long breath, shaking her head in disbelief. "Can I move this now?" she asked, indicating her glands.

"Look, sorry about scaring you," Honey said, helping Bisma wipe away the nectar. "But you know... this is all, er, quite new for us." She looked at her two friends. "We've never rescued anyone from a hornet nest before."

That made them all giggle. Even Bisma.

"So, you know where Wiggy is?" Anton asked.

Bisma nodded. "It was somewhere I was hoping not to see again. But, well, I suppose this is important."

Moments later, Bisma stepped into the passageway. She paused, listening carefully. The only sound was larvae breathing. She touched her temple, but there was nothing on the intranet. All clear, she signalled the others to follow. They turned left and started towards the centre of The Nest.

Soon, they reached dormitory 4C. They crept inside. At the fifth wall of cells, Bisma spotted a colleague halfway up a stepladder fussing over a larva. She walked confidently down the corridor, sparking up a conversation with the nurse, drawing her attention so Anton, Spyder and Honey could dart across the gap to the safety of the next cell wall.

Crisscrossing dormitories and passages, they managed to evade four nurses and two separate work parties of older drones making their way to interior maintenance sites. Bisma explained, in careful whispers, that she'd been born in The Lowlands, but pollination work was hard to come by – too many workers for too few jobs. Her family earned a little money producing their own honey, but not enough to get ahead. So, she had made her way to the capital hive. Honey knew of it. Informal settlements on its outskirts were growing rapidly. Bisma had ended up in one. Rather than beg or steal, she'd successfully applied for a migrant visa as a nurse in The Nest.

The shifts were long, but she enjoyed caring for the little ones, and she'd made some nice friends. Apart from bees, the Yellow Jackets were the only other non-hornet species approved for The Nest. Bisma sent money home but wasn't allowed to leave The Grove until her work permit expired. So, she was effectively a prisoner. They were right about her neuros. The Nest's intranet had been installed on her first day. She was used to the constant flow of messages. At least the AI spoke soothingly. It regularly reminded her that it was illegal to tell anyone about The Nest. Punishments would be severe.

"The next passageway is where the prison cells are located," Bisma said as she reached the end of her story. She stepped through the exit of the dormitory.

"Whoa there, young lady." She had walked straight into the path of two FSS officers.

"Sorry. Sorry, sir," she responded, bowing slightly in deference, as one of the officers reached for the identity card that hung from a lanyard around her thorax. He pulled her closer and read her credentials.

"Bisma Bee. Dormitory Nurse. Authorised to access Corridors 4, 5, 6, and Public Areas only."

"Yes, sir," Bisma replied nervously, not daring to meet his gaze.

"Do you know where you are?" the second officer asked aggressively. Without waiting for a reply, she continued. "Well, I'll tell you where you're not. You're not in Corridor 4, 5 or 6. And you're not in a public area. This is a restricted zone," she growled.

Bisma apologised again. These hornets weren't regular FSS officers; even worse, they wore the badge of the Personal Protection Unit, the Queen's bodyguards. They were the most intimidating and feared section of the FSS, with the power to arrest any arthro on sight and detain them indefinitely, often with brutal consequences. Many prisoners who encountered the PPU never returned, and hornets and migrant workers alike lived in fear of them.

Behind the thin wall of the dormitory, Anton, Honey and Spyder huddled close, listening and hoping their hornet scent was still strong.

"Are you alone?" the first officer asked. Bisma realised that the guards had already sensed others nearby, but before she could answer, Honey called out to clarify they were together – glancing quickly at Anton and Spyder as if asking, 'What's the plan?'

"Show yourself," the second guard ordered. "Now!"

Honey hesitated. Then called out in desperate improvisation: "I can't. I fell off a ladder, and I think I may have broken my ankle. Bisma was helping me to the medical centre."

The officer threw Bisma's ID aside and ordered his colleague to guard her. He squeezed through the narrow entrance into the nursery.

"Here's my ID, officer," Honey said, immediately splattering nectar on his alarm glands. Before the officer could react, Anton jumped on his back while Spyder sprayed him with web. It took all three of them to wrestle the furious hornet to the ground.

"Is she good?" the officer guarding Bisma shouted, eyeing Bisma suspiciously.

As Spyder wound more silk around the struggling officer, Anton, seemingly taking control, signalled to Honey that they should rush through the door and attack the other hornet. Honey gave him an anxious thumbs up. Anton grabbed his guitar strap from his bag, indicating she should give him hers. He buckled them together to make a leash with a loop at each end. Then, he pulled out two packs of guitar strings and tied a knot between them to make a rough whip. Honey pulled her bass lead from her bag, not quite sure what to do with it.

"Hassan?" the officer called when there was no reply.

Just as the officer dropped two light spheres onto the ground, Anton burst through the entrance, smashing straight into Bisma, and then the officer. All three crumbled to the ground. In the confusion, Anton managed to loop the coils at the end of the guitar straps around the hornet's upper wings. When the officer tried to use them to regain her feet, the straps tightened, knocking her off-balance. The more she tried to use her wings, the tighter the nooses became, so she had to back up against the wall to find her feet. Finally standing, she felt a run of blood at the back of her throat. She spat it out and grinned wickedly at the three insects in front of her.

"Well, well," she sneered at Anton and Honey. She licked the blood off the back of her hand. "Let me guess – come for the earwig, have we?"

She turned to Bisma, smiling sadistically. "You! Mmm. I'll enjoy torturing you later... Then I'll find your mother and your father. And after I've executed them, I'll take your siblings, one by one. Mmm." She licked her lips. "I'll start with the youngest. I'll make them scream for mercy. You can watch. Oh, yes. That'll be sooo nice."

Maintaining the crazed smile, she shifted her gaze back to Anton and Honey and stepped forward, her stinger pointing at them, indicating her temple. "Don't worry," she grinned. "I haven't called this in. You know why? Because I'm going to deal with you all myself. Mmm." She spat. "Parasites!"

He should have been frightened, but Anton felt oddly calm as he held his guitar strings tight in his two top hands. Beside him, Honey swung her lead nervously.

Suddenly, the hornet sprinted at Anton. In defence, he raised his strings and cracked them at her. But as he did, his momentum caused him to slip on some runny nectar that Bisma had accidentally secreted. Losing his balance, he fell backwards, limbs flailing, and slid under the hornet like a slapstick actor. His whip, however, maintained its momentum and snapped around the hornet's stinger, pulling her off-balance. For the second time in quick succession, the combat-trained hornet found herself on the ground. Honey reacted immediately by flicking her lead at the hornet. It coiled around one of her legs, and Honey pulled with all her might.

The PPU officer had been made to look a fool. Now apoplectic, she bounced back to her feet and began to rage, hopping around the enclosed space without a shred of caution. Anton and Honey, now aided by Bisma, clung desperately to their leashes, dancing from side to side to keep the hornet directly between them.

"I'm going to kill you!" seethed the hornet, gnashing her teeth and becoming more furious with each failed attack.

"I can't hold on," Anton mimed fearfully to the two bees, the wire now cutting into his hand as the hornet swung the three insects around the corridor with increasing violence. The pain was too much, so Anton was forced to release his grip on the tether, and it immediately whiplashed back at him, smacking him across his thorax and knocking him, dazed, against the wall.

The hornet licked her lips. The wire held by the two bees was now only a minor annoyance, the need for her wings' speed no longer essential. Very slowly, Bisma and Honey felt themselves slipping forward as the hornet pushed her way towards the prostrate Anton. Her stinger was ready.

"Vermin!" the hornet hissed.

Honey wanted to scream Anton's name, but could only stammer a whisper. She could find no purchase. No grip. Nothing to hold the hornet back. Nothing to force the stinger away from Anton. She was being pulled, sliding, hopeless, towards Anton's painful death.

"Eeeeee! Eeeweee! Eeeeweeeeeweeeekreeeeek!"

The sound was deafening. Not because it was loud, but because it was so high-pitched – painfully high-pitched. Honey automatically dropped the lead and rammed her hands against her ears, squeezing hard against the sides of her face, desperate to keep the sound out of her head. She swung around towards the source to see Spyder grinding a tiny bullet microphone into the face of Anton's mini amp, where everything was dialled up to ten. Feedback!

On the floor in front of them, the noise knocked Anton back into full consciousness. It was a noise he recognised, but not at this pitch. He, too, clapped his hands over his ears.

So did the hornet. But while Honey and Anton knew the sound, it was new to her. Suddenly disoriented, she also flung her hands to her ears, trying vainly to decipher the wail and where it came from.

This gave Spyder just enough time to cast a web net over the hornet and pull as tight as they could. As the hornet scrambled manically, she became more entangled, until finally she fell flat on her face. Honey whacked nectar over her mandibles.

Anton staggered back to his feet and, with Honey and Bisma, dragged the hornet, who was now spasming like a shrimp at the bottom of a boat, into the dorm. They set her beside her motionless colleague.

The four arthros stood staring at the incapacitated creatures, not quite believing they'd overcome two highly trained hornets.

"What shall we do with them?" Spyder asked.

They reminded Bisma of two oversized pupae in cocoons. She aimed her stinger at them. "We can't let them live," she said, her voice calm and serious. "If we do, well, they know who we are. They'll track us down. And they *will* kill us."

"But will they?" Honey asked. "Will they want to admit they've been overpowered by us? Really? If it were me, I'd keep quiet. Better that than run the risk of humiliation."

"And maybe even a court martial," Spyder added.

Anton reached out to Bisma. "They're right. Look, we can't tell you what to do, but all I know is that you shouldn't do something you may later regret. Like, do something that might haunt you for the rest of your life."

Bisma, her face grim, ignored Anton. She stepped up to the two hornets. She stood over them for a moment, as if considering what to do. Then she lifted her stinger and placed it very deliberately on the face of one of the hornets. Pressed slightly. The hornet groaned. She pressed a little harder, ready to release the poison that would end the hornet's life.

She stabbed the first hornet. And then the other.

Then, to the surprise of the others, she reached down and pulled away Spyder's webs. "Help me," she said as she started to unbutton the hornets' tunics.

"They're not dead," she added, "just unconscious. But we can use their jackets and caps." Bisma handed a PPU ID lanyard to Honey. "And this may come in handy."

With Bisma and Honey at the front, now dressed in the uniforms of the FSS, the four arthros ducked back into the passageway and moved away from the central hub. On the left side of the corridor, the first door was labelled E. They tried it. It was locked, so they knocked, but no one answered.

They did the same at doors G and I with the same result. However, door K was different. It was sturdier and featured a small viewport at head height.

"This must be it," Bisma whispered.

"Let me handle it," Honey said, stepping forward. "You two, stay out of sight." She pressed the ringer and waited. After a moment, the porthole slid open, revealing the face of an FSS officer. He could make out the odour of two hornets.

"Yes?" he asked curtly, his gaze flicking from the darkened faces under peaked caps to their PPU badges.

"We've come for the earwig," Honey grunted. "Bring him here now," she ordered firmly. The hornet on the other side of the door eyeballed her back.

"IDs!" he barked. Honey held up her lanyard, then moved aside to let Bisma do the same.

"Wait here," the hornet growled. He slammed the porthole shut. The four insects waited nervously in the dark until a series of bolts were drawn back, the door swung open, and an insect was shoved through. He tumbled into the arms of Honey and Bisma, and they wrapped his upper arms around their thoraxes, then led him staggering down the corridor away from the cell.

After a short distance, Honey nodded towards an entrance. Anton took over from Bisma as she checked the other side of the door. It was a storage room. She waved them through, and Anton and Honey carefully set Wiggy on the floor, leaning him against the wall.

Wiggy's head lolled forward in semi-consciousness as his friends gathered around him.

Honey gently stroked the back of his head. "Wiggy, it's me, Honey. Can you hear me? I'm here with Anton and Spyder."

"H-Honey?" Wiggy responded weakly, trying to open his eyes. "Wh-what?"

"It's okay, buddy," Anton reassured him. "It's us. We've come to get you out of here. Do you think you can walk?"

Wiggy managed to open one eye, then the other. He let out a pained giggle. "Honey... ew! You look so... hornet." He stretched an arm towards her. "Brie would love that cap."

Honey glanced up at Spyder. "He's totally out of it."

Wiggy reached out awkwardly. "Anton! Hi!" he giggled. "You really shouldn't have left me with those insects... Naughty Anton. Naughty!"

Anton hugged Wiggy. "I'm sorry, man. Are you ready to get out of here?"

Wiggy braced himself against the wall and pushed with all his might. He rose onto his feet and stood unsteadily before slipping down the wall again, sniggering.

"We really need to get going," Bisma said, her voice tense with urgency.

Anton slapped Wiggy's cheek lightly. "Wiggy! Come on, man. Can you walk?"

Spyder and Honey helped Wiggy to his feet again. He wobbled but managed to stay upright.

"Sure, guys. Let's go!" he said enthusiastically.

"How do we get out of here?" Anton looked at Bisma, a note of desperation in his voice.

She suggested they could cut back the way they had come, return to the service entrance, join the lines of insects back down the branch and trunk, and then figure out how to get out of the Exclusion Zone.

"I can't see any other way," Spyder suggested. Honey nodded.

"W-wait," Wiggy slurred, his eyes still glazed. "There's just one thing."

The four insects stopped, turning towards him.

"D-do you know why they brought me here?" he mumbled.

Anton held Wiggy around the abdomen. "It doesn't matter, mate. So long as we get you out of here. Come on now." Anton started to walk Wiggy towards the door.

"No. Wait. You don't understand. It does matter," Wiggy insisted, stopping and unwrapping Anton's hand from around him.

"The password." Wiggy sighed, sitting down again, holding his head in his hands. "I think I gave them the password."

"The password to what, Wig?" Anton asked.

"The password to The Cloud."

"Cloud?"

"Yes. It's a, er, super-large hard drive."

"Okay," Anton said slowly. "And what's in this Cloud?"

"They call it UniSynCom."

"They? You mean Insecterpol?" Spyder asked.

Wiggy looked at Spyder uncomfortably. "Y-you know about Insecterpol?"

Spyder nodded. "And Terry."

"We know everything," Anton replied. "Terry told us everything. Said you'd been kidnapped to create some security system for the hornets. Said you were the best at that sort of stuff. Look, it's okay – we can talk about it later. But for now, yeah, we all just need to get out of here."

Wiggy held his hands towards Anton, who pulled him back to his feet. Wiggy brushed himself down and swept his fringe back over an ear. He pursed his lips. "But did he tell you about UniSynCom?"

Anton raised his eyebrows towards Spyder and Honey. They all shook their heads. Terry hadn't mentioned UniSynCom.

Wiggy sighed. "Of course not. Listen, you guys, if the hornets have accessed UniSynCom, then..." He trailed off. "Then that's bad. Really bad."

"Okay, so what is this UniSynCom stuff?" Honey asked briskly.

"Universal Synthetic Communication. It's synthetic pheromone. You know that before our intellectual revolution and the development of our universal language, we communicated by chemical signals?"

"Pheromones," Honey nodded.

"Back then, we responded to the world unconsciously, didn't we? The release of a particular pheromone from one would stimulate a specific response from another. But as we evolved into intelligent, conscious creatures, pheromones became redundant. The thing is, pheromone remains stored in our genome, dormant.

"Insecterpol has enlisted an army of scientists to utilise the latest AI in generating code for every single pheromone. Ever. That's what's stored in The Cloud. Synthetic pheromone code. UniSynCom.

The mood had turned dark.

"Okay, so... why do the hornets want all these codes?" Honey asked.

"Well, let's say that the synthetic pheromone could be transmitted into a host. What might happen?" Wiggy's question was for anyone.

"It could stimulate an unconscious response. I suppose that essentially you could control... another animal's behaviour."

Wiggy nodded slowly. "*Exactly*. And what is Insecterpol working on right now?"

"A UniSynCom transmitter?" Spyder asked rhetorically. The arthros exchanged nervous glances.

"So, what if the hornets have already invented it?"

It was Bisma who finally said what everyone was thinking. "They could make us do what they wanted. They could take over the world."

Each arthro swore quietly to themselves.

"You see," Wiggy said, "That's why we can't just leave. If they have this transmitter, we have to destroy it."

"Yeah, right," Spyder spluttered. "And how are we supposed to do that? We don't know where it is or what it looks like. Even if we did, it'd be heavily guarded. Do you think we can just walk in, switch it off, say cheers and, er, walk out? I don't think so!"

Bisma held up a hand. "I might know where it is."

The others turned to her. "The neural intranet tells us where anyone can and cannot go. The only place even Yellow Jackets are banned from is a recently built annex at the very top of The Nest. It can only be accessed by FSS and approved senior officials. There's still construction work going on up there. Maybe we can get in from outside?"

Anton nodded. "What do you think, guys?"

"It sounds like our best bet," Honey whispered.

"What!" Spyder exclaimed disbelievingly. "We're actually going to do this?"

"Do we have a choice?" Anton replied.

Nobody said anything.

"Bisma's right," Anton said finally. "There's no way we can get to it from inside. If we can get outside, maybe join a line of workers..."

"... cause a distraction, break-in..." Honey added.

"... overwhelm the heavily armed guards, find the 'off' button. Escape," Spyder continued.

"And be back in time to play the gig!" Wiggy finished cheerfully.

"Now, *that*'s a plan." Anton smiled at his friends.

18

The Control Centre

Sure enough, at the very bottom of the corridor, they found a ventilation shaft set high up on the wall – but it was too narrow for them to crawl through. Without a word, Anton unshouldered his pack, handed it to Honey, and rolled up his sleeves. After termites, ants are the most effective tunnellers in the insect world; but Anton had never dug anything before in his life.

Facing the wall, he paused, steeling himself. He tried to scrape the wall using first his antennae, then his legs. Neither was particularly effective, so he switched to his mandibles, twisting and screwing until he finally broke the surface. He stood back to admire his work, then smiled a 'told you so' at his friends. Spyder punched the air jokingly with their top arms, while Honey gave him a 'keep going, then' look.

Anton soon got into the swing of it. He used his mandibles to saw and scoop, pushing the fragments behind

him with his legs. The others cleared away the debris dis-
lodged from the hole, scattering it across the floor. A little
further back down the corridor, Bisma kept watch, although
she had no idea what to do if a guard came. But she stayed
alert, ready to raise the alarm.

The Grove's capital hive was an impressive engineering
achievement. The original nest, now serving as the central
hub and royal quarters, was built by Vespa's ancestors and
was designed to last. Over generations, as the population
grew, The Nest expanded in all directions.

Until recently, tree hives were made from chewed-up
wood fibre. The resulting material was spread across a frame
in sheets, paper-thin. It hardened into an expanding network of chambers and connecting tunnels. As the number
of available workers increased, hornet architecture shifted
from framed extensions to hollowed-out spaces. This modern approach sacrificed the careful craftsmanship of older
times for speed. Today's builders, many of whom were migrant workers, were driven by financial returns. Volume
equalled money, and potentially a bonus. But quantity over
quality also led to rough finishes, haphazard layering, and air
holes.

As Anton dug steadily through the wall, he regularly
came across small cavities, which made the material crumble
more easily. It didn't take long before he was able to push
his antennae through the final layer. Fresh air rushed in,
and Anton paused to breathe in the afternoon breeze. He
then fashioned a more usable exit before shimmying half his
body through the hole. He slowly rotated around, taking in

the outside of The Nest. It looked alien and lifeless. Bands of greys and browns, like the grains of weathered wood, rippled across the surface. This section was rough and unkempt, with bulbous humps interspersed with craters and hollows. The entire area was cast in a dull, eerie light – he had emerged well beneath the mid-point of the dark side of The Nest, a place that never saw direct sunlight. Below, he could make out the edge of the platform, beyond which was a section of the Exclusion Zone and some workers' villages.

His antennae probed the air. There were no signs of hornets or WASPS on this cold side of The Nest.

Bisma and Honey were the first to join him on the surface. Still dressed in their PPU uniforms, they hovered close to the ground, scanning the air and keeping watch as the other three crawled out of the hole. The group then moved upwards in complete silence, using the nooks and crannies to stay out of sight as much as possible.

They made steady progress until they felt their equilibrium readjust to the other side of the midway point. Now walking the right way up, their pace quickened, and for the first time that day, Anton thought about the band. Their future. Thinking about the future of the band was Anton's favourite pastime. Whether he was in a hotel, travelling to a gig, trying to sleep, walking in the countryside, that's what he was always doing – plotting and planning and considering. *This isn't the time, Anton.* No. But, well, band stuff was a welcome respite.

It had been full-on since the big meeting. All four releases had fired, and the band was working on a further two. They'd tested them live a few times without introducing them, and they seemed to go down well – lots of followers wanted to know where they could hear them, so they had teased sections of them on Insectagram. Anton thought there were a few bootlegs doing the rounds, but that was normal for many bands.

The thrill of touring, however, was wearing thin. Not the stage – that was still incredible – but the never-ending stream of anonymous hotel rooms, restaurants, vehicles, and faces. Anton knew he had behaved badly more than once, but everyone else had, too. Even Honey! Anyway, what's the point of being a rock star if you can't behave like one now and then? They were a guitar band, for goodness' sake, and guitar bands got into trouble. That's what the fans loved about them. That's why the conservative media didn't... which only made them more loved by fans!

After Flutterbury, they had a few more dates, but after that, nothing. That would be holiday time, and he couldn't wait. He and Honey hadn't really spent more than a day or two together alone, and even then, there was the next gig or rehearsal or recording session to think about. He turned to her and saw she was also lost in thought. He felt his chest flutter right in the middle, so he took her hand. She smiled at him and squeezed, and they walked hand in hand, like a regular couple out for a walk.

He loved her. Even more, now. Since they became official, he couldn't help but feel responsible for her wellbeing. His role was to keep her safe. But now that he thought about it, he understood that thinking like that also disrespected her.

Of course, he wanted her to be safe, but she was perfectly capable of looking after herself. Would she have been able to sting a fellow insect? Kill it? Would he? *What am I even thinking about!* He released her hand to run his hand over his head, shaking it wryly. Would they ever be able to get back to normal? Would they ever get back? What if they were captured? Would Terry send a team? He tried to block out these thoughts and think about the band. He had some new songs he was keen to try out...

"What?" Honey asked.

"Nothing. The band. And..."

"What?" she asked, digging him playfully in the abdomen.

"Ow! I was just thinking... about how much I love you."

Without stopping, she reached over and kissed him clumsily.

Definitely some time off. Where would they go? The beach? A safari, maybe. An incognito trip in some faraway land. *Mmm – time to chill. Imagine that! Rising late, early to bed. Well, not too early...* Then Anton reckoned they'd be ready for an album. Should they consider a project, try to write in a particular style, or just more of the same? Their compositions seemed to be developing naturally, so trying to force them somewhere new could backfire. Wiggy had such an important part to play in the feel of the music.

Wiggy.

How would it be when – *if* – they returned home? *How do I feel about him?* Anton was about to consider this, then told himself again that this probably wasn't the time. And then, as if he was listening to Anton's thoughts, Wiggy murmured: "Guys, I'm so sorry."

He had wanted to say something the moment they emerged onto The Nest's surface, but had only now found the courage. It was barely a whisper, but they were all close enough to hear him. For a while, no one said anything.

"Okay, I'll say it... You used us, Wiggy." Spyder stared hard at the forlorn earwig. "I mean, the idea was whack. Using a band as cover? I get it. I do, really. But, you know? Now? Here?" Spyder turned all the way around, their mouth grim, before falling back into line.

Wiggy sniffed back a tear.

"Should we be doing this now, guys?" Anton said.

Spyder ignored him. "None of us could believe it. When Terry said you were a spy. I mean... a *spy*. You? Like, when we first met you, when we went out on tour, you were so..." They tried to think of the right word. "...unspyish. I mean, no one could be less spyish than you."

"Well, strictly speaking, I'm not a spy, I'm an..."

"Asset. We know. And the greatest hacker in the world," Spyder aped, flicking two speech marks in the air.

"Well, maybe once," Wiggy replied innocently. "But what I'm really good at is writing code. And coming up with unbreakable security systems."

"Yeah, right! Like the one for The Cloud?" Spyder said sarcastically.

"But, but... do you know the technology the hornets created to do this?" Wiggy said with childish excitement. "Truly amazing! Years ahead."

"Shhh." Bisma turned to the four band members sternly, finger at her lips.

Wiggy bowed his head submissively, realising he was being inappropriate.

"Sorry," he said. "Sorry." Wiggy returned his stare to the ground. "It's j-just, I n-never thought it would come to this." Wiggy wiped away another tear. "You've put your lives in d-danger to save me."

"It's okay, mate," Anton said, putting an arm around Wiggy's thorax and stopping. "It's okay. It is what it is. You're a spy or an asset, or whatever you are." Anton's tone was gentle now. "But you're also our friend. A member of Them Creepy Crawlies. Of course, we forgive you. Don't we guys. Because that's what friends do."

"So, we're okay?" Wiggy asked sheepishly. "Spyder?"

Spyder hesitated and then smiled. "Yeah, man. We're good. Come here, you freak!" And there, on the surface of a hornet's nest, the four members of Them Creepy Crawlies came together in a group hug.

"Sorry to break up the love," Bisma said curtly, "but can you hear that?"

Anton, Honey, Spider and Wiggy turned to where Bisma pointed, their antennae pulsing gently. There was a very gentle, late-afternoon breeze. And on it was a *shick shick shick* sound.

"A worker's column." Honey was the first to recognise the marching sound.

The five arthros crawled along a hollow towards the noise. At the end, Bisma very carefully lifted her head to see two lines of creatures, one heading upwards to the left loaded with material, the other moving to the right, downwards, to collect the next load from the platform. There didn't seem to be any WASPs, FSS officers, or Yellow Jackets around, so after a quick discussion, Honey and Bisma simply marched Anton, Spyder and Wiggy to the line and pushed them into place, one behind the other. If anyone was surprised that two PPU officers were on the surface of The Nest with an ant, a bee and a spider, they didn't show it. Neither did they think anything about the fact that they weren't carrying anything. PPU officers could do what they wanted. Marching in parallel, Bisma and Honey tugged their caps a little lower over their eyes and pushed their dark glasses a little closer to their faces.

The surface had levelled off to nearly horizontal as they neared an area of intense activity. The route took them through a large team of arthros working shoulder to shoulder, spreading out piles of recycled aggregate. Then, behind them, other teams, clutching large spreader brooms, brushed the mix as flat as possible. A final team layered sticky gloop across the newly prepared site, securing it with a series of balletic jumps and hops. It was as if they were spreading grey icing over the top of a big truffle cake. To his left and right, as far as Anton could see, the activity was the same, each field split by carrier lines.

Up ahead, the destination of the carrier lines seemed to be mounds of material. Behind the mounds, temporary shelters opened towards them. Butted up to each other, they completely encircled a partly hidden inner area behind. It reminded Anton of one of those old-fashioned ruffs that some aristocratic ants wore as a decorative collar. He saw that the shelters were refreshment stations. In the central circle behind, Anton could just make out the rounded, shiny top of a circular tower. It was bright white and quartz-like – unlike anything he'd ever seen. Anton, Spyder and Wiggy took their turns pretending to dump something and followed the other arthros into the nearest rest area.

Everyone sat around long rectangular tables, drinking cups of tea, eating some sort of bread, and getting ready for the journey back to the platform for another load. Hardly anyone spoke. Security, as usual, looked casual, and no one was paying any attention to the few Yellow Jackets who lingered nearby – although some nervous eyes were now flicking towards the two PPU officers who stood watching the crowd.

Anton, Wiggy and Spyder filled a cup, grabbed some cake, and found themselves a spot at a vacant table. They sat quietly, surreptitiously taking in their surroundings.

"Any thoughts?" Anton asked.

"Didn't notice any vents," whispered Spyder. "But did you see that strange, shiny tower-thingy? That must be something, right?"

Anton nodded. "I agree. It looks pretty impenetrable, though. I'm thinking they must get fresh air from somewhere, yeah?"

"Air-conditioning?" Wiggy wondered out loud.

"These temporary structures seem to encircle it," noted Spyder. "I wonder what's on the other side of that wall?" They nodded towards the back of the structure.

"Wait here," said Wiggy, leaping up before anyone could stop him. He had spotted the sign to the restroom, located at the back of the refreshment area. From there, he might be able to take a closer look at the tower. When a unit became free, he locked the door and looked up. There was no window, but because of the structure's temporary nature, there was an opening between the wall and ceiling, with just enough room for him to squeeze through. He pulled himself up and peered out. He could see a security fence with relay boxes, which meant it was electrified. It circled a dead zone, empty apart from a few humps and hollows, and beyond that was the weird-looking tower.

Moments later, Wiggy, Anton and Spyder stood motionless, their backs pressed hard against the restroom's outer wall, surveying the space beyond the fence, looking for some sort of access point to the tower.

And then, from the wall above, Anton heard some scrabbling. He looked up to see two legs and two wings appear from the gap beneath the roof. He swore inwardly. Had they been followed? Surely not. He hadn't seen any Yellow Jackets or FFS anywhere. He held his breath.

"Bloody hell, Bisma." Anton exhaled a rush of relief. "You scared the life out of me. I could've... well, I could have..."

"What's up?" Honey interrupted, landing right beside them.

"Nothing," Anton replied, regaining his composure. "I see you've got rid of the uniforms."

Back together again, the five arthros gazed at the tower. From where they stood, it looked more like an upside-down saucer with an elevated central dome. There was a dark blue strip of something around the rim and the structure was smooth and shiny grey, steep at the ground then flatter against the base of the dome, which sparkled as if millions of tiny moving tiles were catching the light. Above the summit of the dome, some whorls of leaves pulled down smaller branches, but above these wispy outliers, the great canopy of the baobab tree stood strong and full. Through the foliage, dappled light fell from the late afternoon sun. Dark, oblong shadows swayed over the humps and hollows of the fenced-off area – except off to the left, where the dome's shadow darkened a section of the ground.

"So, what now?" Wiggy asked, surveying the scene uncertainly.

"You reckon that fence is just a fence, and not a canopy shield?" Honey asked.

"An electric one, yeah," Wiggy replied.

Shortly afterwards, Wiggy sat nervously cradled between Honey and Bisma, an arm around each of their thoraxes and another pair around their abdomens, his legs dangling perilously near the fence as they flew him over it.

Once the bees had lifted Spyder and Anton over the fence, they spread out, hunched over, carefully staying within the shadow of the dome, searching for anything that resembled a vent. The ground was rough and littered with abandoned piles of building clay, craters, and boulder-like mounds. There was plenty of cover but no shafts anywhere to be seen.

There must be a way inside. Anton tried to remember some of the spy movies he'd avidly watched, and the control centres of all those villains who wanted to take over the world. *Where did their air come from? What did those vents look like? They wouldn't be noticeable – they'd be disguised.* Anton looked around the area. *The rocks?* He kicked one. Then another. *One of the hollows, maybe?* He stepped into one, scraping the ground forlornly with his foot.

He considered the dome. It looked ominous. He'd never seen any building with glistening walls. *Pretty threatening.* And the saucer... from a distance, its convex side seemed smooth, but up close, there appeared to be an impassable network of beams. *Whatever's inside, the hornets definitely don't want anyone getting to it.* And the moat. An actual moat! *Medieval and modern technology side by side!* Anton knelt at the edge and peered into the inky water. It was dark and foreboding. *I wonder where the water comes from.* He looked around. There were no obvious storage tanks.

He reached a hand towards the moat's surface to cup a drink, and his arm slipped through thin air. Shocked, he pulled back; there were no drips, no wetness. He submerged his hand again, and it disappeared. He shook it around, and the water seemed to crackle with mild distortion. *It's a hologram!*

"Over here!" Anton called softly, waving a hand.

He demonstrated his new discovery by submerging an antenna. It disappeared under a ripple of silent static. The others, stunned, dipped various limbs through the surface, shaking their heads in disbelief as the illusion sizzled.

"I'm going to have a look." Spyder held Anton's hands as he lowered himself through the hologram. Underneath, the sides were vertical, black and smooth, apart from hundreds of tiny light sources that threw holographic lasers across the cavity. It seemed safe, so he urged them all to follow. At least they couldn't be seen beneath the image. He edged towards some LEDs and felt a vibration that, as he got closer, turned into the faint hum of an engine. A motor sucked in air through a grate. It was secured to the superstructure of the dome by bolts. Anton searched his pack. He had a screwdriver and a small pocket knife with attachments. But he didn't have a socket spanner.

Anton sat down and swore quietly to himself.

"What about this?" Spyder asked, handing him a set of drum keys.

Anton grinned back at Spyder, grabbed the set, found the right socket, and unscrewed the bolts.

"You guys wait here – I'll take a look." Anton crawled into the horizontal duct. After a while, the tunnel turned vertical, so he had to use all his limbs to shimmy upwards, where he discovered a rubbery aperture kept open by the rush of air sucked in from below. Beyond the aperture, he emerged into a tiny control room for an air conditioning system. Further ducts, each with rubber apertures, led left, right, and straight up. A control panel, housed in an opaque case, was mounted against a wall. It was unlocked, so Anton swung it open to discover various pressure gauges and a bank of red and white buttons. There were four directional settings: 'In', 'Out', 'Up' and 'Down'. The temperature indicator was set to 'Cold' and the airflow speed to 'High'.

Leaving the switches untouched, Anton chose the left duct and immediately felt colder air blowing powerfully at his back. The duct was circular, so he presumed he was circumnavigating the top of the saucer. Having crawled through three more identical control chambers, he returned to the first, confirming it was a closed loop.

This time, he pulled himself into the ascending duct. He used his back and legs to climb vertically, and when the tunnel levelled off, the rush of the air became much louder. Anton could see that the end of the tunnel emptied into a brightly lit area.

What he found there was astonishing.

Thousands, maybe millions, of tiny branch-like arteries filled the space, radiating out from a central trunk that rose through a cloud. The fibres spread in flawless symmetry, each stretching out with linear precision, arching like a waterfall to create the illusion of the glowing dome Anton had seen from outside. They pulsed and quivered with occasional fizzes and sparks of light. Anton could feel the heat from the nearest arteries and realised that the air conditioning was keeping them as cool as possible.

From his vent, Anton could see three more openings, spaced equidistantly around the dome. His attention turned to the cloud that formed a fluffy floor across the base of dome. He carefully touched it with an antenna. It felt dewy, airy and weightless, and seemed to shy away from his touch. He guessed it was formed by the meeting of warm air below with the colder air from the air conditioning.

Steadying himself, he submerged an antenna very slowly into the vapoury substance until he sensed it break through to the other side. He scanned the room below with his up-side-down periscope. *A control room!* When he was satisfied that he hadn't released an alarm, he cautiously dipped a second antenna through the cloud and memorised as much detail as he could – technicians; computers; panels; screens; equipment he didn't understand.

Very quietly, he backed up the ventilation system until, much to his friends' relief, he reemerged into the moat. He sat down, gathering his thoughts before describing the dome and the layout of the control room beneath.

"So, this tree thing. You think it could be the hard-drive for the UniSynCom data?" Honey asked.

"I don't know," Anton replied. "It could be. But why do the branches – the artery things – like, end so perfectly?"

Wiggy turned to Anton. "Could you see the base of the trunk thingy?"

Anton shook his head. "No. It appeared to come from below the control room. There was a sort of control panel around it blocking my view. I assume the tree, or whatever it is, is attached to that panel."

They all looked at Wiggy, waiting for him to say something. Wiggy brushed his fringe repeatedly from his forehead. They knew when he was thinking. He started pacing in a circle. He looked totally uncoordinated, hunched over so his head wouldn't break the hologram's surface, his legs bent at the knee, each wanting to go in a direct direction.

"Of course!" A wry smile spread over his face, and he stopped, facing his audience.

"What, Wiggy? What is it?" Spyder asked urgently.

"Oh, my. Oh, my goodness." He chuckled, nodding slowly, cementing his thoughts. "It's the delivery system. The, er, transmitter. Anton – how fast does light travel?"

Anton grimaced. He had no idea.

"It's about 300 million metres per second," Honey volunteered.

"Two hundred and ninety-nine million, seven hundred and ninety-two thousand, four hundred and fifty-eight, to be precise," whispered Wiggy.

"So?" Spyder said.

"Well, that's the speed at which pheromone can travel. UniSynCom is going to hitch a ride on light waves. Of course! Brilliant!"

No one said anything.

"Quite brilliant," Wiggy continued. "You see, the trunk? It's a luminal aorta. But instead of blood, it carries light created from… a homemade sun! I assume its somewhere under the control room. I wonder how they store the Uni-SynCom?" he wondered, before continuing, "Anyway – the branches? Ha! Well, they're photon veins – they're the gun barrels that will shoot out the light waves. Think of a sunrise. But in this case, as soon as you see it, you've already been shot with UniSynCom."

"The hornets have made a sun?" spluttered Spyder.

"Yup."

"That can be switched on at any time?" asked Bisma.

"Yup. But it needs to warm up. Like a tube guitar amp. You first switch on the power, and after the tubes have warmed up, you flick on the standby."

"At which time we'll all be under the control of the hornets?" Honey said matter-of-factly.

"Well, it depends on what pheromone they transmit, but potentially er, we could be, yes." Wiggy flashed a resigned smile.

"So, how do we switch it off, Wiggy?" Anton asked, with a serious tone to his voice.

"Or back to standby?" Spyder added.

"No idea," Wiggy replied, simply.

"Right. Well, start thinking about it, Wiggy," Anton urged.

"Hang on! Hang on!" Spyder said, rolling their eyes and turning to Anton. "So, this is actually not a joke, yeah? I just want to get this absolutely clear. We're going to jump through the weird cloudy stuff, overpower the evil technicians, turn off the doomsday machine, and escape back down the ventilation shaft."

Anton raised his eyebrows up and down, while pulling an ironic grin.

"Cool." Spyder nodded repeatedly. "Just checking."

Anton stood with his hands on his hips, surveying his friends. "Look, if anyone else has a better plan, let's hear it. Maybe if there was more time, we could better understand the comings and goings of the guards. Or even find out the location of the off or standby switches. But we don't have time. The UniSynCom might be broadcast at any time, and we are all aware of the likely consequences.

"We've all got our unique skills, and the hornets are bound to underestimate us. And, critically, we have the element of surprise."

"And guitar leads," smiled Honey, holding one up and swinging it seductively.

"Wiggy," said Anton, "we know that when it comes to it, you'll work out how to switch this thing off." He stared at Wiggy intently. "There isn't a cleverer insect on The Nest."

As he led his friends into the ventilation shaft, Anton sensed a steely, if nervous, determination among the friends following him. They'd managed to overcome a bunch of weird new challenges. Now, they had to be proactive. Now they were on the offensive – and possibly about to engage an armed, highly-trained enemy that would kill them in an instant. What he'd give to be watching one of the acts at Flutterbury right now.

When they reached the control room, they split up. Honey and Bisma turned left and made their way to the vent on the opposite side of the dome. Wiggy crawled to the vent on the right and Spyder to the left. Reaching his outlet first, Anton smiled as Wiggy and Spyder marvelled at the neural tree and the flickering arteries. He then slid his antennae through the cloud.

In the middle of the room, there was a circular console. It was flat, smooth and matte black, emanating a menacing simplicity. At its centre, the luminal aorta gleamed brightly, with countless veins extending up through the cloudy ceiling, pulsing with the initial shocks of energy. Two technicians in white overalls and clipboards were engaged in a deep discussion beside it.

A transparent control panel stretched around the circumference of the room at, Anton calculated, about thirty degrees off the horizontal. Like the central console, it seemed to float on its own. Above the panel was an advanced Quantum Dot OLED flexi-monitor that also ran uninterrupted around the room. The screen was alive with shifting data and overlays. Two more technicians sat at points around it, pressing buttons and examining the constantly shifting information on the screen.

Directly below him, a pair of FSS officers stood on either side of the only door, legs apart and heads held high. Their upper arms were behind their backs, while their lower arms held automatic weapons.

The time had come.

19

The Escape

As Anton and his friends were discovering the dome, Colonel Hendrix waited in an anteroom. He stood at ease, hands behind his back, although his gaze appeared distracted, a little out of focus. That was strange for him.

While the earwig's interrogation had been successful, Hendrix still felt uneasy. He was unable to recall anything about his experience inside the earwig's subconscious. However, the technicians had retrieved and downloaded the data, and that was all that mattered. It had been an extremely lengthy process – the passwords had been well concealed. One technician had told him there had been an extraordinary amount of sub-cortical activity towards the end of the journey, and his heartbeat had spiked considerably. Maybe that's why I feel distracted, he thought.

"Colonel Hendrix," the equerry summoned him.

Without acknowledging the attendant, Hendrix entered the chamber and marched towards the Queen.

"Your Majesty." He took Vespa's hand and bowed his head, so his lips hovered just above the back of her palm.

"Colonel," Vespa greeted him coolly. Hendrix took two steps back and stood at ease. "I trust everything has gone to plan?"

"Indeed, it has, ma'am." He smiled. "We successfully accessed The Cloud. UniSynCom is downloading into Helionix as we speak."

"Excellent, Colonel. You have done well," Queen Vespa said without emotion.

"If I may say, Your Majesty," Hendrix replied, "the Helionix project would not have been successful without your input. The work you did with the scientists was most impressive."

"Thank you, Colonel," Vespa responded. "I had always suspected that the cellulose microfibrils in plants could serve as dense storage units. We already know that plasmodesmata channels connect plant cells into a continuous network." Vespa brushed off a couple of creases from her jacket.

"Indeed, my Queen." Zir Hugh emerged from the shadows at the back of the chamber.

"But it was you who demonstrated that the entire plant kingdom can work as a single, networked hard drive."

Vespa bowed slightly. The challenge, however, had been how to input data and then retrieve it on a major scale. The solution was Helionix. Essentially, Helionix was a server contained in the space under the control centre. It sat alongside the light generating extension to Sol, the photonic system capable of transmitting massive amounts of data via light.

Zir Hugh turned to Hendrix. "How long until Sol reaches its transmitting capacity?"

The colonel looked at his watch. "Precisely fifteen minutes and... twenty-three seconds, Zir."

"And can you confirm that the appropriate pheromone packets have been uploaded?" The old retainer's voice was deliberate and grave.

"Yes, Zir Hugh," Hendrix replied tightly, a slight hint of impatience creeping into his voice.

Hendrix turned back to his Queen. "With your permission, ma'am, may I proceed?"

Vespa gazed at the Head of the FSS, then turned to the mantle and the photographs of her assassinated family. They had become her silent guides, their echoes helping steer her decisions. But she had chosen this path a long time ago, and her determination was undimmed.

"We will accompany you, Colonel Hendrix," Queen Vespa said, starting towards the door.

"Your Highness, there is no need. Do not trouble yourself with the mechanics of Sol," Hendrix said with a courteous bow, his voice smooth with deference. "Entrust this command to me, and I shall see it fulfilled. It would be my honour."

Vespa was not used to being challenged. "Colonel Hendrix. We are on the verge of changing the course of history. I will most definitely be there!"

She glided out of the chamber, followed by Zir Hugh, with Hendrix bringing up the rear. When the High Council had appointed him to coordinate the Helionix project, Hendrix had worked tirelessly, harder than anyone, to reach this point. Not everyone had agreed with his methods, but he was proud of what he had achieved. He had coordinated every element of the project, and it was he, through his spy network, who had discovered that Insecterpol had beaten them to developing a full synthetic pheromone dataset. But critically, he knew that no one else had Sol.

The colonel smiled politely at the hornets that bowed in respect to Queen Vespa as they made their way through the corridors towards the control room. After UnsiSynCom had been transmitted, everyone would finally recognise him.

#

Spyder and Wiggy locked their gaze on Anton, their focus wound tight as a drum. With his antennae focused firmly on the control centre, Anton raised his top right arm and three fingers in a prearranged gesture. When he lowered one, he could feel his heart beating just a little faster. Then he lowered a second finger.

Just as he was about to signal 'go', the door to the control centre opened. Three hornets entered: two males and a female at the front. One of the males was older, while the other wore a black zip-up jacket, pants, and a peaked cap with the stinger emblem. The female was smart in a trouser suit, her hair perfect and held in place with a bejewelled circlet.

Anton swore and frantically waved his hand to hold back the attack. With his antennae acting as eyes, he watched the older male and the female shake hands with a technician, who then began showing them around the OLED flexi-monitor, pointing out different things on the display. The female seemed especially interested, interrupting and asking questions. At one point, the technician gestured upwards towards him. Anton's heart lurched, and he quickly withdrew his antennae. *Did they see me?*

No alarms sounded, and no one shouted a warning, so he guessed their attention had shifted elsewhere. He carefully lowered his antennae to see what the technician had pointed at. A digital clock. It was old-fashioned with red italic numbers that read...

4.55

He hadn't seen the clock before, but he understood what the numbers indicated. He relayed the info to Spyder by tapping his wrist and holding up five fingers. They nodded back. Then he held up three more fingers and mimicked a gun. It was the best way he could think of to show there were more people in the room. Spyder gave a 'what now' look. *I'm thinking!* Anton indicated the other side of the space. *Tell the bees.* He glanced at the other vent. *Any ideas, Wiggy? No, of course not.* He refocused on the room below. *How are we going to do this now?* He watched the demonstration, trying to figure it out. *The techs are showing the female a lot of respect. She must be someone important.* He thought for a moment. *That's who it is! Queen Vespa!*

Now, above the central console, a dome-shaped hologram appeared. After a few glitches, it stabilised into a clear, three-dimensional map of a valley. *The Grove.* Anton could see the camps, the river, and in the centre, a large baobab tree. He watched, mesmerised, as the tech 'squeezed' the air in front of him. The hologram shrank to focus on a tree. *The Nest!*

The tech then expanded the view to show... *the entire continent!* He used four arms to pull away a smaller section for a closer look, spun it 360 degrees, then dismissed it with a swipe, leaving the hologram to return to its original Grove setting.

Queen Vespa looks very pleased. Anton checked the clock.

4.15

Another technician was now talking to the Queen. *She could be trained in combat, but... nah – unlikely. Same with the older hornet.* Anton considered the other male. *The scar. Hendrix!* Anton cursed just loudly enough for Spyder to hear. They gestured frustratedly at him. Anton held up his hand. *Just wait, Spyder.* Anton still believed that he and Spyder could take out the two FSS officers at the door. They had surprise on their side. He'd have to land squarely on his officer. There'd be no second chance. *No holding back, then.* Anton had never knocked someone out before. How hard would he need to hit them? *What about Spyder?* Anton imagined Spyder could handle themselves. He recalled the story of Spyder meeting Honey. *Seems I'm the only one who's never been in a fight before today.*

He watched the technician guide Queen Vespa to the other side of the console where she raised a transparent control panel roughly the size of a tablet. It hovered in the air perfectly still. She prompted the Queen to tap a spot. Anton saw a multitude of tiny black dots appear across the map. Most were on the ground, but some floated in the air. The tech squeezed her hands inward, zooming in on the holographic view, and peripheral features disappeared until only a cluster of black dots remained.

Anton strained to listen. He'd only caught bits and pieces before, but this time the words were clear as day.

"Hornets, Your Majesty."

3.45

The black dots vanished. Another tap, and green ones replaced them. The tech twisted and turned the view to display the camps, then the trunk, and finally the platform. Lots of green dots with gaps between them. *A different species.* Then, a scattering of them moved across the surface of The Nest. As the view shifted to the top of The Nest, it became clear there was a single green dot right at the very apex. On its own.

The tech looked surprised and tightened the image as far as it could go. He tapped. The green vanished and was replaced by nine black dots. He tapped again. There was definitely a green dot. Anton understood. The green dots were ants. And the single green dot? That was him. He saw the Queen and the technician suddenly look upwards.

Anton glanced to his right. Wiggy had dipped an antenna through the mist. *I hope he can work out how it all works.* To his left, Spyder was still focused on him, holding multiple loops of thread, waiting for the order. They were ready. Anton pointed to Spyder and then the guards at the side of the door. Spyder nodded. He pointed to the bees – Spyder should prepare them. Spyder nodded again and turned to Honey, who'd been watching her friend with the same intent as they'd been watching Anton. She threw Spyder a thumbs-up. She and Bisma were ready.

3.19

Anton jumped.

His feet crashed into the head of the FSS guard. Anton managed to roll out of his fall and, regaining his feet, leapt into an 'en garde' position. The hornet had smashed backwards into the door and crumpled to the floor unconscious. The other officer was grappling at his neck, gasping for breath as Spyder pulled on the threads they had lassoed around him. Without thinking, Anton lashed out, catching the astonished hornet in the abdomen. Spyder let go, and the hornet collapsed.

To his right, about a quarter of the way around the circular room, an outraged Hendrix was now shielding the older male, with a technician cowering behind the pair. To his left, directly opposite Hendrix but hidden behind the luminal aorta of Sol, was Queen Vespa and another technician. They were staring at Anton in disbelief. He couldn't see the third and fourth technicians. *They must be on the other side of the trunk.* In his peripheral vision, he saw Hendrix draw his weapon. Instinctively, he ducked, yanking Spyder down to the floor with him.

The shot rang around the room, but the projectile ricocheted harmlessly off the door. Hendrix pushed the older hornet further behind him, his weapon aimed at Anton for another shot.

"GET THEM!" he screamed.

2.52

An alarm sounded. A loud, old-fashioned whoop. Heavy bars crashed through the inside of the door, sealing the room. Someone shouted. Another shot rang out. Anton and Spyder had just enough time to throw themselves to their left, only feet now from Vespa and the frightened tech. Instinctively, Anton lunged at the white coat while Spyder shot a web at Queen Vespa. A third shot exploded near them. Then, in a flurry of wings and legs, Bisma and Honey swooped across Anton's line of sight. Another shot. A scream. Anton grabbed some of Spyder's silk and wrapped it hastily around the tech, who was very happy to lie still.

"Don't shoot!" someone yelled. "The Sol!"

Hendrix ignored the appeal and fired again, repeatedly, this time upwards towards the bees. The bullets whined through the cloud, zipping and zizzing through photon veins.

"Stop firing! You'll destroy the Sol!" a technician shouted desperately.

Bloody alarm! Anton tried to concentrate. *Two FSS officers down. One technician. How long?* He glanced at the clock...

2.14

In his peripheral vision, he could just make out a hornet flying directly at him, white lab coat flapping, stinger ready. Anton leapt out of the way, narrowly avoiding her. The hornet jammed on her wingbrakes and tried a U-turn, but she was not used to attack flight patterns and careered sideways, wings fluttering hopelessly. Honey was on her in an instant with a well-aimed sting to the abdomen. The hornet managed to stop her slide, but the stun-sting made her wings slow to a halt, and she fell helplessly to the floor.

Spyder, meanwhile, had wrapped a sturdy thread around the wings of the still-shocked Queen. When Honey landed nearby, they both looked at each other in panic.

The alarm's wail was all-consuming, but Anton sensed a slight change in tone, which made him instantly wary. The third hornet came at the three of them with a crazed scream. Honey and Anton avoided it, but Spyder was knocked to the floor. It may not have been trained to use its stinger in hand-to-hand combat, but fuelled by adrenaline, it flashed and slashed manically at Spyder, who was struggling to fend it off. With Anton now restraining Vespa, Honey realised it was up to her to save her friend. She plunged her hand into her pack. The first thing she felt was a guitar lead. She tried to flick it out, but it stuck, so the entire pack set off in a slow arc. To avoid the bag, the hornet adjusted its flight path. Instead of taking evasive action to the left, it winged right and crashed into the protective sheath around the Sol. The force of the collision set off a series of electrical shorts, which triggered the Sol's defence system. The hornet, screaming in agony, was electrocuted.

Three techs down. A captured Queen. Anton wondered where Bisma was. Then his focus shifted. Wiggy was crawling through the mist, over the flexi-screen and into a chair in front of one of the terminals.

"You're two officers and three technicians down," Anton called to Hendrix, watching Wiggy activate a terminal. He began creeping round the central console, holding the Queen, now gagged, in front of him. "And we have your Queen, so... let's negotiate."

1.24

Hendrix had assessed the situation. The alarm added to the chaos in the room, but that was a good thing. No one could get out, and that was good, too. The technicians and officers were unfortunate. The Queen a hostage? That was also unfortunate, but the Sol was one minute and twenty-four seconds from activation and that took preference over everything. All he had to do was keep the bloody ant talking. Of course, he also now had an excellent bargaining chip. A sinister smile spread over his face.

"As you wish," he called back. "What did you have in mind?"

1.15

With his arm around Queen Vespa's thorax, and careful to keep her between him and Hendrix, Anton edged slowly into view. What he saw made his heart sink. Standing facing him was Hendrix, a wry smile on his face. Behind him was Zir Hugh. To Hendrix's right was the fourth technician. And in front of that technician, with a gun pointed at her head, stood Bisma.

"I must commend you, ant," Hendrix said, "for getting this far."

"Stop the countdown, Hendrix, and I'll hand over your Queen." Anton tried to sound forceful. "If you don't..." Anton tightened his grip on Vespa.

Hendrix laughed. He grabbed Bisma and pulled her to him, so close that she could feel his breath on the side of her face. "Why don't *you* let the Queen go, and I promise not to execute the bee?"

1.09

Anton could see the tears welling in Bisma's eyes. "Let her go, Hendrix," Anton shouted, anger creeping into his tone, "or I swear..."

Hendrix chuckled. "Let her go? Stop the countdown? I don't think you really know *what* you want, ant. Tell me, would you sacrifice the bee for Sol? Would you give up both bees? I tell you what: hand over the Queen, the spider, and the other bee, and I'll turn it off." Hendrix was enjoying this.

On the other side of the Sol, Wiggy had been scanning every inch of the console. He knew that a wrong tap could trigger an alarm or, worse, cause a lockout, but now he leaned in closer. He was certain there would be a pattern. Most of the icons pulsed brightly, inviting interaction, but a faint line of duller, slower-blinking symbols hugged the bottom edge, nearly blending into the background grid. The security system that guarded the Sol's operating system was 3-Gen.

He leaned back and looked up at Honey, anxiety in his eyes. "You got this," she nodded reassuringly. He shifted uncomfortably. He wasn't usually nervous in front of a computer, any type of computer, but he wasn't used to working against a clock.

He got to work, frantically tapping and watching words and characters and numbers come and go from the screen. He eyed the clock off to his left and then focused back on the console and the tangle of information racing down the screen. Recognition. He selected a symbol. A submenu unfolded – an operator's log. He tried another. Maintenance protocols. A third led to calibration routines. His pulse quickened. He was in the right territory. He started typing again, faster this time. Tracing one submenu into the next, beginning to map the arrangement in his head, and then translating it across the flexi. This was Wiggy's world, the place he felt most comfortable: cyber mazing, dead ending loops, digging up redundancies, reinstalling redundant redundancies. He knew that everything was built to make the shutdown impossible to reach. But Wiggy also knew that everything had a back door.

He tapped return. At first, the screen looked the same as before, but then the display stuttered. The smooth overlays and sleek menus collapsed instantly, leaving only a flat grey field. In the centre of the screen, a single line of green text blinked faintly.

MAINT-ACCESS://SOL 47B >> UNAUTHORISED ENTRY

Wiggy swore. A dead end. But then, as he wondered what to do next, the text fractured and faded, leaving a blank screen. Moments later, five root instructions appeared:

>> CORE CALIBRATION

>> DATA REDUNDANCY

>> TARGET

>> EMERGENCY PROTOCOLS

>> ROOT OVERRIDE

There were no confirmation prompts, no layered permissions. Just five lines of stark, blinking text. He scrolled to TARGET *and clicked.*

{A} ALL [EXCLUDED: HORNETS] **LOCKED**

{B} BY CLASS [EXCLUDED: __________]

{C} BY SPECIES

He sucked in heavily and exhaled slowly. Option 'A' was highlighted in red. He tried to move the cursor, but it was locked.

"Keep going," Honey urged, rubbing his back, "you're nearly there."

Wiggy nodded and returned to the previous menu. He selected EMERGENCY PROTOCOLS and clicked. The screen shifted again, opening into a short, three-choice menu:

[1] SHUTDOWN

[2] REBOOT

[3] PURGE CACHE

The cursor blinked expectantly. At the bottom of the screen was a progress bar and a clock:

HELIONIX PROTOCOL ENGAGEMENT — 0:14

As the alarm continued to wail, Wiggy sat transfixed as the four flicked to three, then two.

When Hendrix shut down the control centre, he was determined that nothing would stop Sol. He'd assumed that the ant, the bees, and the spider were Insecterpol agents sent to destroy Sol and the Helionix project. He hadn't considered that they had first rescued the earwig, who, for the past minute, had been working to disable it.

Hendrix wondered why the ant hadn't made a move. He seemed content talking and threatening. But the clock was ticking down, so why wasn't he more desperate? An elite agent wouldn't have thought twice about sacrificing a nursing bee. Why didn't he act? And where was the spider? The other bee?

For the first time, Hendrix felt uneasy. His smile faded, and he stopped speaking. He noticed the ant looking at the clock, a faint smile on his lips. Something wasn't right. And the noise had started to irritate him. He tried to shake away the racket, but as he did, he heard a shout from the other side of Sol.

"It's done, Anton! Wiggy's stopped it!"

He looked instinctively at the clock.

0:11

His eyes stayed fixed on it, waiting for the 11 to change to 10. But it didn't. He looked at Anton, puzzled. Then back at the clock. It hadn't budged. He turned again to Anton. On the outside, he appeared calm, but inside he was seething. Speaking very slowly, he addressed Anton.

"You have no idea what you've done."

He held Anton's gaze, and, unblinking, addressed the technician with two simple words:

"Kill her!"

The technician's grin spread across his face. With a sharp twist, he wrenched Bisma against him, one arm clamped around her thorax, while the other jammed the gun barrel into her forehead.

But before he had time to pull the trigger, Honey dropped through the misty ceiling in a streak of black and gold, wings shrieking through the air. She hit the technician full force. The collision drove him to his knees, made him release Bisma and whipped the gun from his grasp. It skittered, clunking end over end almost in slow-motion, across the polished floor.

For a moment, the technician, Zir Hugh, and Bisma froze, eyes darting between one another. Then Zir Hugh moved first – pivoting with startling speed for an old hornet. The technician, still on his knees, scrambled after the gun and into the Queen's advisor's path. Zir Hugh tried to leap over him but clipped the tech's shoulder instead, sending both of them tumbling.

"Enough," Bisma ordered, grabbing the gun and pointing it at the hornets.

"Hands," she ordered, flicking the gun up and down. "Now!"

Anton had watched this unfold so never registered Hendrix's first movement. He came at him with a singular fury like a sprung trap. Anton crashed to the floor, holding his abdomen and gasping for air. Moments later, Hendrix loomed over him, eyes cold, his stinger twisting ominously towards the prostrate ant. Anton knew it was primed to kill.

With the alarm keening like a blade in his ears, he shut his eyes and waited for the inevitable.

It never came.

Hendrix felt an intense shock of pain shoot down from his head, through his exoskeleton, to the tips of his six limbs. He knew he should have employed an alternative strategy, but he couldn't help himself. He'd been driven by something primeval. He didn't care that there were two bees armed with venom. And he'd completely forgotten that one of them had his gun. As he fought desperately against losing consciousness, he realised he'd been struck over the head with it.

When he came to, the alarm had been replaced by the sound of drilling. His head throbbed, but he remembered what had happened. Hendrix swore violently and tried to get up, but none of his limbs responded. He wasn't sure why. He struggled with increasing desperation to stand until, exhausted, he lay back helpless on the ground. His arms and legs had been securely tethered. Honey and Bisma, stingers primed, stood over him. He tried to shout but only managed a muffled groan through the web-gag. Twisting onto his side, he saw Queen Vespa and Zir Hugh also securely bound and gagged. He turned to his other side.

"Mm-uuh!" Hendrix exclaimed, shocked to see the earwig smiling at him. He writhed for a moment before giving in and lying still.

Anton knelt beside the hornet, chuckling. "Got something to say?"

Hendrix winced when Anton ripped off the web from around his mouth. "You have no idea who you're dealing with," he growled, stretching his jaw. "You and your pathetic friends. Pitiful species."

Anton stood up and tutted. "Is that all you have to say? Ha! Someone shut him up, please."

As Honey slapped sticky nectar roughly over Hendrix's face, Anton turned to Wiggy. "All good, mate? The system's shut down?"

Wiggy nodded.

"Right, then. Let's get out of here." Then, as a second thought, he added: "We should bring the Queen."

Honey held the end of a web tether, and with Bisma pressing her stinger into Vespa's back, she forced her to take off. The two bees and the hornet queen flew through the mist and into one of the vents with Spyder clambering closely behind.

Wiggy, though, lingered. He stood over Hendrix, expressionless. Anton touched his arm. "Come on, Wiggy, let's go," he said gently. "He's not worth it."

Wiggy was still. He looked at Anton and then back at Hendrix, prone at his feet. And then, quite deliberately, he clasped his pincer around Hendrix's throat. He squeezed, watching Hendrix's expression flood with a mixture of anger and fear. Another squeeze made the hornet choke. A little more, and Hendrix's eyes widened in desperation.

And then, without a word, Wiggy let go. Anton helped him clamber up the wall and into the vent. "Proud of you, man," he murmured as they crawled along the shaft.

When they caught up with the others at one of the air con control rooms, Honey had a suggestion. "They're going to follow us, yeah?"

The others nodded.

"So, we need to turn the temperature up as high as it will go. They won't be able to handle the heat. It might give us a bit more time."

"And with a bit of luck," Wiggy added, "the insulation of the photon veins will crack."

Honey flashed a grin and cranked both the dials to maximum.

Outside, Anton pulled his phone from his pocket and turned it on. Two percent battery, one bar. He dialled Terry's number. No signal. He handed the phone to Bisma and told her to fly to the highest point of the tree before redialling. Then she should keep going.

As Bisma disappeared into the foliage, Honey took off with one of Spyder's threads and looped it around the lowest hanging stalk. The arthros pulled it down to the surface so Wiggy, Anton and Spyder could clamber onto a leaf. Honey and Vespa landed beside them. At the end of the leaf, they tiptoed across the stalk and hopped onto a branch, then another, and started to wind their way upwards and into the canopy. Their only plan was to reach the top and hope against hope that Bisma had reached Terry and he had sent a rescue team.

Below, FSS engineers finally cut their way through the door into the control centre to discover six unconscious hornets, the Queen's chief advisor bound and tied to a chair, and the Head of the FSS cocooned in a net of spiderweb. Just a dull throb of limited energy, Sol no longer sparkled.

Two engineers struggled to rip away the network of threads around Hendrix's body. He wriggled and cursed until he was free, then picked the nectar out of his mandibles, at the same time barking orders for his squadrons to search the upper sections of the tree.

"Shoot on sight," he snarled. "Any arthropod."

He rounded on a technician who had regained consciousness, demanding they reboot Helionix. When the tech explained that the UniSynCom data was leaking quickly, Hendrix smashed the hornet's head against the console, screaming at her to find a solution or they'd all be executed.

As he stormed from the room, roaring commands into his wrist unit, a first drop of condensation fell onto the floor.

\#

Spyder led the way, weaving a route up through the branches, over knolls, and, wherever possible, under leaves. Every so often, they would sling a web across gaps in the foliage, hoping to catch or slow the wings of hornets that would inevitably follow them. Behind, Honey's patience was fraying as Vespa dug in with every step, and at the rear, Wiggy was blowing hard. He'd never cared for exercise or sport and was probably still under the effect of whatever drug the hornets had used on him. Anton urged him on, lending him a steadying hand here, a helping push there.

"Shh!" Spyder stopped suddenly, raising a hand. "I'm picking up lots of new vibrations."

Anton saw it first. He turned to the others, urgently signalling for them to hide. They watched the lone hornet scout rise steadily and hover just inches from where they were concealed. Like a periscope, it turned slowly, scanning the surroundings.

"Hmmph!" Vespa's half-muted cry was just loud enough to catch the scout's attention. It turned at the sound and moved towards it. In the early evening light, the shadows made the web invisible, and the hornet flew straight into one of Spyder's traps. As it tried to back out, it only managed to entangle itself further in the sticky strand.

The trap gave the friends time to crawl away through a bunch of leaves and onto the underside of a branch. But the pathfinder had reported its position. Glancing down, they could see a squadron of hornets that had been hovering in and out of the labyrinth of branches and leaves, stop. They regrouped into formation, turned sharply, and shot up to the position of the tangled hornet.

Anton swore. "They're onto us. Come on, we haven't much time."

The group set off again, desperate to reach the top of the baobab before the hornets caught up. Spyder, still in front, scanned the darker spaces in the canopy, looking for a route the hornets wouldn't spot. Honey dragged Queen Vespa, cursing and tugging the tether hard each time the queen faltered. Wiggy clung to the rough wood, his breath now coming in sharp, panicked gulps. Anton, at the back, kept glancing down, catching flashes of yellow and black flicking through the branches. The hornets were climbing quickly, and he could feel the chase gaining on them.

Just as they reached a fork in a branch, a scout veered into their path. The last thing they wanted was to split up, but they had no choice. Anton angled towards a narrow limb that curved back towards the tree's heart, then turned upwards. Stopping briefly to glance back over his shoulder, he saw Spyder slip into a side chute of vines that twisted upward like a hidden staircase. Wiggy darted for a jagged spur leading to a less exposed ascent. He strained left and right but couldn't find Honey. For a moment, he considered going back to look for her, but quickly decided against it. Suicide. Anyway, with a cloak of hornet scent, she had a better chance than any of them of reaching the top. Looking up, the final stretch through a lattice of thin twigs loomed.

Honey had taken the same branch as Wiggy and was well ahead of him when she veered onto yet another adjoining limb. She stopped briefly to wipe her brow.

"Eu shld surrnder now. Onla mattime fore mm swrms fnd eu," Vespa hissed, the gag now only half covering her mouth. Honey ignored her, snapping the lead upwards toward a steep ridge of bark where shadows pooled. Having battled to drag-fly the Queen every step of the way, she was exhausted. But, almost at the top of the tree now, Honey reasoned she no longer had any need for her. Under the nearest clump of leaves, Honey pushed Vespa to her knees and reached into her pack for her guitar strap and leads and started to secure the Queen to a twig.

"I know you have royal blood," Vespa whispered, also exhausted, the gag now hanging around the top of her thorax.

Honey didn't respond. She started to rearrange the gag, but Vespa persisted. "We're all connected. Did you know that, my dear? It's the pheromones. Tell me, how did a girl like you get caught up in something like this?"

Honey snapped back: "You know nothing about me. But I know about you... what happened to your family. Your husband. I'm sorry for that. But taking revenge against the whole world? Changing the future of civilisation? Wiping us all out?"

Vespa appeared shocked. "What do you mean? I don't want to wipe out anyone, whatever you've been told. And revenge?" She shook her head. "I've dealt with the assassins of my family. And one day I will find the arthropods who planned it."

"But you stole UniSynCom. You created that transmitter thing to fire it into us – so you can control us."

"You?" Vespa said sharply, fixing Honey with a hard stare. "You? I'm not interested in controlling you," she sneered. "What do you think I am? A megalomaniac? Yes, we stole UniSynCom, but only because no one has the right to hold our pheromone – or anyone else's for that matter."

Honey shook her head. "I don't believe you. When Wiggy hacked into your computer, I was there. I saw the target with my own eyes. It was highlighted in red. It said 'All – hornets excluded'."

"Impossible. That's impossible." Queen Vespa seemed perplexed. "I was there when Helionix was programmed...

only for hornets. I locked it myself. The password was protected. No one else had access. Unless..."

"Well, I know what I saw," said Honey. "But why would you want to control your species, anyway?"

Vespa, deep in thought, only half-heard Honey's question. "What was that?"

"Why do you want to control hornets?"

"Before liberalisation swept the world, every species knew its role. We were the cullers. You were the pollinators. Ants were the engineers. Now, everyone can be whoever or whatever they want. Let me ask you – would you rather work on a building site or kill other insects?"

Honey remained silent.

"Exactly. The culling workforce is down significantly everywhere. The packet of synthetic pheromones was meant to be transmitted to hornets to stimulate our culling instincts."

"But I don't understand why they wouldn't give you the packets you needed. Surely, they know the risks to the ecosystem if populations grow or decline unchecked?"

"Of course they do!"

The revelation stunned Honey, but before she could process it, a hornet swooped overhead. Then another. She ducked, feeling Vespa's antennae around her, shielding her.

"You'll be safe while my scent is on you," the Queen yelled over the rising buzz of hornets. "Now, go!"

Honey nodded, smiled at Vespa, loosened her ties, and flew to the top of the uppermost leaf. There, she crouched as low as she could. Searching the sky. Waiting. The thrum of hornets filled the air around her. The first squadron had reached the top. They had broken their formation and split into smaller divisions, hunting. For the moment they ignored her, but a flight had discovered Spyder at the top of a neighbouring cluster of leaves. Honey watched her friend rush back and forth, jabbing and stabbing and firing whatever silk they had left. Honey thought she was going to be sick. There was absolutely nothing she could do.

Further across the canopy, a line of four hornets came zizzing at Wiggy, one after another, just nanoseconds apart. Wiggy slashed and sliced with his pincers and limbs, and his uncoordinated methods seemed to confuse the hornets as he managed to disable two. The remaining pair circled around for another attack. It would only be a short time before Wiggy was totally drained of strength.

On the highest leaf, Anton had run out of options. Hornets came at him relentlessly from all directions, and his muscles cried out with every defensive parry he made. His head told him to surrender, but his heart kept him fighting. *Bloody hornets! COME ON!* The screech of each attack had become overwhelming, consuming all his thoughts. It made him furious. The combination of sweat in his eyes and growing exhaustion started to play games with his vision, until the attacking hornets were just blurs of rushing light. But they couldn't get him. Despite being hardly able to stand, he'd be damned if he was giving up. He slashed and sliced, every last morsel of energy feeding his limbs. He cried out at the pain until, exhausted, he fell to his knees, beaten, head lowered, arms useless. He was finished. Waiting for the end.

Waiting.

He sensed somebody beside him.

"Get up," the voice growled. He recognised it instantly; the venom in it. There was a hand on his antenna, pulling. He couldn't resist. Forced back on his feet, now he was being pulled viciously across the leaf. He fell. Got up – sensed other hornets nearby. With his one good eye, he could make out the black uniform, and the back of a cap. He tried to keep up with the pull, but he couldn't. Fell again, but the grip refused to let go. Anton tried to get back to his feet. He was being dragged now. The other hornets laughed. Some cheered. There was shouting. Then suddenly, the noise quietened and Anton couldn't feel anything, although he sensed movement away from him. The pressure on his antenna had gone. He wondered if it had been pulled out of his head. He thought of Honey. He squinted. *Honey?* He smiled at the thought.

The light! He was forced to turn his head away from the streaks of reds and oranges, greens and blues, zigzagging across his blurred vision. He was on his knees now. He reached up to his antennae – both there, thankfully. The pain was starting to fade. He could feel his limbs again. He wiped the back of a forearm across his soaking face. But he was confused. Why? Why had the pulling, the pain and the noise stopped? Then came a voice he didn't recognise.

"Get on!" it bellowed. "Get on!"

Anton looked towards the voice. Blinking, he could see two shapes, perched horizontally and silhouetted against the setting sun. He tried to focus.

Dragonflies?

"Get on. NOW!" With his last bit of strength, Anton pulled himself onto the back of the creature.

"The strap!" the dragonfly shouted. "Fasten it tight!" Anton buckled the belt around his abdomen and held on as the dragonfly took flight. It weaved and then soared upwards into the evening sky. So high that Anton struggled to breathe in the thin air. He twisted around to watch The Nest grow smaller and smaller. Three other dragonflies swooped down and settled into formation beside him, Honey, Spyder and Wiggy astride their shimmering backs.

20

The Festival (2)

The dragonflies landed in the same small clearing from where they had set off the previous morning. Anton, Spyder, Honey and Wiggy slid down the backs of their elegant rescuers, ran to each other, and hugged. They held each other tight, embracing their security, their friendship, the incredible fact they had made it back. Then they just stood back, quiet for a moment, before bursting into unrestrained giggles of relief and fatigue.

Terry watched from a distance. He knew that each of the friends, in their own way, would go through a period of processing. It wouldn't be easy. There would be nightmares as they reflected on what had happened and what might have happened. What they'd done and hadn't done. There might be some guilt, or elation, or depression. Terry vowed to himself, there and then, to look after each one of them.

The four bandmates thanked their dragonflies warmly, waved and watched them fly off into the night. Even when there was no trace left of them, they continued to stare into the distance, images of The Nest and hornets haunting their thoughts.

"Come on, you guys," Anton said finally. "Let's get out of here."

They turned and walked towards their manager.

"Terry." Anton greeted him with a slight nod as they drew near.

"Anton," Terry replied, extending his hand. Anton hesitated, staring at it before finally accepting it. When he did, Terry clasped it firmly, placing a second hand on top. Anton wasn't sure whether that second hand was a show of warmth, relief, or something else. Terry enthusiastically shook Spyder's, then Honey's, before embracing Wiggy warmly.

He led them away from the landing strip and through the surrounding trees. Nothing was said. It was Terry who finally broke the silence. He stopped and turned to the band.

"What you did was downright irresponsible. You could have been killed! All of you!" Then his tone softened. "But what you achieved... well, you saved this earwig's life. And possibly saved the entire arthropod race from a life of servitude. And for that, I could not be more grateful."

Honey was about to say something, but Anton got in first. "What about Queen Vespa and Hendrix?"

"Did you not see them?" Spyder interrupted.

Anton looked puzzled. "See them? What do you mean? I never want to see them again."

"On the leaf, Anton." Honey put an arm around his shoulder. "At the end. From the dragonfly. We saw Hendrix

– with you. Dragging you around the leaf. Don't you remember? He was about to..." Honey's sentence trailed off.

"He was about to kill you, Anton," Wiggy continued, straight to the point.

Anton rubbed his eyes wearily. "I-I remember thinking of you, Honey." He held her hand. "At the end. I-I was so sure it was you." He shook his head and frowned. "It must have been an hallucination."

"It wasn't me, Anton. It was Queen Vespa. She was the one who saved your life. She flew in with some other hornets. They grabbed Hendrix. Arrested him."

Anton stared at Honey and the others. "I-I don't understand."

Honey explained the conversation she had had with Vespa. "Somehow, he had managed to change the target." She turned to Terry. "Why wasn't she granted access to hornet pheromone?"

Terry either didn't hear or chose to ignore her. "Now then, let's get you to a hotel. Some hot food and a shower. Then we can have a proper debrief."

Before Honey had a chance to press Terry further, Spyder blurted out a thought that had snapped into her head. The words spilled out, tight with panic. "Bisma! Terry? Did she make it?"

Immediately, thoughts of Hendrix and Vespa and pheromone evaporated as everyone turned to Terry.

"The bee? The one who called me?"

They all nodded.

"She was picked up by one of the first dragonflies. She's safe."

"Thank goodness," Honey exhaled. "We wouldn't have succeeded without her." They all nodded solemnly.

They had now reached the vehicle park, and Terry ushered them towards a black arthro-carrier. But just as they were getting in, Spyder's antennae pricked up. They paused and then remembered. Music!

"Oh my God! I'd completely forgotten about the festival. Amazing!"

"Ha! Me too!" Anton exclaimed, climbing out of the vehicle to listen. The booming beat echoed clearly over the fields.

"Are you thinking what I'm thinking?" Spyder called to her friends.

A smile lit up Honey's face. "I reckon!"

"I'm up for it," Anton shot back eagerly. "Wiggy?"

"I think I'd really like that," Wiggy replied.

Terry looked surprised. "What? No. Seriously, guys? You want to go back to the festival?"

"Absolutely!" they all shouted back as one.

"Okay, if that's what you want. Hang on a tic..." He pulled his phone from an inside pocket but then stopped. "Bugger!"

They all looked at him in surprise. They'd never heard Terry swear.

"I forgot to tell them that you'd become, er, unavailable."

"Really?" Honey gasped playfully. "You actually forgot? Terry, seriously? You mean everyone's still expecting us to play?" She paused, letting the revelation ring around the band. "Well," she beamed, "does that mean... we'll just have to play?"

"Yes. Yes. YES!" Spyder laughed. "Anton?"

"Seems like the best sort of debriefing," Anton chuckled. "Wiggy?"

"I think I'd really like that," Wiggy replied, this time strumming an air guitar. The four of them cheered and yeh-ed and jumped up and down, clapping and high-fiving with childish excitement, completely forgetting the trauma of the past 36 hours.

"Well, all right then," Terry grinned. "Excellent. Let's do it!"

#

The four band members sat together around the table in a small trailer at the back of the stage, feeling a little self-conscious in their new costumes. Earlier, they had shut the door and asked not to be disturbed. There were a few things they needed to discuss.

But when the conference was finished, Brie and Blake were the first inside. "Where have you been?" Brie exclaimed. "Insectagram's abuzz with speculation! We need new content! You've been isolating, yeah? Possible virus. All clear now. Quick chat?" She nodded eagerly at the band, seeking their approval, which they gave – if somewhat unenthusiastically. "Blake, love," she called out. "Bring the camera, will you? Now, darlings, outfits..."

You didn't go to see Them Creepy Crawlies for their out-fits. But now that they were fully-fledged rock stars, Brie had insisted they move away from any old jeans and tee-shirts to a more glamorous and coordinated look.

"Darlings," she'd told them, "It's my 'Three Ss' look: simple, subtle, and superb."

"I feel a bit silly," said Wiggy, inadvertently adding a fourth 'S'. He wore a dark brown silky shirt that hugged his thin abdomen, topped by a russet-coloured collar around his thorax. His pants were almost black but shimmered orange when the light caught them.

"No man. You look really cool," Spyder insisted. "But not as cool as me, hey?" They did look amazing. Raven hair, bigger and curlier than ever. Large silver hoop earrings. A tight, lime green spidersuit, covered in sparkles. A yellow scarf flung around their thorax. And, of course, enormous goggle sunnies.

"Or me!" Honey gave everyone a twirl before she sat down quickly, a little embarrassed at her peacocking.

"Wow, you look super-sexy! But you always do, Hon," Spyder added, flirtatiously.

Honey blushed. She wore a thin, high-cut black jumper with her signature white Peter Pan collar and cuffs. The jumper doubled as a miniskirt, and she wore black patent blocks with a silver buckle. Her wings were accessorised with dark blue and yellow faring, ready to shine in the spotlight.

When Anton joined them, head in the setlist, Spyder giggled. "Hey, man! Who's plugged you into the zeitgeist?" Anton pretended not to hear them, but he felt good in the baggy black street pants and low-cut white vest under a faded black leather jacket with red stripes up the arms.

"Whoo!" Spyder joked, roughing his hair and jangling a necklace of beads – the first jewellery that Anton had ever worn.

There was a knock at the door, and Terry poked his head in. "Everyone okay? Ready for this?" he said a little over enthusiastically.

"Feeling good, Terry, feeling good," Anton replied distractedly, studying the setlist.

He looked up. "Listen, have you got a moment? There's something we want to talk to you about."

Terry sat down at the table, maintaining his usual erect posture, stick held in two hands in front of his abdomen. He turned his head to each band member and then focused on a spot above Anton's head. "You have every right to feel let down by me," he said. He continued staring straight ahead, then coughed. "Therefore, I offer you all my resignation. I was untruthful, and I, er, well... Worst of all, because of me you put yourselves in mortal danger." He lowered his head and groaned. "I can never forgive myself for that."

"Shut up, Terry," Spyder interrupted, enjoying his discomfort. "We want in."

Terry shot a surprised look at Honey.

"That's right. We want to join Insecterpol," said Honey, smiling serenely.

"Look, Terry," continued Anton, "we don't condone what you did by keeping your plan from us, but we understand why you did it. When we set off to find Wiggy, we had no idea what we were getting ourselves into. The naivety of youth, I suppose. But, although we've learned we're not bulletproof, we've also learned that together..." He smiled warmly at his friends. "... together, we make a damn good team."

"Damn right!" Spyder added.

Honey pitched in. "You know, in our own ways, we've each been looking for a purpose in our lives. And working to ensure the safety of our world... well, there isn't a bigger purpose than that!"

"And we don't want to lose you as our manager," Anton added, touching him on the forearm. "Without you... well, we wouldn't be here waiting to play Flutterbury."

Somehow, Terry found a way to straighten his back even further, to hold his stick a little more firmly. Behind his dark glasses, he could feel something welling, which he quickly wiped away. He cleared his throat.

They had totally taken him by surprise. He hadn't expected them to reach The Nest, let alone rescue Edward and return home relatively unscathed. He had listened, shocked and impressed, as they explained snippets of their experience.

Terry pursed his lips. "That's an interesting proposal."

"Come on, man. The band cover thing is totally cool," Spyder said. "But, you and Wiggy... well... you're a bit, like, limited in your abilities." They cracked a small smile.

Terry rubbed his chin and gave a brief nod. There was no doubting that.

"And to be a team, a real team..." Honey leaned back in her seat, raising her top arms to encompass her bandmates. "... Everyone needs to know what the other one is doing before they do it. It's like being in a band."

"Yeah, girl," said Spyder, "you're so right. It's weird, isn't it? Like, I knew you were going to say that." They both giggled.

Terry turned to Wiggy. "You've been quiet, Edward. How do you feel about all this?"

Wiggy gazed out of the window. He still felt guilty for abusing the band's trust, probably would do for a while, especially as they had risked their lives to save his. He wondered if the interrogation and the whole kidnapping experience would come back to haunt him. Meanwhile, there was no one else he'd trust more than Anton, Spyder and Honey – no one else in the world. And, weirdly, a phrase kept nagging at him, an earworm that captured how he felt: 'Strength through unity'.

"For me, er, working for Insecterpol was a bit of a game, really," Wiggy said softly, still staring out of the window. "Like I was in a film. The geek, sort of locked away in a windowless room, saving the world. But having been through what I've... what we've been through, well, my perspective has sorta changed. Bad guys no longer just exist in video games. They're real."

He turned to his friends. "I know I've got stuff to work through, with myself and with each of you, but right now all I know is that I feel a deeper bond with you guys than I ever did before."

He broke into the broadest smile any of them had ever seen before. "And you guys were totally awesome at The Nest. So, yeah, I say *yes*."

"Yeah!" Spyder slapped hands with Wiggy.

Anton stood up. "Come on, everyone. We've got a gig to do – and I need to warm up."

"Yes, sir!" Spyder and Honey replied in unison, leaping to their feet with a childish salute.

"You see!" they said to each other, again in unison, before falling about in laughter. They skipped out of the trailer, hand in hand, followed by Wiggy, a little less coordinated.

At the door, Anton turned to Terry, who hadn't yet moved. "Look, we know we'd need training, but, well, I think you know we'd be good, Terry." Anton smiled at their manager/handler, hopped through the door, and jogged across to the green room, a spring very much in his step.

#

The crowd had been growing throughout the evening. Rarely had the Second Stage commanded such interest. It only happened when a new band had a bunch of awesome songs *and* a fresh new sound, *and* when the audience knew the musicians had the same loves and hates, convictions and challenges, dreams and aspirations as they had themselves.

Anton stood on his own at the side of the stage. He was early, so he watched the crew set up – changing amplifiers, moving drums, repositioning speakers. His gaze shifted to the audience, where the mood was joyously festive, bubbling with anticipation. Despite it being the biggest crowd he had ever played for, Anton felt calm. A bit nervous, certainly, but there wasn't any of the dread he had felt before. Now, there was only excitement, and he was dying to get out there and play the songs that he knew everyone loved. He was confident and in control. For the first time in his life, he knew who he was and what he was supposed to do.

"You okay?" From behind, Honey wrapped her top arms around his abdomen and kissed his cheek.

Anton turned around and held her close, staring intently into her eyes. "I thought I'd lost you," he said. "On that leaf. At the end." He shook his head at the thought of those moments, then kissed her gently.

"I thought I'd lost you, too," she replied, smiling. "Several times." She pulled him to her, and they stood for a moment, just hugging.

"Oi! Stop it you two! Say hello to my friend, Salama. Sal, this is Anton." Anton broke away from Honey with a final kiss, and shook Salama's hand. "Very pleased to meet you," he said, beaming broadly.

"And... this is Honey."

Honey took Sal's hands in her own and looked at her, grinning. "Salama! What a beautiful name. I'm so glad to meet you." Honey kissed her on both cheeks, then shot Spyder a playful smile.

"Darlings! Yoo-hoo!" Brie swept across the backstage area, the ever-dutiful Blake in tow. "We must have photos to preserve this special moment. Blakey!"

Click, click, click.

"Gorgeous! Now, my sweeties. Sy, you too. And Terry. Lovely!"

Click, click, click, click.

"Beaumont! Belle! Come on, sweeties. And, of course, the gorgeous George! Beautiful!"

Click, click, click.

As the gang stood around chatting, a beetle wearing headphones and a mouthpiece approached them. It was time to go on. No more photos. Please. Come on. The crowd's waiting.

The roadies had left the stage; the last-minute sound and light checks were complete. The stage was dark except for a single red spotlight highlighting the drums. The crowd was hushed, expectant. Everyone was focused on the stage. Only seconds now.

A single spotlight followed a celebrity to the centre of the stage, and the crowd gave a polite cheer. The celebrity said something inane. There was some impatient shuffling. The celebrity held up their arms...

"Insects! Arachnids! Myriapods! Please put your hands together and give a huge Flutterbury welcome to...

"THEM. CREEPY. CRAWLIEEES!"

Acknowledgements

330

Thank you to Jason Fischer for providing shape, Ralph Johnstone for editing and proofreading, and Hermann Lauss for the cover design. And to Adam, Toby, Rick, Mike, Jim and Nick, without whom there would be no Them Creepy Crawlies.

About The Author

Neil Mackenzie grew up on the shores of Strangford Lough in Northern Ireland, where he dreamed of becoming a famous rock star. Despite playing in bands across Ireland, England, Kenya, and Australia, fame and fortune remain elusive. Along the way, Neil has worked as a teacher, event manager and CEO. Semi-retired, he now combines disability support work with driving a school bus. Neil is married to Victoria, a devoted teacher and bookworm, and together they serve their two grown-up children.

neilmackenzie.com

www.ingramcontent.com/pod-product-compliance
Lightning Source LLC
Chambersburg PA
CBHW040515170726
48295CB00012B/214